IT CAME EVEN TO ME

A Novel by

DREW HILL

www.EvolvedPub.com
Evolved Publishing LLC
Butler, Wisconsin, USA

Books by Drew Hill

Crossing the Tracks

It Came Even To Me

Dedication

For Dad,
A father's love, a pastor's heart,
and the courage to change.

Introduction

"I do not at all understand the mystery of grace — only
that it meets us where we are,
but does not leave us where it found us."
~ *Anne Lamott*

Chapter 1 – Nightmare

> "Thou shalt not be a victim,
> thou shalt not be a perpetrator,
> but, above all,
> thou shalt not be a bystander."
> *~ Yehuda Bauer*

"Sorry to call so late, Reverend. Sheriff Wade here. It's your boy, David. He's been in an altercation out at the truck stop. Not sure how it happened. There was a fight your boy tried to break up, but I'm afraid he got a beatin' for his trouble."

I glanced at my alarm, trying to shake myself awake: 1:47. "Where is he, Sheriff? Can I talk to him? How bad is he hurt?"

"I think he'll be all right, needs stitches for sure and some x-rays. I had my deputy take him on to the ER. You can sure talk to him there."

I winced as I pictured our son beaten and bloodied. "We'll head over there right now, Sheriff. How did this happen? David's never been in a fight in his life."

"I don't have the answers, Reverend, but we'll get to the bottom of it, I can tell you that. There's another boy, that Summers kid, he's hurt worse. I called the ambulance for him. We'll have to sort this out. I'll need a statement from David when he feels like it."

"I understand. We'll get on to the hospital. Thank you for letting us know, Sheriff. Goodnight."

Sally had heard every word and was already pulling on her jeans and stepping into her sandals. Her questions came in a stream, with every breath. "Who could have done this, Bart? How bad is David hurt? What does the sheriff know about medical things? David's no fighter, never has been. What was he thinking?"

"Sheriff says David was trying to stop a fight. At least he didn't start it." I scrambled for my shoes and grabbed my wallet and keys from the dresser.

Sally reached for her sweater as we hurried down the hall and on our way, but her questions kept coming. "Well, why didn't he call the sheriff in the first place?" Her voice began to tremble. "How could this happen, Bart?"

I put my arm around her shoulder and kissed her forehead. "C'mon, Sal, let's get over there."

I drove in silence to the hospital, except for Sally's intermittent sobbing and whispered prayers. Most of the stoplights along Benton Avenue blinked yellow in the late hours, no one on the streets. How many times had I made this drive to the hospital in the past sixteen years at all hours of the night? More than I could remember. Being a pastor in a small town like Joppa, Georgia, means you double as an on-call chaplain at the local hospital.

No telling how many visits I had made to Joppa Memorial or all the hours I had spent in that dinky waiting room, holding worried hands, praying and helping others to pray. Usually, it was routine stuff, but when the call came from the ER, I knew the situation was critical, sometimes tragic. I thought of that horrible fire at the chemical plant, speeding to the ER to be with those three men so badly burned, including one that didn't survive. What a horrific night... for everyone.

But this was my own nightmare. My boy, my son, lay somewhere in that ER on an examination table. As I pulled into the nearly empty parking lot, I noticed the sign, "Reserved for Clergy," next to those marked, "Visitors." This time, I chose the visitor's spot. This patient belonged to me.

***

As Sally and I hurried up the walk to the ER entrance, the growing roar of a helicopter neared. I leaned away from the building and spotted the Medivac helicopter, lights blinking, settling over the concrete slab beside the new wing of the hospital. I turned to Sally, trying to get her inside.

She shouted over the noise, "Have they come for David?"

"Let's find out. C'mon."

We stepped inside and found no one at the information desk—no staff in sight—but we were in no mood to wait. I pushed through the doors and we hurried to the nurse's station.

"Excuse me, excuse me," I said, trying to get someone's attention. "There's no one at the desk and our son is in here, David Sheldon."

A nurse in purple scrubs looked up from her clipboard. "Yes, just a moment. I'll be right with you."

Sally couldn't contain her questions. "How is he? What's wrong? Are you sending him in the Medivac?"

The nurse checked the dry erase census board behind her. "David Sheldon, yes, he's here. Let me get his nurse for you."

As she spoke, a familiar face appeared from behind a patient curtain.

"Amy!" Sally cried. "Have you seen David? Is he all right?"

Amy Morrow, a longtime ER nurse, had been a friend since our kids were small. "It's okay, Sally." Amy gave her a hug. "David's banged up. He looks pretty rough right now, but he'll be okay."

Sally began to calm as Amy reassured her. "We saw the Medivac and were afraid it might be for David. We don't know what's happening."

"No," Amy explained, "the Medivac came for another patient, the boy we brought in before David. We're sending him on to Emory. As soon as he is on the way, the doctor will come talk to you."

"Can we see David now?"

"Sure, this way."

We stepped behind the curtain to see our son gazing up at us through one eye, his left eye a swollen mass of purple. A wide bandage wrapped much of David's scalp and his hair above his left ear was caked with blood. His chin, upper lip, and left eyebrow were tracked with stitches. His nose looked broken, swollen and bent.

"My God, David, what happened to you, son?" I asked. "Who did this to you?"

Sally moved to his side and leaned down to kiss his forehead.

David flinched when she touched his shoulder. "I'm pretty sore, Mom."

Sally couldn't stop the litany of questions as she tried to make sense of a senseless situation.

I had my own questions for our battered son. "David, you're no fighter. What were you thinking? You've never been in a fight in your life. I couldn't even get you to take Tae Kwon Do when you were a kid. You said you didn't want to hurt anybody." I regretted my words as I heard myself speak them. This was no time to scold our son.

"I'm sorry, Dad. I know I'm no fighter. The evidence is all over my face." His words came slowly, painfully, as he tried to explain. "This kid was in trouble, a guy from school, Daniel Summers. I came out of Rigby's and heard someone call for help, screaming. I ran around the side of the building and two guys had Daniel on the ground, stomping on him, on his face, kicking him—killing him, Dad. They were killing him. What was I supposed to do?"

His mother broke in. "Did you call the police, get help?"

"I left my phone in the car. There was no time. I don't think Daniel was conscious when they turned on me."

Wiping a tear from her cheek, Sally said, "I'm so sorry, honey. I can't believe anyone would do this to you."

Dr. Swearngin stepped in pulling the curtain aside, and picked up the patient clipboard from the foot of the bed. "Pastor Sheldon, Mrs. Sheldon, sorry to see your son in this condition, but we're going to take good care of him."

I became well acquainted with Donald Swearngin through Joppa Rotary Club, sometimes working on projects that were assigned alphabetically—Sheldon, Swearngin. He had a family practice, but also covered the ER on rotating weekends.

"David," he said, "I'm going to give you something stronger for pain and we'll keep you here overnight. You may have a concussion with all the rest, and we want to keep you here in case you have any problems."

"Thanks, doctor. These stitches, are they going to heal up?"

"You mean will they leave a scar? Very negligible, hardly noticeable, really. I'm pretty good at this—too much practice, I guess. When the swelling goes down, we'll set your nose and make sure your sinuses are clear. You've got a rough few days ahead of you, but you'll be fine."

We stayed with David another hour, unable to pull ourselves away, still trying to absorb the reality of what had happened to our happy-go-lucky, tenderhearted, peace-loving son—nothing like this in his twenty-four years, nothing close. Sally and Amy tried everything to make him comfortable, adjusting his pillows and giving him sips of Sprite.

Sally dabbed away the dried blood from David's hair with a warm, wet cloth, still unable to stop the flow of her own tears, her heart broken for her son. "I can stay, David, to be here, in case you need anything. Do you want me to stay with you?"

David waved his bandaged hand. "I'll be fine, Mom. You guys go on home, get some sleep. I'll see you tomorrow."

As we were getting ready to leave, Sally glared at me. "Aren't you going to pray with David? You pray with everyone else in this place. What about our son?"

I don't know why it hadn't occurred to me to pray with David, though I wasn't feeling much like a pastor that night. The anger simmered in my gut, a slow burn I should have been expecting. How can any father see his child victimized with no rage, no urge to protect and avenge?

I took David's bruised hand gently in mine and reached for Sally. Amy completed the circle. I closed my eyes to my battered son and tried to pray. "Father, thank you for preserving David's life through this terrible ordeal. Take care of him tonight. Ease his pain and help him rest. We pray that you would grant him full healing from his injuries. And may justice be served to those who do such things. In Christ's name, Amen."

I was finished, but David was not. Through his swollen lips he prayed on. "And God, take care of Daniel. Please let him live. Let him heal, God. And be with his family tonight. I am thankful to be alive. Amen."

***

We crawled into bed an hour before the alarm would signal a new day. Sally's countless questions finally brought her to exhaustion, as she sobbed herself to sleep, but I had too much on my mind, too many questions still to answer. Who would attack a kid like David, so violently and brutally? This went way beyond boys being boys. An argument? An old grudge? Some thugs trying to prove their manhood? And why? For what? What could Daniel Summers have done to deserve such treatment? And why lay into David for trying to stop it? Sounded like the fight was pretty much over by then.

I punched my pillow and tried to get comfortable as my musings continued. I didn't know the Summers well. As I recalled, they were Methodist folks. Mr. Summers taught school in Edgerton, ten miles out, and his wife worked at Walgreens. Seemed like they had a son older than Daniel and younger ones still in high school or junior high. I remembered David and Daniel played on the same soccer team back in their elementary school days. David didn't stay with soccer, but Daniel starred through high school, having headlined the local sports page more than once.

Daniel seemed like a good kid, respectful enough, and I had never heard of him being in trouble, nor being one to pick a fight. He and David had that in common. So, how did these two come to this, both beaten to a pulp, Daniel nearly killed? I struggled to make sense of it.

We needed to get some answers. This kind of thing didn't happen in Joppa, Georgia, at least not to white folks. Sure, from time to time, there had been incidents, black people put down or run off, sometimes worse. The racism of the Old South was alive and well in a town raided by Sherman's cavalry on his march to the sea. The Stars and Stripes flew over the town square, but a framed Confederate battle flag adorned the courthouse lobby next to the faded picture of the regiment that Joppa sent off to fight in the War of Northern Aggression. A bronze statue of General Joseph E. Johnston, turned an ugly turquoise with the years, dominated the courthouse lawn.

So, our little town was no stranger to violence, but this episode baffled me, a real mystery. Drugs, alcohol, some drunken brawl? A case of mistaken identity?

I almost lost my son tonight, and another boy is clinging to life. My God, why?

***

Sheriff Clayton Wade was waiting for us Monday morning when David and I arrived for the interview. We sat at a table in a drab, gray room, with only coffee and a tape recorder.

The sheriff wasted little time getting started. "Reverend Sheldon, we took two men into custody early yesterday morning. We are confident that these two are responsible for the attack on Daniel Summers and your son. They will be arraigned this afternoon, so it's important that we have David's statement on record."

"Thank you, Sheriff. I'm glad to hear it."

Sheriff Wade switched on the recorder and began. "David, walk us through it, as best you can remember what happened two nights ago at the truck stop."

David grimaced as he recounted the ordeal. The swelling was down, but the stitches twisted his lip with every word. His eyes were both open though the bruising had deepened and spread across his cheek and forehead. He looked more like a plum than a person, but determined to tell his story in every detail.

David retraced the moments: leaving the truck stop, hearing the screams, the beating he witnessed and the beating he received.

"David, did you recognize the two young men who did this? Have you ever met them before?"

"No, Sheriff, not personally, but they seemed to know me. I've seen them around town, but never met them, never had a conversation."

"Did they know Daniel? Did you ever see them together, arguing or anything?"

David sat back in his chair and sighed. "No. Never."

The sheriff shook his head. "I don't get it. What's the motive? Do you have any idea why these two roughnecks chose Daniel?"

"I think I do, Sheriff," David answered. "I know why they did what they did. Daniel Summers is gay, maybe not officially, but everyone knows he is. He wrote a paper for his current events class supporting gay rights. Word got around and he never denied it. They know he's gay. That's why they attacked him."

"How can you be sure, David?" the sheriff asked. "What have you not told us about what happened that night?"

David glanced at me and took a deep breath. "It was what they said and what they did, and it's not pleasant."

The sheriff checked the tape recorder and said, "Every detail, David. We need the whole story. What else did you hear?"

David began, "When I came around the building, one of them was yelling, cheering on his buddy. He said, 'Kill that cock-suckin' faggot. Stomp his queer ass.' He said, 'Kick his fuckin' face in.'" David fell silent for a moment. "That's it. That's what he said while the other guy stomped the life out of Daniel. He was helpless down on the pavement, couldn't fight back, but those bastards wouldn't quit." Tears welled up in David's eyes. "So I tried to stop them."

"My God," I gasped. "That's what this was about?"

"You might've saved his life, son," the sheriff said as he put his hand on his shoulder. "Anything else, David?"

"One more thing, the last thing before they heard the sirens and took off. I had collapsed between the two trucks where you found us. Daniel was close to me, but not moving. They urinated on us." David struggled to say the words. "They pissed on us, Dad, and then they ran away." His voice broke and he fell silent.

The sheriff reached over and shut off the recorder.

I had no words... no words for my son's pain.

"Well, they didn't run far, David," the sheriff said. "We picked them up a few hours later at that bar out on

45, already braggin' it up. Apparently, there were some witnesses at the truck stop who saw at least part of what was going on, but with your testimony, we got 'em for assault for sure, or worse if that Summers kid doesn't pull through. Sounds like a hate crime to me."

I couldn't imagine such brutality toward relative strangers. "Who could do such a thing, Sheriff? Who are those boys? Are they from here in Joppa?"

"Richie Towns and Mark Hampton, two sons of the South that oughta know better, but don't. They've been bullies before, but not like this. They're gonna pay this time."

***

While David recuperated from his injuries, he stayed at home with us. His mother would not hear of him going back to his apartment until he fully recovered. With our daughter, Dinah, away for a summer internship in Chattanooga, the house was too quiet anyway. Sally settled David into his old room, still filled with his high school memorabilia, his speech and debate trophies, his posters and artwork. Nothing had changed in the six years since high school.

Friday morning, I cooked breakfast, bacon and eggs and some store-bought biscuits made tasty with Mrs. McCann's apple butter.

David shuffled in and found his familiar place at the table. "That bacon smells good, Dad. I haven't had any in a while. Good thing I still have my teeth."

"Let me get you a plate, son. Glad you're hungry."

David was eating again, his sore lips becoming more manageable.

"How did you sleep?"

"Not too bad. I woke up a few times, but the pain meds help."

Sally marched in with a beaming smile, kissed my cheek as she passed the stove, then gave a gentle embrace to David from behind. "Good morning, gentlemen. Good to see you this morning. How's my husband and my hero?"

"I'm good, Mom, but I'm no hero."

Sally poured a cup of coffee and sat down. "That's not what I hear. Now that Daniel is doing better, some folks are saying you saved his life. Those thugs might have killed him if you had not come to his defense."

I chimed in, "It was a brave thing you did, son. I'm not sure I told you, but it's true. We are proud of you, risking your life for a friend."

David shook his head. "All I did was give those guys another target. Maybe that slowed them down a little, but it's hardly heroism. I keep replaying those moments and wondering what I might have done to stop them. But honestly, if I had had a gun in my hand, I'm not sure I could have used it even then, and that makes me feel more like a coward than a hero."

"Still," I said, "what you did for Daniel was selfless and noble. No one can ever question your courage."

"Or your love, your compassion for people in trouble — all kinds of people," his mother added.

"You mean even gay people, don't you, Mom?"

"Well, yes, in this case. Daniel is gay, and that's why he was attacked, right?"

David nodded his head. "Mom, Dad, I guess now is as good a time as any to deal with this. We've needed to have this conversation for a long time. You may already know what I'm about to tell you, but either way, I need to say it. I didn't defend Daniel because he is gay. I defended Daniel because I am gay."

The words hung in the air for a long moment.

"Oh, David, you don't mean that. You can't mean that," his mother exclaimed. "I know you care about people, especially those who are put down or excluded. You have a kind heart. You stood up for Daniel, probably saved his life. You fought for your gay friend, but that doesn't mean you're gay."

"Mom, it's not just about Daniel. I've known I'm gay for quite a while, since high school."

"High school?" Sally's frustration was rising.

I turned off the stove, poured a cup of coffee, and sat down next to David.

"David," Sally continued, "in high school you were surrounded by girls. You dated all the time. You always had a girlfriend. You took Shanna to the prom."

"You said it, Mom: girl-friends—lots of girls were my friends, close friends, and they know the truth about me. My friends know I'm gay. My sister knows I'm gay."

"Dinah knows! I guess we are the only ones kept in the dark on this." Sally wiped her eyes with a dish towel, trying to compose herself.

"David," I said, "why are we just now having this conversation? When you were figuring this out years ago and deciding you were gay, why didn't you talk to us, tell us what you were thinking, so we could help you work through this."

"Do you have to ask that question, Dad? I know what you think about gay people. That's no secret. Everyone knows. I understand this goes against what you believe and everything you want for me."

"But, son, you know we love you. We want God's best for you. Your mom and I want you to live a life true to your faith, true to the Gospel. We pray for you every day, David, that you will follow God's path for your life."

"I get that, Dad, and the last thing I want to do is to hurt you or embarrass you. But please understand me: this isn't something I've decided to do. It's knowing myself. It's being aware of who I am. I hope you can accept that."

"How can I, David?" And then, thinking out loud, I said, "How can we accept it if we don't believe it? How can I condone in you what I have always condemned in others?"

Sally rallied from her shock to say, "We love you, David. You're our son and we'll always love you, even if we don't understand your decisions."

"That's just it, Mom. This is not a choice I made, like deciding where to go to college. This is just knowing who I am, understanding myself."

"You're a Christian, son. That's who you are!" I nearly shouted. "You've always had a heart for God. How can you turn your back on him now? You should be ashamed of yourself."

My words struck him like the blows of a dagger, and his eyes fell to the floor as he struggled to gather his emotions. "God and I are just fine, Dad. I am not ashamed. I know this is who I am, who God made me to be."

"How can you say such a thing? It can't be. You may believe it, but it is possible to be sincere and yet mistaken."

"That works both ways, Dad. What about you? Have you thought about your view of homosexuality? What if you are the one who is sincerely mistaken?"

I felt my face flush as the tension continued to rise. I pushed back from the table, trying to control my growing frustration. "The scriptures are clear, David. I'm bound by the truth of God's Word."

"Is it crystal clear, Dad? How about you look again? You check it out, and if you still believe people like me and Daniel are an abomination to God, then we'll both know where we stand. Funny thing, though: I know God still hears my prayers and loves me like He did when I was a little boy."

"Don't you lecture me. I know what I believe. I've studied the scriptures all my life. God's Word is true, whether we like it or not. The truth doesn't change. You can't just ignore it." I stood up in an attempt to calm myself, moved behind Sally's chair, and took her shoulders in my hands.

David looked up as tears streaked his purple cheek. "This is who I am, Dad. I need you to try to understand. Just try. Think about it. Give me a chance."

An uncomfortable quiet settled over us as we sipped our tepid coffee.

A broken-hearted mother broke the silence. "Sometimes I wish you were still just a little boy, David."

"Everybody grows up, Mom. Even your little boy."

Chapter 2 – Blind Eyes

"Hatred is blind,
as well as love."
~ Oscar Wilde

"Good morning, Pastor. How are you this morning?" Donna, my administrative assistant at First Baptist Church, entered the conference room and sat down with her clipboard of assorted notes and forms, all the details of church life. Monday morning staff meeting, the one constant on everyone's schedule, was soon to begin.

In Joppa, First Baptist Church had a dominating presence, just two blocks off the square on Main. It loomed over the landscape with its familiar colonial design of red brick, white columns, tall windows, and a towering spire with recorded chimes calling the community to worship. The new sanctuary covered most of a city block, and the family life center with a high school-sized gymnasium sat just across Poplar on the west side.

I liked to think of First Baptist as the leadership church, filled largely with managers, executives, and professionals who carried a great deal of responsibility in Joppa. Those on the outside referred to our congregation in less flattering ways, such as the boss's church, the rich people's church, or the country club church. I'll admit that we did seem to focus on the upper crust of our community, but even the up and out need a church. At least that's what I always told myself.

"I'm fine, Donna. Did you have a good weekend?" Donna had served on my staff for nearly ten years. From time to time, she might drop a detail or two, forget something important, but I appreciated her gentle spirit, never cross or critical.

"We had a fine weekend, Pastor. Saturday, we were down at the lake, beautiful day. We heard the news. How's David doing?"

I knew it wouldn't be long until someone asked about David. They meant well, but I couldn't help the knot in my stomach when friends asked about our son. Part of me wanted to talk about David's improved condition and the rest of me wanted to hide the dark secret he had revealed to us. No one would understand, and I feared what would happen if it ever came out.

"David's doing much better, thanks. He's healing up well. He gets his stitches out next week."

Randall, our worship leader, walked in with his tablet in hand, in time to hear my update.

Brian, my associate pastor, came in just behind Randall. "I guess you all read Oliver's editorial in the paper yesterday," Brian said. "Everybody's talking about it."

Randall responded as he sat down at the far end of the table. "Honestly, why does anybody read his column anyway? Nobody agrees with him on anything. Oliver is stuck with a podunk paper in a small town, so he tries to create controversy out of every scrap of news. He's the devil's advocate."

"Or the devil himself," said Brian. "Did I read him correctly? When he characterized the assault against Daniel Summers and David as a hate crime, I figured he was right on the money. But the way he wrote the story seemed to suggest that both Daniel and David were gay, not just Daniel. You should demand a clarification or a retraction."

Randall answered before I could speak. "Yeah, that might be a good idea, to set the record straight, because that's the talk on the street, that Daniel and David are both gay and... uh... know each other. I'm sorry, but that's the talk, that David stood up for his gay buddy."

"That's shameful," Donna added, "to twist a courageous act into something sordid and ugly. Anyway, I'm glad David is doing better. Just don't let the poor boy read the paper."

I wanted to confide in them, my own staff, some of my closest friends, but I couldn't do it. I couldn't bring myself to say the words, to speak the truth that I had not yet admitted to myself. I wanted to share my own heartbreak, but instead I buried it in the details and demands of a busy week at First Baptist Church. "Thanks, guys. I appreciate your thoughts and prayers for David. We can't control what people say or write, so we're trying to move on. Let's get to our agenda."

***

I walked back to my study after staff meeting and pulled the door closed behind me. Normally, my door always stood open, but on this day, I needed to be alone with my thoughts. I sat behind my desk, leaned back, and tried to make sense of this new reality confronting me. The words played in my mind: *David is gay. My son is gay.* How did this happen? What did I do wrong? All of David's life, he heard me teach and preach the truth of God's Word, and he certainly knew what was right and what was wrong. Why would he say such a thing? He'd convinced himself of something that couldn't be true.

I glanced down to the bottom shelf to the left of my desk, where I kept all the various translations and editions and paraphrases of the Bible I had accumulated through the years, arranged from my old King James Version to the modern paraphrases. Nearly two dozen Bibles rested there, and on the shelf above was my Greek New Testament and my Hebrew Bible, along with my lexicons and interlinear editions. On the end of my desk sat my pulpit Bible, the faded gold letters imprinted on the black cover: "Dr. Bart Sheldon." I picked it up and ran my fingers over the cover and breathed the faint smell of old leather.

It was hard to explain how I felt about the Bible, its overwhelming significance in my life. The Word of God, divinely inspired, the very breath of God, had always been for me the highest law and the final authority. To question or dispute or ignore the truth of scripture was to risk the judgment of God, temporally and eternally. And what could be more obvious than the Bible's condemnation of homosexuality, an abomination before God? Homosexuality was sin and worthy of God's righteous condemnation. I couldn't just rewrite the scripture or tear out the pages I didn't like.

The words kept repeating, unrelenting, a storm in my mind, an ache in my chest: *David is gay. My son is gay.*

He said it was who he was. "It's not a choice, Dad. It's the way God made me."

How can that be? How can he say such a thing? How can he turn his back on everything he has ever been taught, everything he knows I stand for as his father and a minister of the Gospel? And how can he claim God's acceptance, condoning his behavior, God affirming an abomination? Unthinkable.

But this was David, my son. He was no deviant or pervert or molester. He didn't fit any of the sordid stereotypes of gay people.

How do I make sense of this?

One thing must have been true: either David was dead wrong or I was. David had chosen the path to judgment and damnation, or I had been preaching a false Gospel all these years. There was no way to reconcile one with the other.

I blocked out some significant time to pull together everything the Bible had to say about homosexuality, so I could show David in the clearest terms where I stood. I was anxious to begin, and yet an underlying dread lingered, a fear that the Bible I so treasured would be the painful wedge that separated me from my son.

***

"Daddy, I'm home."

There is something about the sound of a daughter's voice in her father's ear. My attention is captured, and my heart softens a bit when my baby girl, though now a young woman, calls me "Daddy." From her lips, it's my favorite word.

"I'm in here, Dinah."

She bounded into the dining room with her usual enthusiasm, making every homecoming like a holiday. Her sleeveless pink top highlighted the colorful wings inked down to her elbows.

I reached down to put my arms around her tiny frame, not quite five feet tall and barely a hundred pounds. "Good to see you, Sweetie."

"What's all this? Do you need some help?"

The dinner table was strewn with wrapping paper and ribbons as I was trying to get Sally's birthday presents wrapped.

"Glad you made it. Your mom will be so pleased, and I'm no good at wrapping this stuff. Can you give me a hand?"

"Sure. You did the hard part, the shopping and the buying. I got this." I sat down as she made short work of her mother's birthday presents. "Great stuff, Daddy. You did well. Mom will love that sweater. Hey, how is she doing with all this? David filled me in on your conversation."

"She's doing pretty well, I guess. Better than me, for sure. She seems to have accepted David being gay, or at least resigned herself to it. A mother's love never ends, right or wrong, no matter what, and that's how it should be, I guess. Dinah, I don't know what to say to David or how to help him understand. He knows what I believe and what I've always taught."

She sat down and pushed the packages aside. Her carefree expression told me she was not troubled or disturbed by this crisis.

I asked her, "How did you come to accept David's decision, or pronouncement, whatever you call it?"

"It's not such a big deal, Daddy. You make it sound like it's the end of the world. David's gay, you're not. I'm short, you're tall. We're different, so what? It is what it is. That's the way I see it."

I shook my head, wondering how my children grew up in our home and could so easily dismiss the beliefs we had tried so hard to instill in them. "How can you say that? Don't you remember anything we tried to teach you? It's all there in black and white."

"I remember, like the part that says 'For God so loved the world.' That sounds like everybody to me. The truth is, I know David better than any of those Bible guys do, and I'll bet if Moses or Paul ever met my brother, they would like him just fine and honor his faith. David is as much like Jesus as anyone around here, and that matters more to me than all of those primitive prohibitions that don't make sense today."

I shook my head. "Dinah, I can't just write off the Bible and ignore what it says."

"Sure you can, Daddy. People do it all the time. Everybody picks and chooses, ignoring parts of it, and beating people over the head with the parts they decide to keep. You know it's true."

Our daughter always packed more punch per pound than anyone, but sometimes it exasperated me. "Okay, you may be right about that, and I know what kind of person your brother is. That's what makes this so difficult for me."

Dinah sat down with a shrug of resignation. "Maybe it's not so tough after all. Do you really want to let the old Hebrews who lived three thousand years ago tell you the score about your own flesh and blood? You know David's heart. Why can't you trust him on this? Why can't you just believe what he's telling you?"

"Dinah, someday I'm going to stand before God and answer for my actions, my teaching, my faithfulness to the Bible. What will I say if I have thrown it all away?"

"Beats me, Daddy, but rejecting your own son won't look too good on the big screen either. Your choice."

***

"Hey, George!" I yelled so my neighbor could hear me over the roar of his big John Deere mower as he mowed along my driveway.

He shut it down as I got out of my car, and looked up with a friendly smile. "How are you doing, Bart?" Neighbors don't come any better than George, one of the few people who just called me by name, leaving off the formal designation.

"Hey, can't you keep that big green monster over in your yard? You're trespassing."

"Just not enough grass to cut in my yard. Thought I might munch on yours, too. I noticed David had been mowing for you this summer and figured he wasn't going to be up to it for a while." George was pushing sixty-five, a retired navy chaplain, devoting his retirement to hospice work and family counseling. He and Linda moved in eight years before and I valued his friendship, always a listening ear and a level-headed perspective.

"Thanks, George, but you didn't have to do that. I would have got around to it."

"Yes, but you don't mow worth a damn. David's much better. He does the detailing, always looks nice. How's he doing?"

"He's good, stronger every day."

"I've been thinking a lot about David, such a good kid. There's lots of talk around town, and I read the paper like everyone else. It's a difficult time for him, and I'm sure it's tough for you and Sally, too. Do you mind if I give you a little unsolicited advice?"

"Of course not, and since when do you ask permission? What's on your mind?"

"Here's the deal, Bart. I suspect you and David are facing some tough personal issues that have a lot of implications for your place in this community. Whatever you do, hang on to that boy, Bart. Don't let him slip away from you. Don't turn loose of him for all the tea in China. The rest isn't worth a damn if you lose your family. And don't let anyone tell you otherwise, my friend. I'm here if I can help, you know that." George had a way of cutting through the fog, like the old sailor he was, to see things clearly.

"Thanks, George, I hear you. It is a tough time for us. I've got some things I need to work through. I appreciate your thoughts and what you said about David. Thanks. I've got to run, have a meeting tonight. Make sure you do a great job on my yard." I turned and headed inside.

"I will. Just make sure you take care of that boy. If you lose him, I'm not mowing your damn yard for you." With that, he turned the key and the mower roared back to life.

***

One of the hazards of serving as a pastor for a long tenure in a small county seat town like Joppa is that jobs and responsibilities tend to accumulate. During my sixteen years at First Baptist Church, I had served on the school board, the hospital trustees, the chamber of commerce, and the ministerial alliance, not to mention PTA and the high school booster club. Most of those jobs had come and gone as my terms gratefully expired, but my involvement with the ministerial alliance was a constant, no re-election required.

Monthly meetings rotated among the large downtown churches, a more convenient location for everyone, and the bigger churches could afford to buy the donuts. Each month about two dozen ministers would gather, representing the full spectrum of Christian faith and practice in Joppa, from Sacred

Heart's Father Tom and the liturgical mainliners, to Pastor Frieda Smith of the Full Faith Gospel Fellowship, and all points in between. Some of our conservative brethren looked askance at the female pastors who participated. It made for lively discussion and sometimes a difficult consensus.

The agenda for these meetings consisted of the obligatory minutes, the treasurer's report, discussion of benevolent needs and projects, and planning for our two annual combined community services, Good Friday and Thanksgiving, which nearly half of the pastors refused to attend or promote because of their doctrinal differences. The meetings could get dicey, or unpleasant, depending on who showed up.

Roger Holcomb served as pastor of Bethany Baptist Church on the highway just north of Joppa. Bethany split from First Baptist many years before I showed up, and I was never clear on the cause of the conflict. Anyway, Bethany had become the home of the true children of God, representing the right end of our theological spectrum. Brother Holcomb was like the prophet Elijah reborn among us, long and lanky with boney fingers always pointing as he talked. During these meetings, and in his occasional newspaper columns, he never hesitated to pass judgment, always ready to denounce and condemn the latest offender of God's holiness. And that week, he came cocked and loaded.

"God will judge this nation for the sins we tolerate and the evils we choose to allow. We have compromised with this godless culture and sold out the Gospel to the liberal, homosexual agenda. If we don't stand up and speak the truth, God will judge us for our cowardice. If we compromise on homosexuality, everything crumbles."

There were nods of approval around the room and a few hearty "Amens" from the like-minded brothers.

Roger rolled on, caught up in the moment. "I say we should choose one Sunday and all of us get up and preach against the gay agenda on the same day, and let the whole county know where we stand, and where this nation is headed if we don't turn back to God's Word. I so move." Roger glared around the room as two pastors offered seconds to the motion.

Then the discussion began.

Lonnie Turpin, from Joppa Assembly of God, spoke first. "I say let's do it. Finally, we stand up for the truth and begin to turn this town and this country back to God."

"Back to God?" said Pete Helms from Countryside Methodist. "It sounds to me like you want to go back to a time when gay folks stayed in the closet and black folks stayed in their place. When was God ever calling the shots around here? Certainly, not back then."

The tension mounted as Roger stood to his feet with fire in his eyes. "Make no mistake, brothers... and sisters, what's at stake here is not just our churches but our homes and our families as well. If we cave on this issue of homosexuality and the sanctity of marriage, we lose the whole ballgame, our homes and our nation. The judgment of God will not only be upon this godless and perverse nation, but also upon the spineless, compromising preachers that refuse to stand up for the truth. We must be the prophets of God. This is our Mount Carmel, and we must be on the Lord's side." The room fell silent as Roger retreated to his chair, his red face beginning to cool.

Then, in a quiet tone, Yvonne Meadows of the United Church of Christ broke the silence. "While I can appreciate your sincerity, Pastor Holcomb, I do not share your views, and I do have one question for all of us to consider. What will become of the gay people who attend our churches—not just mine, but all of our churches? Make no mistake: whether you know the truth about them or not, they are in our pews as we worship. How will they hear these pronouncements? Are you ready to ban them from your church? Where will they go to find the grace and love of God?" She let that question hang in the air for a moment as all eyes turned back to Roger.

He cleared his throat and said, "Jesus came not to call the righteous but sinners to repentance. Those who are sinning and in danger of God's judgment must be warned, or else their blood will be on our hands."

Nods and murmurs of approval rippled around the room.

As for me, I didn't know what to say, so I kept still. In the past, I would have supported Roger's motion, but what if it became known that my son was gay? The rumors had spread all over town. How would I explain my hypocrisy? Renounce my own son? Silence seemed my only option.

When we voted, I raised my hand in favor of the motion, partly from conviction and partly from fear that if I did not, they would guess why. Most of the pastors agreed with Roger, anxious to participate. The mainliners bowed out respectfully, but indicated that they would focus on home and family in their own way. Nonetheless, a strong majority approved the motion, and September 20th was chosen as the special Sunday.

But what to call it? Should we give it a name? Suggestions included 'Salvation Sunday,' 'Return to God Sunday,' 'Revival Sunday,' and finally, 'Gospel

Truth Sunday,' which carried the day. On that one Sunday, fourteen Bible-believing pastors would be preaching the Gospel truth about homosexuality, and calling for repentance and sexual purity.

As I was leaving, Roger shook my hand and gave me a long knowing gaze. "I'm sure praying for your family these days, Brother Bart. Praying for your son, that he will follow in the Lord's ways and not stray from the truth. We've got to show the way and be godly examples to our people. We men of God must rule our own households or be disqualified. You know what the scripture says."

I nodded, having no desire to extend this conversation. "I appreciate your prayers, Roger. Thanks."

When I walked out to my car, Yvonne Meadows stood waiting for me. "I wanted to tell you, Bart, that I'm praying for David and the other boy who was attacked. Your son is a brave young man. You must be very proud of him."

"Thanks, Yvonne, that's kind of you to say. I appreciate your prayers and concern."

As I drove across town, a troubling question confronted me, pointing an accusing finger in my face: *Am I proud or am I ashamed?*

***

On the way to the church, I noticed Luther Gray sitting in his usual spot on one of the large stone planters that marked the intersection of Benton and Main. Luther was dressed, as always, in his ragged jeans, muddy boots, and his army surplus jacket pulled over layers of dirty t-shirts, no matter the temperature. His gray hair and beard framed his dark African American features.

His ensemble never varied, probably all he had, always topped off with his black "Colt 45" cap.

Nobody knew Luther's story. Neither did he. No family around now. He'd finished the eighth grade all those years ago, and it seemed like he'd been sitting at that four-way stop ever since. He had a little landscaping business that he ran out of a concrete shed by the animal shelter. Since he volunteered at the shelter, they let him use the space — probably slept there, too. Other than landscaping, Luther's other skill was parking cars. At every high school game or event, the county fair, or the July 4th picnic, he stood his post, flashlight in hand, directing traffic. Everybody knew him and most folks appreciated his friendly demeanor, though as you might expect, a few were mean to Luther, targeting him with various forms of cruelty.

I worried about his health, knowing that he didn't eat often or well. I pulled to the curb and lowered my window. "Hi, Luther, how are you doing today? Keeping busy?"

"Hey, Brother Bart. I'm okay. You know me. I work hard every day they let me."

I reached in my cup holder for an envelope and pulled out a ticket. "Luther, did you hear about the chili supper that the booster club is putting on tonight before the game?"

"Sure did. I'm in charge of the parking at the high school, you know, so I'll be there."

I handed him a ticket. "Here you go, Luther. After you finish your parking duties, go on in and get some dinner. They're serving pie, too."

He took the ticket and shoved it in his pocket. "Thank you, Brother Bart. You're a kind man. I love pie, all kinds, don't matter to me. What do I owe ya?"

"Oh, nothing, Luther. I have these extra tickets I need to use, and besides, when you park all those cars, you've earned your chili and pie."

"I guess I have. Didn't think of that. Hey, I heard what happened to your boy. That's a terrible mean thing they did to him."

"Yes, it was, Luther."

"You know, they done mean things to me, too. I got scars to prove it. Once, I thought they was gonna kill me, but someone came along and shamed 'em out of it. Sounds like that's what your son did. Some folks think being mean is their job or something. They got nothin' better to do—all filled up with hate. I'm sorry about your boy, Brother Bart. I hope he's better soon."

"Thanks, Luther, I'll tell David what you said. You take care of yourself."

Luther nodded and smiled as I pulled away.

***

I tried to take Fridays as my day off. It didn't always work out, but that was my plan. In nice weather, the golf course beckoned. Over the years in Joppa, I had found three golf buddies who did not attend my church, an easy-going trio who didn't mind letting me be just one of the guys. Our rounds at the country club were always good medicine for me, and never more needed than that particular week.

"Hey, Dud, nice shorts. Did you sleep in those? Did they come with a matching top?" None of us were great golfers, but we were world class talkers, and we showed no mercy in our weekly two-man scramble.

"Nice drive, Flips. Does your husband play this game? Better play the reds next time."

Greg Phillips was a local dentist and the shortest hitter among us. Steve Dudley was a Remax agent who matched my slice with his hook. Cory Moss managed the Winn-Dixie in Joppa. Cory was the best golfer in our foursome and I was the worst, so we were always paired up against Steve and Greg.

Cory coached me around the course in a laid-back, good-natured way. He made it a habit to stand behind me as I prepared to hit a shot and whisper, "Slow, Bart. Nice and slow." Sometimes it helped, often it didn't, but he never quit trying to improve my game.

After the front nine, we grabbed a hot dog and sat down for a few minutes.

Steve brought it up. "Bart, what are you going to do about David? Man, people are talking. First everyone said he was a hero, and I think he was. Now they say he's that Summers kid's queer lover or something. It's ugly, really ugly. What are you going to do about it?"

Greg followed with, "What can he do, Dud? You can't sue people for gossip, and Oliver was too damn careful in the paper. There's no way to get him on that. But you're right, it's ugly. It's shameful."

"What about your church?" Cory said. "There's bound to be trouble there if this talk keeps going. You've got some people in that church who don't take prisoners, Bart. You know it better than I do."

"All I know is I love my son and I love my church. Beyond that, I can't say what will happen."

My partner summed it up as we picked up our clubs for the back nine. "Well, we're with you, Bart, hell or high water, whatever we can do. We'll stand with you whatever happens. Just don't leave. Dump the church if you have to, but stick around to play golf."

I tried to chuckle but couldn't manage it. "Thanks, guys. Hopefully, it won't come to that."

***

When my sister, Janice, called from Memphis to say she wanted to come for a visit, I should have known something was up. We had always been close, but we rarely got together except for the annual reunion on Memorial Day weekend. A phone call once a month or so, a few pictures or posts on Facebook, kept us in touch. But here she was, taking time off from her demanding job as a hospital administrator to spend nearly a week with her little brother and his family in Joppa, Georgia, not exactly a prime vacation spot.

Sally and Janice took a drive up to Chattanooga to see Dinah one day, and another afternoon they shopped in Atlanta. We all went to the Braves game on Friday night, which was David's first real outing since the attack.

Janice asked me to go to breakfast with her on Saturday, and I sensed that whatever she wanted to talk about, this was likely her main reason for visiting us. We settled into a booth at the diner and after our breakfast plates were cleared and our coffee cups refilled, she came around to her agenda.

"Bart, I want to talk to you about David. You guys have always been close. I remember how he followed you around when he was little, how he mimicked your walk, and even pretended to preach to Dinah when she would sit still for it. Remember that?"

"Sure," I said. "David was always a little man, in a hurry to grow up and do grown-up things."

She looked down as she stirred her coffee. "He loves you, Bart, and respects you as much as any son could respect his father. You know that's true. He needs your love and respect in return."

"David knows I love him. That's never been in doubt."

"I know, but he needs you to love and accept him as he is, who he is. He can sense the tension, the distance between you. We all can. He feels like he's lost you, lost your respect as a son, as a man, and as a person of faith."

I leaned back with a deep sigh, unsure how to answer. "I don't know what to say, Jan. I don't know how I should act towards David. He feels rejected and I get that, but so do I. He has rejected me, my beliefs, my life's work. How can things ever be the same between us?"

"Well, little brother, I have a theory about that, but first let me ask you something. Why do you suppose homosexuality is such a sink or swim, life or death issue for you? On lots of other subjects, you are more open-minded, respectful of different points of view. I would never call you a hardline fundamentalist, Bart, but you certainly are on this subject. Yet you do know, don't you, that there are many devout, God-loving Christians who are accepting of gays and lesbians?"

"I can't answer for them, Jan, but I have to be true to the scripture, to my faith, to the Gospel as I understand it. I can't turn my back on the truth."

"Okay, I hear you, but this is not one of your deacons sitting here this morning. I'm not here to argue about the Bible. This is your sister, and I wonder if there might be something else driving you, something deeper that you may not have considered."

As she spoke, I sat up straight, moving my cup to the side. I wasn't prepared for what came next.

"Bart, have you ever talked to anyone about when we were kids, what happened to you when we lived in Merrifield?"

A wave of nausea washed over me as she called to mind the deepest secret of my childhood. "No, no one. Only you."

She reached for my hand and lowered her voice just above a whisper. "I'm wondering how what happened to you might be affecting you, influencing you, without you even realizing it. Could David's coming out be bringing some of that nightmare back to the surface? You know, Bart, not every homosexual is a pervert or a child molester."

My sister was suddenly calling to mind images and feelings that had laid dormant for decades. Against my wishes, an old dark movie began to play in my mind.

***

Out of the deep fog, an old clapboard garage emerged, one side standing open with room for a car or a lawn tractor, and the other side closed in as a tool shed with a workbench. It was just across a dead-end street from the house where we spent our early childhood. A divorced woman lived in the accompanying house with her son, Ronnie, and her father, Mr. Keller.

As kids, Janice and I and our little brother, Jerry, had the free run of the neighborhood, often invited back and forth for meals and overnights with neighbors and friends down the street. My parents, like most moms and dads back then, gave little thought to their kid's security, let alone any potential abuser lurking about.

It began innocently enough. Mr. Keller was kind and friendly, me being just a six-year-old boy. He liked to talk and usually spent much of his time in that dark garage, tinkering at his workbench, so I would stop by. Sometimes he had fruit or candy bars. He would show me how each tool worked or tell me stories of his past. Strangely, though, every conversation ended with an awkward hug, and later, with a kiss, which made me uncomfortable.

After that, my memories were largely repressed, just a series of frightening snapshots, blurry images of his hands on me, his mouth on me, my penis. The sight of his erect penis in my face and his prodding to give him a kiss. The horrid smell. His grip on the back of my neck, his hold on my pants when I tried to run away. His stern threats if I told anyone about our kisses. The fear and shame. Lying awake at night and staring at that garage from our bedroom window.

I had no way of knowing how long or how often such things happened to me. Only our move to another town finally delivered me from his clutches.

My parents never knew what Mr. Keller had done to me. I only told Janice years later, and as she suspected, I had confided in no one else, not even Sally. I broke every rule of good mental health, ignoring the counsel I myself had given countless victims through the years, and now my sister had the audacity to suggest that the abuse I endured as a small boy might impact how I viewed homosexual behavior in general, and in my own family.

I'd heard it said that naming the demon was the first step in the process of exorcism. For me, reviewing those haunting images was my first step to finally escaping that dark garage and knowing my own heart.

***

"Pastor, you have a visitor. Pastor Yvonne Meadows is here to see you."

I was just back from lunch and catching up on some correspondence. "Show her in, Donna. That would be fine." I stepped to the door to greet my unexpected guest.

Yvonne greeted me wearing her clerical collar with a satchel of books under her arm. "Good afternoon, Bart. Thanks for seeing me. I know I didn't have an appointment."

Though I had known Yvonne for several years through the ministerial alliance, I could not recall a conversation apart from those meetings. "No problem. This is a nice surprise. What can I do for you? Would you like some coffee?"

"Thank you, but no, only two cups in the morning. I won't stay long. I've just been thinking of you since last month's meeting. That whole discussion had to be painful for you. I read the paper and I hear the talk like everyone else. I want you to know I'm praying for you and your family, especially David. Here he is, a young man who does a noble deed, and it gets treated like a scandal. Such a shame." Her sincerity shined through her warm smile.

"Thank you. That's thoughtful of you. These are difficult days for us, but we are muddling through, trying to make sense of this whole situation."

Yvonne had her satchel on her lap debating what to do with it. Before I could ask, she continued. "Bart, did I ever mention to you that I grew up in a Southern Baptist church?"

I was thoroughly surprised. "No, I had no idea. Where are you from?"

"I grew up in a small town, Freeport, Virginia. My father was a deacon and a Sunday School teacher in the church. My mother taught the children and sang in the choir. She still does. Dad's been gone a few years now."

"Really? That's something. I have to ask. How does a Southern Baptist girl grow up to be a pastor in a UCC church?"

"Well, that's probably a longer story than you want to hear, so I'll give you the short version. When I was seventeen, I became aware of two surprising realities. First, I felt a call to ministry, which my pastor would not acknowledge or encourage. Second, I realized that I am gay, which my church would never accept. So, I had no choice but to find a new place to worship and serve."

"I had no idea, Yvonne. I don't know what to say." I had struggled enough in recent years, adjusting to women in ministry, and never even considered the possibility of gay women as clergy.

"It was a painful, disillusioning time for me, rejected by my family and shunned by the congregation that had been my spiritual home since I was a toddler."

"I can't imagine," I said, thinking out loud.

"I guess that's why I am here, Bart. I wouldn't want anyone to go through what me and my family experienced. It took years to reconcile with Mom and Dad, and I'm still the daughter my mother doesn't talk about. She's still embarrassed and ashamed."

"I'm sorry. That sounds awful."

"It was as bad as it sounds." She dabbed a tear from her eye and cleared her throat. "Bart, it's not my place to interfere or to judge, but there's something I need to say. If your son David is gay, please don't make the same mistake my parents made. Don't reject him. Don't send him away."

My defenses cracked and crumbled as she spoke. "Honestly, Yvonne, I don't know what to do. I feel torn and confused. I love my son more than my own life, but if I turn my back on my beliefs, then I'm a fraud and a failure as a pastor, as a Christian."

"I'm not so sure about that," she said, lifting her satchel to her lap. "I believe the Bible as surely as you do. I don't question your integrity or your sincerity, but maybe it's time for you to take a fresh look."

Her face radiated genuine concern, and I could not take offense.

"I have something for you, Bart. I hope I'm not being presumptuous when I loan you a few books that you may not have on your shelf, which might be helpful these days. They all deal with sexuality in the scripture. Keep them as long as you like, and use them or don't, as you wish. But, if you would like to talk about what you find here, I'll be happy to discuss it with you. Give me a call."

I took the satchel from her hands as she stood to go. "Thank you. That's thoughtful of you, Yvonne. I am not offended, though I might have been a few months ago. I'll look these over and maybe we can talk. We may not always agree, but we will both be wiser from comparing notes. Thanks, again."

When we got to the door, she turned and extended her hand. "You are welcome. You and your family are in my prayers."

"I appreciate it. Thanks for coming by."

***

I sat in my office with books and Bible commentaries scattered across my desk, two weeks' worth of reading and study. Since David's confession, I had to admit to myself that I had never done a careful study of homosexuality in the Bible. Knowing how David felt served as a strong motivator for me, and I wanted to be able to tell him I had done my homework thoroughly and fairly. With Yvonne's resources I was able to study a wide variety of scholars and interpreters, a broader spectrum than I typically read. This was helpful to me, even refreshing.

For most Christians growing up in the sixties and seventies, homosexuality was considered perverted and twisted, certainly sinful. None of my fellow students in seminary seemed troubled or confused on the subject. It was never seriously discussed or debated, not where I went to school. So, this was a first for me and I tried to approach my research with an open mind. I was surprised, even stunned by what I found and what I didn't find. What had seemed clear and straightforward was not so simple after all. I needed to reconsider my old assumptions.

I thought about all that I had written and said through the years, sermons and lessons. Those blanket statements, my confident pronouncements and high-handed condemnations, replayed in my mind. My face flushed hot with embarrassment as I remembered those counseling sessions through the years, the advice I had given to parents, the troubled teenagers that felt broken, unwanted, and unloved, rejected by God. What did I say? What had I done? Like Job, I wanted to put my hand over my mouth and admit that I had spoken of things I did not know. With painful regret, I had to admit that any honest look at the biblical evidence must at least leave room for greater openness and understanding toward gay people.

As I sipped my coffee and reflected on the results of my study, I thought of what I should do now. How could I as a pastor suddenly change my mind on the most emotional and controversial issue in our culture? But how could I keep it to myself? If I opened my mouth so freely when I was mistaken, how could I keep silent now?

***

As I was finishing up my sermon for Sunday, Donna buzzed me. "Pastor, Stanley Pulliam is here if you have a minute."

Stanley was a longtime deacon of the church, one of our prominent Bible teachers, always leaning to the right, politically and scripturally. Through the years, I never had to worry about Stanley straying from the straight and narrow. He stood for the literal truth of the Bible with little room for discussion or debate. Stanley was tall and gray, retired military, in his early seventies, but still stood ramrod straight and looked at me with steely blue eyes. I couldn't put my finger on it, but for some reason, I never felt like I quite measured up to Stanley's ideal of a 'man of God.'

"That's fine, Donna. Send him in." I met Stanley at the door and greeted him with a friendly handshake. My welcome seemed to slow him down a bit, but Stanley was all business. I offered him a chair and, as he got comfortable, he came straight to the point.

"Pastor, I've been hearing things around town, disturbing things, things that grieve my spirit. I had to come see you to let you put my mind at ease if you can." He was visibly distressed, his brow furrowed with concern.

"How can I help you, Stanley? What is troubling you?"

He looked down for a moment and shifted in his chair. Then he lifted his gaze to mine. "I'm just going to ask you directly, Pastor. Is your son a homosexual? I'm sorry to ask, but I've been hearing the talk all over town. Is it true? Is David a homo?"

"I guess it's no secret at this point. David told his mother and I that he is gay. He told us after the incident at the truck stop, but he said he's known that he is gay for several years. His friends have known for a while, but this was all new to us. We had no idea. But that's what he said and that's what he believes."

Stanley leaned forward shaking his head. "Oh my, I'm sorry, Pastor, so sorry for you and Sally. Gosh, we never know what kind of trouble our kids will get into in this godless world. I'll pray for David, I sure will. He always seemed to be a good Christian boy, and then to go and get caught up in something like that.... What a shame."

"I'm not sure how we will handle this, Stanley. We never saw it coming."

He slowly got to his feet, standing tall in front of my desk, and I stood up as well. "Pastor, we can't control everything our kids do, we all know that. The Bible says that those who lead the church should rule their families well, and I know this doesn't look good for you. It's not a good witness to our community, but you just keep preaching the Gospel, and we'll stand by you while you work this out. Whatever David does, you just stand up for the truth of God's Word. That's what your son needs, what the whole world needs." He shook my hand and headed for the door.

"I appreciate your concern, Stanley. Thanks for coming by."

The door closed and I collapsed into my chair, thinking, *What do I do now?*

***

The afternoon drizzle thickened to an early evening downpour as I headed for home. I spotted Luther walking down Benton, still about ten blocks from his place by the animal shelter. I pulled up to the curb and pushed open the passenger door.

"Hop in, Luther, or you're going to get soaked."

He climbed in with an expression of relief. "Thanks, Brother Bart. It's really comin' down. Takes me a long time anymore to dry off and warm up. Appreciate the ride."

"Are you going home, Luther? Can I drop you there?"

"Sure, I had some work this morning. I'm a muddy mess. Sorry if I smell like shit, but that's what I've been doing, putting out fertilizer." He wasn't kidding about the smell, and the rain didn't help.

"That's okay, Luther. I've noticed sometimes you smell like a flower garden and other times you smell like a compost pile."

He laughed and smiled. "Yep, I have some sunny days and some shitty days. I guess we all do, don't we?"

"You're right about that."

"Lately, you been having more than your share of shitty days, haven't you, Brother Bart? I been hearing the talk around town. People ain't bein' kind. They say your son is a faggot and you don't have the balls to deal with it, cause God hates fags. It's what they say."

Sometimes I wished Luther wasn't quite so honest and straightforward.

"I can't help what people think, Luther. We're just doing the best we can." As I stopped my car in front of his shed, he looked at me thoughtfully, and I knew he had more to say.

"Know what I think? I don't think God is a big white man in the sky. I think he's got to be every tribe and color, like a rainbow. And the way I see it, God would have to be a he and a she, not one or the other, our father and our mother. You know, I don't have any family, so God has to be my papa and my mama."

"That's a beautiful thought, Luther. I think you're right about that."

"And if you ask me, I bet God swings both ways, queers and fags just the same as everybody else. I think it's one big family, all God's children. What do you think, Brother Bart? Am I full of shit? I already smell like it."

I put my hand on his shoulder and looked in his kind face. "Luther, you might be the wisest person I know, certainly the most honest."

***

Sally was already in bed when I came upstairs, trying to focus on a novel she had nearly finished. We hadn't talked much since David's revelation at the breakfast table. She had been focused on David's recovery, and with Janice's visit, there wasn't much time for real conversation. Sally seemed to feel better with each passing week, less weepy, a little more comfortable with our situation.

I didn't speak of my conversation with Janice. The time would come to tell her about that dark chapter in my childhood, but not in this present crisis. One revelation at a time. I had shared my study notes with Sally so she could understand what I had learned from my research, but she was not much interested or impressed.

"How I feel about David and how we treat our son," she'd insisted, "will not be determined by your study notes or anybody else's. I may not know Leviticus, but I know our son, the kind of person he is, his faith. That's what matters to me."

So, we didn't talk much then, either.

I set my alarm and crawled in bed, putting my cell phone on the headboard. I reached for a biography of Theodore Roosevelt I had been working my way through, and had read just a few pages when Sally laid her novel aside, turned off her lamp, and slipped over close to me.

"How are you doing, Sweetheart? Are you okay?" she asked.

"I'm okay, except some woman just put her ice-cold feet against my bare leg."

"It's the only way I can get warm, you know that."

"How about those fuzzy thermal socks I bought you?"

"It's summertime. I can't wear fuzzy socks in the summer." Sally always had her own logic to things.

My thoughts turned back to David. "Sal, did you ever suspect that David was gay? Any indication as he was growing up? Any hint of it?"

"I've thought a lot about that since he told us, and in hindsight, maybe we missed a clue here and there, little indications that we didn't recognize or chose to ignore — his relationships, his close friends, his interests. Maybe we were not the most observant and involved parents, Bart."

I put my book back on the headboard and put my arm around Sally as she snuggled in close. "Maybe not, Sal. I never even allowed for the possibility of having a gay child. I always believed that if you raised your child in the faith and tried to be positive role models as parents, then you could count on having a godly, righteous kid."

"I think we did, Bart, and we do. We do have a godly, righteous kid. 'Train up a child in the way he should go....' It's been true for us. Gay or straight, David is still the kind of person we always hoped he would be."

"I know, you're right. We did raise a great son, no matter what anyone thinks or says."

"Have you said that to David? Have you told him that you are proud of him and that you accept him as he is? You know he's struggling. He's facing all the criticism, those judgmental attitudes, all the ugliness, and he's not complaining or whining about it. But what he needs more than anything is to know that you are in his corner, Bart, that you will stand by him. Talk to him. He needs his father right now."

"I guess I've left him hanging all this time while I struggled with my own crisis. I'll talk to David tomorrow." We laid awake for a while pondering the storm ahead.

"What are you going to do at First Baptist, Bart? What's going to happen? You know those deacons. It's black and white to them. If you speak up about homosexuality, you'll be fired the same day. You know it's true. Then what will happen to us?"

"I don't know, Sally. I don't know what we'll do, but I do know this. If David found the courage to confront those thugs at the truck stop, then I can face a room full of deacons. I'm not backing down and I won't keep quiet. After that, it's in God's hands." I turned my head to look in her eyes. "Are we together on that, Sal?"

"Side by side, Sweetheart, side by side."

I reached for the lamp and turned toward Sally. Her arms encircled me in the darkness, my head resting on her shoulder, her warmth the antidote for my fear.

***

The next afternoon, I asked David to go for a walk with me. We took the car over to the city park, following our old routine. When the kids were younger, we would take long walks around the lake at the park, following a wide gravel path used by boaters and maintenance vehicles. The September sun lingered warm and bright, no hint of autumn color yet in our part of Georgia.

"How long since we walked here, David?" I asked as we left the car and headed toward the path.

"A long time, Dad. I can't remember when, before high school maybe."

"Lots of good memories though, when you kids were little."

"Sure. Dinah always running ahead, that time she went skinny-dipping. Me wandering off the trail, getting poison ivy. Mom running from that squirrel."

We laughed as comic scenes replayed in our minds.

"Try to stay on the path today, okay?" I said.

"Will do." We walked on past the first fishing pier. "This was a good idea."

"Yeah. Gives us a chance to talk. I know things have been tense between us. It's been strange not to be able to communicate, to even know what to say to you, Son."

"I hate it, too, the distance between us, the disapproval and disappointment that I feel and you must feel, too. I never wanted it to be this way."

"David, there's something I need to say, something I should have told you sooner, but I had to do some soul-searching of my own. I need to tell you I was wrong, dead wrong, and I've been wrong for a long time. I can't change that. I can't take back all the words I have spoken, but I can be honest about what I have come to believe today."

David stopped and turned face to face, his eyes brimming with tears. "Do you mean it, Dad? You changed your mind?"

I put my hands on his shoulders and looked in his eyes. "I want you to know that your mother and I love you and accept you just as you are. If you are gay, then God bless your gayness. I'm with you, son. I'll stand with you and support you, privately and publicly. You've always made us proud, and I'm sorry for all the pain I've caused you." David stepped into my embrace, and I held my son for a long moment.

"I love you, Dad."

We walked a while without words before David spoke. "I guess you have revised your thinking about the Bible?"

"Certainly, I have a better idea of what it says and what it does not say. But that's not the main thing for me. Do you know what the game changer was for me?"

David shrugged and shook his head.

"It's you, Son. It's you. You are the best argument I know. You are indisputable proof in my book."

"Thanks, Dad. That means more than I can say."

Chapter 3 – Truth Bomb

"If someone is gay and he searches for the Lord and has good will, who am I to judge? We shouldn't marginalize people for this. They must be integrated into society."
~ Pope Francis

Brian brought up the subject in staff meeting. "What's this 'Gospel Truth Sunday' I read about in the newspaper? Roger Holcomb was quoted saying that on September 20, all the pastors in Joppa are going to preach the 'Gospel Truth' about the Bible and homosexuality. Let everyone in town know where we stand, he said. And, First Baptist was listed as one of the participating churches. Is that right?" He was clearly miffed that he had to read about it in the newspaper. "It sure came up suddenly, and I must say, the timing seems more than a little suspicious."

I answered, "It was sudden, Brian, in the meeting two weeks ago. I should have mentioned it sooner. Sorry about that. I was there when it was decided. It was Roger's idea though, like you said. Not all the churches are participating, but most are, including all the Baptist churches. So, we're in, too."

"Since when does Roger Holcomb decide what you preach around here?" Randall asked. I never had to wonder where Randall Shirley stood on things. "I am fed up with Pastor Holcomb's habit of speaking for all of the churches without their knowledge or input. You know he's doing this now because of the rumors about David and the Summers boy."

"That may be, but I'm not opting out. We're going to participate and I'm going to address the subject as best I know how."

No one spoke for a moment as we tried to focus on our agenda.

Then Brian added, "I respect you, Pastor. You are our leader, our preacher, our Bible teacher. But I don't envy you. I mean, how will David hear it? How do you preach the hard truth to those you love? That's tough. I'll pray for you, Pastor."

"Thanks, Brian. I appreciate your concern and your prayers. Keep them coming. I am hopeful that all the people I love will be able to hear and accept what I have to say. We'll see."

***

I decided to hit the gym early that morning, determined to work off some of the stress weighing on me. David had arrived earlier, being more disciplined in his exercise routine. I pounded away on the treadmill for thirty minutes and hoisted a few free weights. I was spent, done, all I could do. David finished his workout while I caught my breath, so we walked out together.

"It's good to see you working out again," I said.

"Yeah, but it was weird, like working out by myself. People cleared out wherever I went—the ellipticals, the free weights, the water cooler, the locker room."

"That is strange. We've been working out here for years. How's Daniel doing by now?"

"He's home now, after eighteen days in the hospital and three surgeries—his jaw, his eye socket, and his eye. They're still not sure how much vision he will have in his left eye, probably not much, but he's in better spirits since he's home. I saw him last night and told him about your change of heart. He was surprised and pleased, I think."

"Give him our best when you see him. Let him know we continue to pray for him as he recovers."

"I will, Dad. I'll see him tomorrow night."

We walked around the sidewalk to the lot behind the gym, the only available parking during the busy hours. We both saw his old silver Honda Civic at the same moment. David dropped his bag and ran to the car, fell to his knees, and frantically tried to wipe off the word sprayed in large letters on his car door, but the black paint was already dry, the word: *FAG*.

***

My morning of study passed quickly. I found myself invigorated as I went about my preparation, searching the scripture with new eyes. How much of what I had preached for all those years was based more on my own assumptions and a selective reading of the Bible. I couldn't help but wonder how much I had missed and how many other "infallible" interpretations needed to be revisited. Donna's buzz interrupted my thoughts.

"Priscilla Larson is here to see you. She called yesterday. I left you a note on your desk."

I had failed to notice the pink slip in the corner of my desk pad with Donna's clear penmanship. "Thanks, Donna, I found it. Tell Priscilla I'll be with her in a moment."

Priscilla Larson had joined First Baptist a few years before, but not for the best of reasons. Forty-two years old and three times divorced, Priscilla was in the market for husband number four. She seemed to exude her sexuality, her blonde hair and voluptuous figure strenuously maintained. I had counseled Priscilla through her two most recent breakups, and I soon developed a new set of ground rules just for her. At first, I had to admit I was flattered by her subtle overtures to me, though I never encouraged her in any way. I soon learned that Priscilla could not resist coming on to any male who would pay her attention.

She came for her counseling appointments dressed to kill, with low-cut necklines and short skirts. She never missed an opportunity to show off her cleavage, and sometimes she would cross her legs slowly, with the slightest hesitation, inviting a casual glance up her skirt. It was pitiful. It reminded me of when David was just a little guy and insisted on showing everyone his new Spiderman jockey shorts. I wondered how emotionally needy a woman must be to hit on her pastor in a counseling session.

Sally found Priscilla's flirting to be sadly humorous. "Don't let Priscilla take advantage of you, old man," she would tease as I headed to an appointment. "Tell her you are not that easy."

I told Sally that I could refuse to counsel Priscilla, refer her to another pastor, if she felt uncomfortable about it, but she never felt threatened.

"No, you are her pastor. You should minister to her and counsel her when she needs help. Besides, it's probably good for your circulation."

So, I learned quickly to stay on my side of the desk during my sessions with Priscilla. My spacious office had a couch and two chairs, but I always directed Priscilla to one of the side chairs in front of my desk. On this day, I had no idea what she wanted to discuss, since our counseling had ended several months before.

She greeted me pleasantly. "Good morning, Pastor Bart. It's good to see you. How is David doing by now? Better I hope." She made herself at home, taking her usual chair in front of my desk

I moved back to my leather desk chair. "I'm fine, Priscilla, and David is getting better, stronger each day. Thanks for asking."

"I feel just terrible about what happened to David and that other boy. You know one of those boys that did it, Mark Hampton, is a cousin to my second husband, at least by marriage, I think. I can't imagine how anyone could do such a thing. It's so ugly and cruel." She seemed sincerely concerned and thoughtful.

"It is hard to believe, Priscilla, but I guess such things happen around here. We know it's true. Usually, it's racism in this neck of the woods, good old boys determined to keep black people in their place, but this time it was different."

"That's what troubles me most, Pastor. I don't think a person should be judged for their sexuality. It seems like that's standard equipment to me. Sex is part of what comes naturally to everyone, something to be celebrated, not denied." She had stated clearly her own approach to all things sexual.

"You're right about the standard equipment part, Priscilla. I used to think of it as a simple choice people make, to be gay or straight, but now I know better. Sexual orientation is part of who we are. It's not an option we choose. On the other hand, how we live out our sexuality is all about the choices we make, and we are certainly responsible for our sexual behavior."

"People are saying ugly things, Pastor, about David and about you, too. They're saying David is gay like his friend, Daniel. Queer lovers, they say. Some of the ladies at the salon even suggested that you might be gay yourself, having a family with Sally just as a cover, so that you could be in the ministry. Such things have happened, you know. I've seen it on Dr. Phil, men who have a wife and children, but are really homosexual and have male lovers on the side."

"Where are you going with this, Priss? Are you asking me if I am gay?"

"Well, I was thinking about my sessions with you, all those times we talked. You did seem uncomfortable at times, being alone with me, a younger woman. Was that it, Pastor? Were you just not attracted to me because you are gay?"

"Priscilla, I'm your pastor and your friend. You are a beautiful woman and a good person, but I'm not attracted to you sexually because I am very much in love with my wife. Sally is not my cover, she is my partner and companion, the love of my life. Our son's sexuality is part of his standard equipment, as you said. Right now, we are all just figuring this out, what it means for our family. I do appreciate your concern."

Priscilla blushed as she rose to her feet and extended her hand. "Thank you for your time, Pastor. That's kind of you to say. I hope I haven't offended you. I heard the talk and just had to ask."

I nodded as I shook her hand. As she slipped out of my office, I shook my head in disbelief.

***

I stopped by Martin's Hardware on the way home from the church. Sally had called about a problem with the garbage disposal, probably too many potato peels. It never did work well, and she wanted to get it replaced.

The church had a fund for the maintenance and upkeep of the parsonage, so I stopped by to get a price on a new one.

Martin's Hardware Store was a throwback to a bygone era, equal parts hardware store, dime store, and general store. Hugh Martin had apparently been dragged into the twenty-first century against his will, refusing to carry anything that smacked of new technology while continuing to carry all the odds and ends of the good old days. Browsing in Martin's was like flashing back to my childhood. He even carried some of the old candies that were hard to find these days — Sugar Babies and Cherry Mash, and real Jaw Breakers. While the store was delightful, the store's owner was anything but pleasant. Gruff and profane, Hugh Martin was not a church-going man. In fact, he often criticized "church people" to the point of ridicule. Nonetheless, for some unknown reason, he was always respectful to me.

"Good afternoon, Mr. Martin. How are you today?"

He was bending over a box of receipts, his ledger opened on the counter. Broad shoulders and a square jaw gave him the look of a boxer or a bouncer. Pushing seventy years old, with just a wisp of sandy hair still standing on his bald head, Hugh Martin never considered retirement. He was all business. He wore long-sleeved, blue chambray work shirts every day, year around, and a canvas apron hung from his neck, tied around his waist. On warm days, he rolled up his sleeves, uncovering his massive forearms and a Marine Corps insignia.

I was certain that no sane person ever considered shoplifting from Martin's, let alone robbing the place.

"Hello, preacher. I'll bet I'm doing a damn sight better than you today. How's that boy of yours? Is he going to be all right?"

"Yes, he is. Thank you for asking. My wife wanted me to come by and price a new garbage disposal. Our old one runs but it gets clogged a lot. Maybe we need a bigger one. How much does a new disposal run?" As I spoke, he moved around the counter and started down an aisle, and I followed.

"About three bucks to begin with," he said as he reached down and picked up a large bottle of Drano. "Try this first. Half a bottle, wait fifteen minutes, turn on the water real hot, run the disposal a couple of minutes, then do it again with the other half. Should open it right up, work like a new one. If it doesn't, come back and we'll get you fixed up." He handed me the Drano and headed back to the counter and cash register.

"Thanks. That sounds like a plan. I've never tried that before." He nodded as he rang up the total and I handed him the cash.

"It's in the book, the manual for the damn thing, but nobody ever reads it." He handed me the change and leaned back against his desk with his burly arms folded across his chest. No one else was in the store. "I'm sorry for what you're going through, preacher, I really am, but none of this trouble surprises me, and I can't imagine it surprises you much either. You know better than anyone what kind of people you have over there at that church. It's the biggest bunch of self-righteous hypocrites on God's green earth. Parading around like the children of God, but all the while living like the devil—crooked businessmen, cheaters and adulterers, and such bigots. You know there are Klansmen in that church, and more than one or two. I've been around this town since I got back from Nam, and I'm telling you, no matter how well they clean up on Sunday, there's some dirty sons of bitches in that church of yours. It's the truth. Huh, sorry if that offends you." Mr. Martin never hesitated to speak his mind regardless of his audience.

"My advice, preacher, is to get your family and get on down the road. You don't need this shit. Your family has enough to deal with now. Don't let those bastards come after you, and you know they will."

I had never heard my congregation described quite like that before. I wasn't sure how to respond to genuine concern and harsh criticism coming all at once.

"I appreciate your concern for my family, Mr. Martin. I won't deny that there is hypocrisy, perhaps quite a bit of hypocrisy, in the church I serve. But I also believe there are some good, devout people. When these difficult times come, I have to hope that the faithful will do the right thing." He nodded as I turned to go. "Thank you for your help. Have a good evening."

***

Later that evening, I turned off the ballgame—had too much on my mind to pay attention. Sally was out with Dinah, and David had gone to see Daniel Summers. Alone in our suddenly silent house, I strolled into David's old room and turned on his desk lamp. His speech and debate trophies needed dusting. On the shelf above, three shoe boxes contained his spiral notebooks, shoved in on their side like big file folders with the spirals sticking up, maybe twenty notebooks in each box. David had always been a writer, keeping a "Top Secret" journal when he was barely able to write. Though he wasn't so concerned with security anymore, keeping a journal had become a daily discipline.

I lifted the middle shoe box off the shelf and pulled out a green spiral from his high school days. Sitting on the bed, I browsed a few pages of typical high school fare, until I came upon these words from David's hand:

> *What's wrong with me? Where do these feelings come from? Are they from heaven or from hell? Am I broken, twisted, corrupted? If I don't understand myself, how will anyone else know who I am? Questions I cannot answer.*
>
> *Do I have to carry this secret all my life or risk the rejection of my family, those who love me most? Dad is quick to judge and condemn, certain of God's wrath on those who struggle like me. How can I be loved and hated at the same time?*
>
> *I sit in church and listen, not to the rejection of my father, but for the welcome of my heavenly Father.*
>
> *"Though my father and mother forsake me, the Lord will receive me." - Psalm 27:10*

I dropped the notebook on the floor as I wept, the first tears I had cried for years.

What have I done? What needless pain have I caused my own son and how many others?

I slipped down on my knees beside the bed, sobbed and prayed. "Forgive me, Father. Forgive me. Let me never speak another word in your name that is not soaked in your love and grace."

***

"You've really got some balls, Bart. Damn!" I had never seen George so animated. "You're going to get up in the pulpit of First Baptist Church of Joppa, Georgia, and tell them you've been wrong all along about homosexuality and the Bible. Turns out, Jesus loves gay people, too.

Holy shit! I'm coming to your church that day. I've got to see this. You might want to have some paramedics standing by, buddy. Gaskets will be blown."

George and I sat on his deck cooling off with some late afternoon lemonade while I filled him in on my plans. Stunned, concerned, and strangely pleased, he could barely stay in his chair.

"Don't get me wrong, Bart. I agree with you a hundred percent. It's the truth, it's the right bomb to drop, but this is a kamikaze mission, my friend. If you take off on this flight, you won't be coming back. They probably won't kill you, but they'll do their worst. Better get you some bodyguards. Yeah, better find you some big gay bodyguards."

I laughed out loud. "George, I appreciate your worry, but don't you think you're being a little overly dramatic?"

"Dramatic? Don't you get it? What you are doing is what every pastor in the country should do. You are breaking the ground, you're sounding the call, leading the charge. Every preacher is this country needs to repent of their narrow-minded bigotry and shout from the top of their steeples—the Gospel is for everyone!"

"I see what you mean, but I'm late to this battle. There are other brave pastors who have tried to get their churches to reconsider their position on homosexuality. I'm hardly the first."

"That's true, Bart, but you are the first one here, in Joppa, Georgia, at a big, traditional Baptist church. I got to hand it to you. I admire your willingness to speak up and not keep it to yourself." He put his hand on my shoulder and extended his other hand to shake mine. "I'm proud to be your friend, Bart, and I'll visit your grave every Sunday."

***

I glanced out the window of my study, and it looked like Easter Sunday. The lots were already full and people were parking on the softball field and up Mercer Avenue. Apparently, Roger Holcomb's efforts to promote "Gospel Truth Sunday" had been effective. And no wonder, with all the talk around town in the weeks since the assault at the truck stop. Everyone knew the subject of the day, and whether they wished me well or ill, they were all anxious to hear what I would say.

I turned back to my desk and noticed two sermons lying side by side, waiting for me to choose one and go preach. Both sermons had the same title, "The Bible and Homosexuality." I set aside the old sermon preached five years before, typical fare for a traditional Baptist church in the South. I had railed against this "godless perversion" and warned of the judgment of God upon our nation for our willingness to condone such deviant behavior. It wasn't quite a Fred Phelps Westboro Baptist sermon, but it struck the same themes. At the time, I believed it—every word.

The freshly printed second sermon struck a different tone entirely. Never had I agonized over a message like this one, asking myself tough questions. Am I being true to the text? Am I fairly and accurately interpreting the scripture? Am I understanding and taking seriously the cultural context? Am I honestly applying the Gospel in a God-honoring way? And more personally, am I preaching the Gospel truth or just trying to defend my son against his critics and attackers?

I realized, as I pushed aside the old sermon and picked up the new one, that I was charting a new course. My ministry would never be the same from this moment. There would be no going back. And yet, as I reached for my Bible, a strange peace came over me. My dread and trepidation began to melt away as I left my study and carried my new sermon to the pulpit. I knew for the first time in all my years of ministry that I was proclaiming the Gospel for the whole world, the love of Christ for all people. No exceptions. No one disqualified. No one turned away.

My fear evaporated under the smile of God.

***

I followed the choir into the sanctuary as the organist chimed the call to worship. In sixteen Septembers, I had never seen such a crowd at First Baptist. The pews were packed, from the main floor to the top of the balcony. The front rows, usually left vacant on a normal Sunday, were jammed. In the narthex, extra chairs had been set out and people were standing. I'm sure the Fire Marshall would have objected, but he was a Lutheran man. One less thing to worry about.

As the overflow crowd elbowed their way into place, the tension in the room was palpable. I could read the anxiety on countless faces, the distracted attempts to sing the hymns and mouth the prayers. All eyes, both the fearful and the hopeful, turned to me. Sometimes, in the past, I felt like a piece of furniture in the sanctuary, hardly noticed, taken for granted. On this day, I met the spotlight of their stares as they waited for my words.

What did they expect of me? What did they want to hear? I guessed that most of my people wanted to hear what they had always heard before. Most expected to have their own views expounded, their biases affirmed, and their comfort level restored. But my son's presence was the wild card. My dilemma was obvious to everyone. Would I stick to my guns and throw my own son under the bus, or would I stand with David and deny the truth as they understood it?

As the choir finished their anthem, I moved to the pulpit and laid out my sermon notes. The congregation fell deathly still, no rustling of bulletins or gum wrappers, none of the usual settling in for the sermon. Stoney silence ensued as I took a deep breath and began.

I never dreamed I would preach this sermon. There was a time when answers to difficult questions came easily to me. It was simple and straightforward, all there in black and white. I would choose a text to make my point and hammer it home. No room for discussion or debate, no tolerance of different points of view. I preached the truth, the gospel truth, as best I understood it. But sometimes I was wrong. I can't change that fact, but I can learn, I can grow, and I can admit my past mistakes. So, I share with you this morning a sermon I should have preached a long time ago.

When you hear the word 'homosexual,' what images come to mind? Do you think of those mugshots of pedophiles on the evening news? Perhaps you remember the gay pride parades in the cities, the rainbow protestors carrying signs on the march. More likely, you think of the increasingly common portrayals of homosexuality on TV and in the movies. Since the Supreme Court's decision, we have seen gay and lesbian couples kissing for the cameras, celebrating their marriages on courthouse steps.

For some of us, this issue is much closer to home, in our own relationships, in our families. When we know, love, and respect gay people, it breaks down our negative stereotypes and causes us to puzzle over tough questions. If homosexuality is a perverse abomination, what do we do with these decent, devout people who claim to be both Christian and homosexual? Is the Gospel invitation for everyone, or are some disqualified?

Several moms and dads scattered across the sanctuary scrambled to gather up their young children and hustle them towards the exits. I caught their exasperated expressions thrown my way as they hurried out, although I couldn't imagine anyone in the county not knowing what the subject of the day was going to be. I took a deep breath and pushed on.

What is the gospel truth about homosexuality? What does the Bible say? You might be surprised. Eight verses. Out of more than 31,000 verses in the Bible, that's it. Eight verses, and only a few of those may have any application for people today. Those verses are found in Genesis, Leviticus, Judges, Romans, 1 Corinthians, 1 Timothy, and Jude. Let's take them one by one.

Genesis 19 and Judges 19 describe a brutal, primitive practice of gang rape. It was an act of violent aggression, intended to degrade and dominate. The Book of Jude refers to the Genesis story and rightfully condemns this violent behavior. It appears that this story has much to say about rape and about hospitality toward strangers, but nothing to say about homosexual relationships today.

A brief survey of the Bible reveals another surprise. The ancient cities of Sodom and Gomorrah were not destroyed because of the practice of homosexuality. On the contrary, the people were judged for their pride (Zephaniah 2), oppression of the poor (Amos 4), and false prophets and priests (Jeremiah 23). Sodom and Gomorrah were condemned and destroyed by God for their faithlessness as well as their violent behavior.

As I spoke, Stanley Pulliam stood from his seat in the third row, shook his head in disgust, moved to the center aisle, and walked out the rear sanctuary doors. As he exited the sanctuary, several others rose to their feet and followed Stanley out of the service.

As I struggled to keep focused on my sermon, I realized a mass exodus had begun. I kept going, determined to finish.

Leviticus 18 and 20 are part of the Hebrew holiness code, the regulations given to the people of Israel to keep them from being corrupted by the pagan Canaanite culture they would be encountering in the promised land. Paul refers to this code in 1 Timothy 6. The problem here is one of context and the rules of sound, consistent interpretation. The holiness code prescribes and prohibits a wide variety of actions and behaviors, much of it in agreement with the Ten Commandments — which also make no mention of homosexuality — and our own understanding of ethical behavior. But while there is much that we can wholeheartedly affirm, there are also rules such as prohibitions on planting two kinds of seed in the same field, wearing clothing of two different threads, having sex during a woman's menstrual cycle, trimming your sideburns, or getting a tattoo. Cursing one's parents is punishable by death. A man who has sex with a man as with a woman was to be put to death, and those who commit adultery must be stoned.

I can't imagine anyone today, even among Orthodox Jews, suggesting that people should live by this ancient code. And, if that's the case, is it fair or appropriate to pick and choose which directives we want to bring forward and make binding today? Certainly, we would leave out the stipulation of capital punishment for such behaviors. Sound biblical scholarship requires a consistent approach to the whole of scripture, not a piecemeal, picking and choosing of what's binding and what's not. No one seems interested in living by the Levitical code today.

Paul wrote to the Romans, in Romans 1, about unnatural desires between men, and with good reason. In the Greco-Roman culture, older men took young boys as their students and exploited them sexually even before puberty. This practice, called pederasty, was likely Paul's reference point for his admonitions to the Christians at Rome.

In Corinth, it was the practice of male prostitution, per 1 Corinthians 6, that Paul condemned. Paul simply had no reference point in his cultural context to consider monogamous, loving relationships between people of the same gender. It never showed up on his radar.

By now, several members of the choir had exited the loft and our pianist was gone as well. The building was about half empty, but the remaining people seemed content to stay. A few appeared to be genuinely moved, some weeping, though I couldn't know the reason why. The tension had exited with my protestors, and I was able to rally and finish strong.

The Book of Proverbs, that long catalog of earthy, everyday wisdom, contains several chapters of warnings about the dangers of adultery, and not one word of caution regarding homosexual people or behavior.

Surprisingly, there is nothing in any of the Old Testament prophets about homosexuality, keeping in mind that the prophets were the ethical watchdogs, quick to condemn any moral failure on the part of the Hebrews or their pagan neighbors. Not one word from the prophets.

Even more significant for Christians is the absence of any mention of homosexuality in the four Gospels. Not one recorded word from Jesus. Not a hint of a mention. I know, it's the argument from silence, but the silence in this case is deafening. Not a word. So, it occurs to me, if the church's stand against homosexuality is the whole ballgame, and Christianity rises or falls on this one issue, funny, isn't it, that Jesus never brought it up? Plenty to say about judging others. Lots to offer about forgiveness and grace, but nothing about gay people.

We are beginning to see that while there is much in the scripture addressing sexual behavior, there is nothing that addresses sexual orientation, other than the truth that we are all created in the image of God. Perverse and violent sexual practices are certainly and consistently condemned, but there is nothing to address a same sex couple in a monogamous, loving relationship.

What does this mean for us as a church and as followers of Christ? First and foremost, it means that the Gospel is for everyone. No one is excluded, no one disqualified, no one cast out. God loves the whole world. No exceptions.

Does this mean anything goes with no responsibility for our sexual behavior? Of course not. It is possible to hold up a godly standard for sexual ethics without condemning people for their sexual orientation. We still recognize that our sexuality is intended for monogamous, committed relationships. Everyone is responsible to honor God with their body, mind, and soul.

The truth, which we are prone to forget, is that we are all broken people seeking wholeness and healing. We are all sinners in desperate need of God's grace. We are prodigals who desire a welcoming embrace. Too often, we have behaved like elder brothers guarding the door to our Father's house, as if we were bouncers rather than brothers. It's time to open the door and invite them in.

Many of our gay brothers and sisters have been keeping their distance from God and his church, feeling only the heat of our hatred, the sting of our rejection. As far as I'm concerned, that ends today. I invite you as followers of Jesus to make the same commitment.

Chapter 4 – Fallout

"The truth will set you free,
but first it will piss you off."
~ Joe Klaas

I poured my first cup of coffee as David came into the kitchen with a tired, worried face, still marked by faded purple bruises and narrow pink scars on his chin and eyebrow. "Morning, Dad. How are you doing?"

"I'm okay. How about you?" I asked as I reached for a second mug. "Coffee?"

"Sure, thanks." He slipped into a chair, glanced at the morning paper and pushed it aside. "Mom still walking with Amy?"

I nodded as I took the eggs from the refrigerator.

"So, what happens now? Are you going to be all right?"

"We'll be fine, David. I'm sure of it, just not so sure if I will need to find a new job. You know how it is in a Baptist church. There are some things that a pastor cannot control." I filled his cup and scooted the sugar his direction. "I understand Stanley Pulliam called a special meeting of the deacons tonight, but he has not notified me directly or asked me to attend, so who knows? After yesterday, I can't imagine such a meeting would have a positive outcome, but we'll see."

"I can't help feeling responsible for all of this trouble, Dad. If I had not told you and Mom about being gay, you never would have preached that sermon."

"That's true. I think God used your whole terrible ordeal to open my eyes and make me think again, and that's a good thing, not a bad thing. Even if half of the church walked out, it was the right sermon, a sermon that I should have preached years back. So, whatever happens, happens. I have no regrets and certainly no blame."

"Still," David said, "after the service yesterday, Mrs. Woods was going out the door as I was leaving. I held the door for her. She nodded and walked past me, and then turned back and said, 'Well, I hope you're satisfied, young man. All this trouble is your doin'. And to think you used to be a fine Christian boy.' I guess she does have a little blame for me."

"Just let that go, Son. We can't control what people say. I'm embarrassed to think I've been her pastor for sixteen years, and she's just giving back to you what she's been hearing from me all these years. It's not your fault, David. It's mine."

***

"Anyone see the numbers for yesterday?" Brian asked as we began our Monday afternoon staff meeting. "Well, when we started the service, the ushers counted five hundred and twenty-seven including the choir and everybody." Brian always had the details and prided himself in knowing the score, whatever the situation.

"I counted from the platform during the sermon," Randall was quick to add. As our worship leader, he sat on the platform through the entire service. "After Stanley got up and left so dramatically, I tried to keep up with the others who walked out while you were speaking, but I lost count. Close to half, maybe two hundred people, left before you finished, and then another bunch exited during the hymn. Hardly anybody was still around for the announcements."

"I can't say I'm surprised," I said. "I knew this would be a stunner for all of our people, for me to reverse my position on homosexuality and ask them to do the same."

"Can you blame them for walking out, Pastor?" Brian struggled to control his pent-up frustration. "To tell you the truth, I don't understand how you can change your mind on this. I guess people can interpret the scripture however they choose. But you know what they're saying, don't you? They think you are just doing this because of David, to stand up for your gay son and defend his behavior. And I'm not talking about the ones who walked out. I'm talking about the ones who stayed, the members who love you and have always supported you. I heard some of the talk afterwards. They were saying your son has led you over a doctrinal cliff."

Donna had a tissue in her hands, dabbing her tears, her glasses lying on her legal pad. "I've never seen so many of our people red-faced and angry, marching out of worship as if they're never coming back."

Randall said, "You can bet on it. Most of them are not coming back." He laid aside his notes for staff meeting and leaned back in his chair.

"I'm afraid you're right," Donna continued. "But there were others who were in tears, those who were not offended, who seemed relieved, even gratified by your words, Pastor."

"Lots of families are dealing with this issue," I said. "People have friends and neighbors who are gay, relationships that they value with people they respect."

Brian shook his head in resignation. "All I know is our church just split right down the middle, and the reality is, most of our leadership people and a majority of our deacons, not to mention our most generous givers, just marched out the door. Stanley has already called a meeting of the deacons for tonight, and you know what he's going to ask them to do. They'll vote to ask for your resignation or your termination, I don't know which, and it will pass, maybe unanimously."

"No doubt about it, at this point," Randall agreed and then turned to face me. "I have to ask. Was it worth it, Pastor? Everything blown to smithereens? Losing your job? Our church split down the middle? Was it that important? Couldn't you just leave it alone, stick to the Gospel? Plenty of other subjects you can preach about, things we can all believe and work on together."

Brian couldn't hold it in. "And what have you done to us? Look at our position in this conflict. We're in the middle of this, too, you know. We've worked together all these years. But now, if we stand with you, we'll probably lose our jobs, too. And what frosts me is we didn't have any choice in the matter. You didn't say a word to us. We didn't know it was happening, but now we are at risk, too."

"I am sorry for your hurt and frustration," I said, "I truly am. I don't expect you to go to the wall with me on this, unless that's how you feel. I think I made it clear that I was speaking my mind as pastor, not representing you or anyone else's views. If I have to go, there's no reason you cannot stay and continue to serve here. I won't think any less of you."

"Less of us?" Brian exploded. "*We* haven't gone off the deep end. *We're* not the one who's torn apart a great church to satisfy your own conscience and justify your son's behavior. Less of us? I'm sorry, Bart, but to be honest, I think less of you, much less than I did before yesterday. If I wasn't so certain that you'll be fired, I would have to resign myself. I can't work with a senior pastor that I don't trust or respect." The words trailed off as he slumped forward, his head in his hands.

"I'm sorry, Brian."

"Pastor." Donna had been forming her thoughts. "I think what you did took great courage, and I know you would never have said what you said yesterday unless you had come to believe it with all of your heart. I went home yesterday so upset. I couldn't cook. I didn't want to eat. I lay down for a while, but couldn't rest, so I just lay there and prayed. I prayed for you and your family and for Daniel and for each person I saw walk out during the sermon. After a while, I got up and reached for my Bible. I turned to the scriptures you addressed in your message. What had seemed so straightforward before seemed strange to me now. It's not so simple, is it? I'm not sure where I'll come down on this, but it's your job to make us examine the scriptures and challenge our preconceived notions. That's your job, Pastor, so I have more respect for you, not less."

"I appreciate that, I really do. Thank you. And whatever happens tonight or in the days ahead, it has a been a joy to serve with you all, and while I regret all the turmoil and frustration my message has caused for you, I do not regret what I said. I know I spoke the truth, a sermon God gave to me, a sermon that had to be preached."

***

I decided to attend the meeting of our deacons whether I had been notified or not. I had always attended our monthly meetings, and saw no reason to skip this one. For sixteen years, I had met with this group of men to discuss the work of the church. Sometimes we talked about weighty spiritual matters and prayer concerns. More often, we spent our time on the mundane business of the church, from finances and fund-raising to furnace troubles and what color to paint the bathroom. Thinking back, I could not remember a time when any significant doctrinal issue was discussed among us, but this might well be the first. I had never felt like I was being 'called on the carpet' for any reason, but this evening was like nothing I had ever witnessed.

We always held our meetings in a classroom, specifically, the room used by the Bible Searchers adult Sunday School class, where Stanley Pulliam, our deacon chairman, taught each week. It gave Stanley an added sense of authority, kind of a home field advantage, to be on his own turf.

When I walked into the room, most of the deacon body was present, and several were visibly startled to see me come in. Stanley Pulliam was just about to begin, but my sudden arrival seemed to leave him at a loss for words. I quickly found a chair in the second row of folding chairs.

Stanley cleared his throat and began slowly, without making eye contact with me. "I would like to call this meeting to order. We will dispense with any minutes, saving those for our regular meeting. Roy, would you keep minutes for us tonight?"

Roy Miles picked up a pen with a nod. Most of the men in the circle sat in total silence glancing back and forth from Stanley to me.

"Well," Stanley continued, "you were all here yesterday. You heard what was said in our church's pulpit about homosexuality. My phone has been lit up with constant phone calls, so many of our people upset, angry that our pastor has suddenly gone liberal, in favor of the gay agenda. And on a Sunday when he was supposed to be preaching the Gospel truth, our pastor tried to twist the scripture to say it's just fine to be gay, men having sex with men and women with women. I have never been more offended in my life." His voice was rising with his emotions, and the other men had begun to respond in agreement as he turned his words directly to me.

"Pastor, it's a sad day when a man like yourself, who has served with us for so long, can suddenly betray your own beliefs, your own Bible, your own church. Shame on you, Pastor. You have done wrong and you did it publicly. There's no way to take back your words. You can't undo what you have done." Turning back to the group, Stanley announced, "It is my recommendation as chairman of our deacon body that we demand Pastor Bart Sheldon's resignation, effective immediately. I don't want him to ever preach or teach in this church again. Do I have a second?"

Calvin Davis seconded the motion.

Before Stanley could call for the vote, I raised my hand. "Stanley, you have spoken directly to me. May I respond directly to you and this group?"

As Stanley stammered and hesitated, one of the deacons nodded in the affirmative.

"Gentlemen, I have served as your pastor for a long time, as Stanley said, over sixteen years. If the church decides that I must go, I will go, but with a heavy heart. We have worked together for a long time, and you have trusted me to teach and preach and model the truths of God's Word for our church. I have done the best I could, not perfectly, of course, but responsibly. I regret that most of you did not hear much of what I said yesterday. You left before I could finish my message. You walked out before I could explain and apply the scripture, and because of your example, many others left early as well. So, before you make your decision, I would ask you to listen to or read the entire message, look up the relevant passages, and decide what you believe it means for us. I brought along some copies of my manuscript. If you would dismiss me because of a sermon, you should at least hear the sermon in question, all of it."

By the time I finished speaking, Stanley was boiling over, the vein in his forehead bulging beneath the skin. "I heard all I needed to hear, sir," he said through clenched teeth, no longer willing to call me 'pastor.' "I am calling the question. We have a motion and second, that we demand Bart Sheldon's resignation effective immediately. Are you ready to vote?"

Mike Decker, principal at Joppa High School, raised his hand.

"What is it, Mike?"

"I guess I'm in favor of the motion, Stanley, but I have a question or two. Can we do this? I thought these decisions required a church vote. And if we can take this action, what about the details of severance? Pastor Bart has been with our church for sixteen years, so what is appropriate severance? I mean, it's not like he molested a child or stole money from the church. He preached a sermon we didn't like. I think we should do right by him, even if we let him go."

Ron Neyland, one of the youngest deacons, seemed to come out of his chair. "Listen, Mike, I had to cover the ears of my own little girl as we left worship yesterday. I didn't want my family to hear that left-wing gay nonsense. And what the pastor approved of yesterday leads to those same sick behaviors, putting children at risk."

"Thanks, Ron," Stanley said. "I agree. Mike, I looked it up and the deacons can call for the pastor's resignation, but we can't actually fire him. If he won't resign, we can recommend to the church that he be terminated. Then the church votes, two thirds required to dismiss him, but after yesterday, I'm sure we have the votes."

Mike raised his hand again to follow up. "So, we are basically asking the pastor to resign to save us the trouble of asking the church to terminate him. Is that right?"

Stanley nodded, looking at his watch.

"And what about severance? Is there some severance policy in place?"

Roy Miles, looking up from his minutes, answered Mike. "There is a policy, so many months pay depending on how many years of service. The formula is in our bylaws."

"That's only if he resigns. If we have to fire him, he gets nothing but his vacation time. I've already called the question. So, we are voting to demand his resignation and the severance details to be according to our personnel policies. Sir, would you please excuse yourself before we vote? You won't want to see this," Stanley said with at least a partial smile.

My course of action became clear in that moment. I rose to my feet and looked at each deacon, though few would meet my gaze. Then, I said, "Stanley, you may vote now, vote later, vote all you like. I will not resign as you may request, not demand. My conscience is clear on this matter. Bring it before the entire church if you like. I will certainly abide by their decision, not yours. Goodnight."

And with that, Stanley's crooked grin disappeared, and I headed for home.

***

A special church-wide meeting was called by the deacons for Wednesday night of that same week, with only two days' notice to the membership. Stanley Pulliam claimed that this was such an urgent matter for the church to consider, the normal protocol prescribed by the church's bylaws could be laid aside. He also enlisted like-minded deacons and class members to make phone calls to those most likely to vote in favor of my termination.

Baptists know how to get out the vote.

I asked Sally to stay at home that Wednesday night, or go get some dinner with Amy, anything rather than witness the ugliness sure to unfold at the meeting, but she insisted on being there with me, whatever might happen. David was equally insistent, feeling at least partially responsible for the whole controversy. About an hour before we were heading to the church, as we were eating some Chinese takeout, the front door opened and in walked our daughter, Dinah.

"Hey, Daddy, how are you?" She hugged me around the waist and looked up at me with clear blue eyes, her cropped blonde hair catching the sun through the bay window. "Thought I better get down here and provide a little muscle for this team." I laughed as she flexed her bicep. Dinah was petite in the extreme, but she never lacked spirit or hesitated to stand up for herself and those she loved.

"You drove all the way from Tennessee today, Dinah?" Sally asked. "Such a long way, but it's wonderful for you to come."

Dinah moved around the table to David, taking his face in her hands, giving him the once over. "Well, big brother, you're not looking as nasty as you did before. I'll bet you'll be back to your handsome self real soon." David and Dinah had always been close, being just two years apart. She turned towards her mother. "How about some of those noodles, Mom. Smells good and I'm starved."

As she finished off a spring roll, Dinah said, "So, I guess it's all out in the open now. Most people around Joppa know that David Sheldon is gay and Reverend Sheldon is okay with that. And now they want to fire you, is that right, Dad?"

"Yes, the church is voting tonight on termination. We're just getting ready to head over there. I tried to get your mother and brother to stay away. It won't be pleasant. But they insisted on going with me. What about you, Dinah?"

"Well, why do you think I drove all the way down here, Daddy? We're a family." She rose from her chair and dabbed her mouth with a napkin. "Whatever happens, we'll get through this together. Let's go."

***

Our monthly business meeting at First Baptist was usually attended by the faithful few, a meager representation of our congregation—maybe forty people—but on this Wednesday night, the large fellowship hall was filled to capacity. Even the accordion room dividers on each side were pushed back to allow space for more folding chairs, room for over three hundred people. When we entered the hall, a handful of friends and supporters stood to greet us.

Donna gave us a worried smile and stepped forward to hug me, Sally, and the kids each in turn.

As we made our way down the side aisle to the front, I could feel the weight of every eye on me and my family—concerned expressions, furrowed brows, angry glares, disappointed heads shaking side to side, looks of pitiful disgust. The rest of my staff, Brian and Randall, were seated with their families toward the back. I knew they were present only as observers, not participants.

Too much to lose, I guess.

Dinah paused as we moved toward the front, wanting to speak to some friends she had not seen all summer, but no one wanted to talk. Nearly every seat was filled, but when we came to the front, some of the deacons moved over to make room for the four of us.

Stanley Pulliam, our deacon chairman, was not the regular moderator of our sessions, but since the deacons had called the meeting, he assumed he was in charge of the meeting. He moved to the lectern and picked up the gavel. "I will call this meeting to order. Let's begin with a prayer." And he began.

"O God, this is your church and we are your people. You expect us to live by your Holy Word, to be righteous and true and to resist the evils of this sinful world. Help us tonight to stand up for what is right and holy and pure. We know that you desire that those who lead your church should set a godly example for our community and never lead others into sin. Help us to stand up for the truth tonight and do what we must do to be faithful to you. In Jesus' name we pray. Amen."

He took a deep breath and addressed the parishioners. "You all received a copy of the recommendation from the deacons as you came in."

Someone in the second row handed a sheet of paper over Sally's shoulder. It read:

> *The deacons of First Baptist Church of Joppa unanimously recommend that Rev. Bart Sheldon be terminated immediately and removed from all duties as senior pastor. The grounds for his dismissal are the preaching of false and worldly views on the unscriptural and sinful practice of homosexuality. We further recommend that Rev. Sheldon receive two week's severance pay plus his remaining one week of vacation, and that he be directed to vacate the parsonage within thirty days.*

Stanley continued. "Coming from the deacons, this motion does not require a second. Are there any questions regarding the recommendation?"

I looked back over my shoulder to see a few scattered hands go up.

Stanley pointed over my head. "Yes, Mavis, do you have a question?"

Mavis Brown, one of our few African American members, had worked in our nursery for nearly thirty years. "Our pastor has been with us for sixteen years. He's been awful good to us. Some of you remember 'cause Brother Bart seen you in the hospital or he buried your loved one. He held your hand when you thought your world was endin'. Brother Bart and Sally have been with us, raisin' their kids with our kids. I babysat them. I rocked them to sleep. They is part of our family. Now, you don't like the sermon he preached on Sunday. You disagree with him. Maybe lots of us disagree with the pastor. So, you want to kick him out. You want to get rid of him, but not me. I can handle a disagreeable sermon now and then, but I want a pastor who shows up when you need him. Where we gonna find another one like that?"

Stanley answered as he glanced at his watch. "Thank you, Mavis. Any other questions?"

Amy Morrow stood to her feet without waiting for Stanley's permission. She was not a loud or emotional person, but she trembled as she gripped the metal chair in front of her. "Two weeks, Stanley? Two week's pay and thirty days to find a place to live? You should be ashamed of yourselves, all of you deacons. Is your fear of gays and lesbians so great that you would destroy this family just to keep them out? I say if our pastor must go, we should give him a month's pay for each year he has served our church, sixteen months."

Mavis raised her hand. "I second Amy's motion."

There was a rustle and buzz of conversation as people voiced their opinions.

Stanley rapped his gavel on the wooden lectern and the room fell silent. "I'm sorry, Amy, but your motion is out of order. We are bound by our bylaws on this matter. If the pastor had been willing to resign, he could have received the severance you suggested, but he refused to resign. Termination is a different matter."

Jim Hinnessy raised his hand. Jim had been the church custodian several years before, until I had to fire him in an awkward situation when he had walked into the women's locker room while a woman was showering, and then returned a few minutes later as she was getting dressed. After losing his job, Jim held a grudge, resentful not only that he had been fired, but that I knew what he had done. He continued to show up from time to time, always looking for opportunities to criticize or undermine my role as pastor, trying to settle the score.

Now he saw his chance. "Some of you remember when I was fired from my job as custodian here at First Baptist. The pastor gave me two weeks and my vacation time. If that was good enough for me, it's good enough for him." I had never publicly disclosed the grounds for Jim's dismissal, so rather than being grateful for my discretion, he decided to play the martyr and complain about his unfair treatment at my hands.

Calvin Davis, probably the wealthiest member of the old guard of the church, asked to be recognized. Mr. Davis had retired as president of First National Bank, but he was still the primary stockholder on the board. His thick gray hair was swept to one side and his stooped and crooked posture made his hand-tailored suit seem ill-fitted. He rose slowly and steadied himself with his cane.

Mr. Davis always spoke in a low, conversational tone, as if he was talking over his desk rather than addressing a large group. "We better let him go. The pastor knew what he was doing, and he knew how we would feel about it. He's brought disgrace upon our whole church. I'm embarrassed to be a member of this church as long as he's here. People are already leaving. You saw them walking out the door Sunday morning. The only chance we have to get those folks back in church is to get a new pastor, one that believes the Bible and won't go changing his mind. I say, let him go."

The growing rumble indicated widespread agreement.

As Mr. Davis sat down, one of the young deacons, Ron Neyland, stood up, nodding to the older man and then pointing at me. "I agree with Mr. Davis. If that man stays, I'm gone. I'm here tonight because we have a chance to clean up this mess and get rid of the problem before it destroys the testimony of this church and corrupts our own children. And I know that many of you folks feel the same way. He's got to go."

Five years before, I had helped Ron keep his marriage together after his wife, Kelly, had discovered his addiction to pornography. It seemed strange to me to hear him taking the moral high road.

"May I say something?"

I turned to my right to see Dinah on her feet. "After all," she said, "it's my family that is on trial here. We are the ones at risk."

Stanley stepped back wiping his brow and looking at his watch. "I think it's time for a vote. It's getting late."

Dinah stepped up on her chair so that she could see and be seen by all the people. "I will have my say, Stanley. I grew up in this church. I know you, most all of you. I grew up watching my daddy serve this church. I know the hours he worked, the things he gave up, the opportunities he missed, the times my dad wasn't there for me and David because he was with you, taking care of all of you." Her voice faltered as her eyes filled with tears, but she gathered herself and went on. "You have no idea what he has given to you, to this church, to God."

Ron Neyland came out of his chair nearly shouting, "Well, we know what he did last Sunday, don't we? That man tried to twist the scripture to say that God approves of all kinds of sexual perversion. He's put our families at risk. Whatever he did before doesn't change what he did Sunday."

Dinah had climbed down from her chair, but still standing, she spoke through her tears. "My brother is not a pervert. You should know better, Ron. You should all know better. You say you feel ashamed... well, me too. I'm ashamed of you."

Sally put her arm around Dinah and the two of them moved to the side aisle and slipped out a side door.

Ron was still standing with his hand raised. "Enough talk! Let's vote. I call the question."

A grumble of agreement arose all around the room.

Stanley struck the gavel again and brought the crowd to attention. "Ron's right. It's time to vote. I think we can do this with a simple show of hands. I don't see the need for ballots." He turned and looked directly at me. "Would you and your son please excuse yourselves from the room? We will inform you of the results in just a few minutes."

I turned away from Stanley's mock courtesy and looked into David's face, still marked from the beating he had endured, and saw the deep hurt and anguish, the pain not so much for himself as for me, his father humiliated and rejected. I reached around his neck and kissed his forehead.

"It's okay, Son," I whispered. I turned and nodded to Stanley, and then stood, facing my congregation for the last time. "I want you all to know that it has been the great blessing of my life to serve as your pastor these sixteen years. Whatever you decide tonight, please understand it was never my desire to harm or disrupt our fellowship. The sermon I gave last Sunday morning is the same message that will eventually find its way to hundreds and thousands of preachers and pulpits. Sooner or later, churches like First Baptist of

Joppa will have to relearn the most basic truth of the Gospel—it's for everyone, for all kinds of people, and that includes homosexual people." I turned to face Stanley. "I'm going home. You may call me if you like. Goodnight."

David got to his feet and we walked side-by-side down the center aisle. Most of the people looked away, and only a few reached for my hand or whispered a goodbye. We climbed the stairs to the main foyer, and found Sally and Dinah waiting for us. Together we walked out the main door, between the tall white columns and down to the car. The call came before we got home.

Stanley didn't bother to sugar-coat the news. "You're out. The motion passed, nearly unanimous. Never mind the numbers. You know the terms. Some of the deacons are boxing up your stuff and cleaning out your office tonight. Your computer stays with us. It's church property. You need to load up your stuff and turn in your keys before Sunday, and pick up your check. Your thirty days begins tomorrow. Do you understand?"

"Yes, I do. Thanks for letting me know, Stanley. Goodbye."

***

When I pulled in the driveway, I noticed George next door sitting on his front steps.

As we got out of the car, he walked over and put his arms around Sally and Dinah. "Are you all right? Can't imagine what that meeting was like for you, but I'm sure it was ugly."

I nodded.

"Come on in, George, I'll make some coffee," Sally said, grateful for a friendly embrace. "It was ugly, like nothing I ever thought I would see at church," she stammered, stunned and bewildered from the whole ordeal.

We had just sat down at the kitchen table when the doorbell rang. Sally went to the door, and I recognized Amy Morrow's voice. I could hear them trying to comfort each other through their tears. Dinah joined them in the living room, leaving George and David at the table with me and five cups of coffee.

George assumed the worst but wanted to know the details. "So, did they do right by you, Bart? Did they at least give you enough severance and time to find something? And what about the house?"

"It's not good, George. Two weeks plus a week's vacation pay, and thirty days to vacate the house."

George set his cup down and shook his head in disbelief. "Are you kidding me? Two weeks for sixteen years? That's unbelievable, unconscionable. What are you supposed to do now?"

"Well, the deacons boxed up my office tonight and changed the lock. I'm supposed to pick up my things and drop off my keys before Sunday." I stared into my cup as I stirred my coffee, feeling equal parts of shame and resignation.

George was having none of it. His voice was strong and firm, like a coach's halftime speech or an officer barking orders back in his navy days. "Hey, Bart, look at me, friend." His face was kind and yet intense as he put his hand on my shoulder. "No matter how those bastards treat you now, you did the right thing. You spoke the truth they didn't want to hear, but God knows they need to. So, keep your head up. You are the man of God in this story, the one who is speaking the truth."

"He's right, Dad," David said as he moved around the table towards me. "You have nothing to be embarrassed about. In fact, I've never been more proud of you. You stood up for the truth, for what you believe. And you stood up for me." He bent down and hugged me, his eyes wet with tears.

George wasn't quite finished. "That goes for you, too, David." George stood up and gathered both of us in his arms. "Don't let anyone get to you, whatever they may say or do. You stand tall. You have nothing to be ashamed of. You are a brave young man."

***

We both tried to read a little bit in bed that night, but it was useless. We couldn't focus or quit thinking about what had happened. We were traumatized, seeing those angry, hateful expressions in our minds, hearing the words over and over again. I lay there in the dark with Sally close by my side, her head on my shoulder, her tears warm on my chest. There wasn't much we knew to say.

"What will we do now, Bart?"

I held her close and kissed her forehead. "It will be all right, Sal. I'll get a job. I'm sure there are some options out there. I can update my resume and send it out for churches looking for a pastor."

"But, Bart, you know how long that can take, even in the best case. But now you've been fired. What church wants to call a pastor who has been fired by his last church?"

"I know, Sal, I know. I'll probably need to consider jobs other than being a pastor. There are things I can do. To tell you the truth, I'm not sure I want to be a pastor again, at least not any time soon."

Sally nestled in close and reached up to touch my cheek. "I can't blame you for that, Sweetheart. Not after this. It does make you wonder what's the point of it all." There was a soft knock on our bedroom door.

"Mom, Dad, are you still awake? It's us." Dinah and David came in through the darkness and climbed into bed, David beside his mother and Dinah next to me.

I had to laugh. "This is just like the old days. Is it storming or something? I didn't hear the tornado siren. What's going on, you guys?"

Dinah snuggled close to me as David put his arm around his mother.

"Worst storm I've ever seen," David said softly.

"Yeah, the worst night I can remember," Dinah said. "Are you okay, Daddy? I swear I'll never set foot in that place again." Her tears came with deep sobs.

Sally reached out to comfort her and began to cry.

Both shoulders damp with tears, I breathed a silent prayer there in the darkness. *God, are you seeing this? Can you see my family here in my arms, crying in the dark?*

"I can't believe it's over," David said. "You've been pastor at First Baptist Church almost our whole lives, and now in one week, it's come to this. What will you do now?"

"We'll survive, David. We'll be just fine. I'll find something, and when I do, the first thing I'm going to buy is a bigger bed, a much bigger bed."

Chapter 5 – Untouchable

"The only queer people are those who don't love
anybody."
~ Rita Mae Brown

Cory Moss left me an insistent voicemail, indicating that I was supposed to meet my usual foursome for golf on Saturday morning at the club, whether I felt like it or not. Having heard reports of what happened at First Baptist, my golf buddies knew I needed some encouragement and stress relief. I didn't feel like seeing anybody, let alone playing golf, but true friends don't take "no" for an answer.

I heard Cory's horn blaring in our driveway at 8:30 Saturday morning and Sally pushed me out the door.

The country club in Joppa was nice, but modest by big city standards, nothing too extravagant. The clubhouse had a decent restaurant that members had to frequent to the tune of two hundred dollars each month. There was a nice pool, nothing like the newer water parks, but well maintained and thoroughly restricted to members and their paying guests. The golf course was laid out like most of the members — short and wide, designed to be easily playable, especially for the older, retired players who made up a majority of the membership.

The best thing about Joppa Country Club for me personally was the ministerial membership policy. All local pastors were granted full membership privileges with no initiation fee, and were required to pay just a fraction of the regular annual dues. It was a very generous policy, although some of the pastors suggested that giving us a discounted membership at the club made folks feel better about underpaying their pastors at church. Either way, it was a nice benefit, and since the rest of my usual foursome were members, I took advantage of the golf privileges regularly.

When Cory and I pulled up next to Greg's Explorer, the guys were sitting on the rear bumper lacing up their golf shoes.

"Hey, Bart, how you doing, man? Rough week, I hear," Greg said. "I'm sorry for what happened, though I don't really understand it all."

"Me too, Bart," Steve added. "Been thinking about you and Sally and David. That kind of shit is not supposed to happen, not to good guys like you."

I nodded as I pulled my clubs from Cory's trunk. "I appreciate it, guys. It has been a hard week, really tough, painful for my family and a lot of people, but we'll get through it. Life goes on." The last thing I wanted was to spend the whole round of golf rehashing the details of the past week, and the guys seemed to understand. "Let's play some golf."

Cory glanced at his watch and said, "We're right on time and the tee box is open. We're up."

Members were not required to check in if we had a tee time and an open box, so we pulled our carts to the first tee. We were loosening up and stretching out when Stewart Lane, the club pro and golf director, stepped out of the pro shop and called my name.

"Reverend Sheldon, can I talk with you for a moment?" Not being a serious golfer, I had little contact with the club pro, so I had no idea what was on Stewart's mind.

"Sure. No problem." I walked towards the clubhouse still carrying my driver, and he came down to meet me on the cart path. "What can I do for you, Stewart?"

He seemed hesitant and confused. "Reverend, did you get a letter from the club this week, just the last few days?"

"No, I did not. No mail from the club this week. I'm sure we're current on our dues. What letter?"

He pulled an envelope from his back pocket, removed a letter, and handed it to me. "It must be in today's mail. Here's a copy of it. I'm sorry, but your membership has been revoked. It's all here in the letter. I'm sorry, Reverend."

I took the letter and began to read it as Cory and Greg stepped beside me, reading over my shoulder. The letter read;

> *You are hereby notified that effective immediately your membership at Joppa Country Club has been permanently cancelled and all privileges revoked as per Article VII of the club's code of conduct: Any immoral or indecent conduct shall be grounds for the termination of membership, requiring a majority vote of the club's Board of Directors. A vote regarding your dismissal took place Thursday, September 24. The motion carried.*

"Are you kidding me?" Greg exploded. "Are you freaking kidding me, Stewart? They're kicking him out of the club because some good ol' boy Baptist deacons didn't like the sermon? That's it, isn't it?"

Cory was just as upset. "That's bullshit, Stewart. Bullshit, plain and simple, and you know it," Cory insisted.

As embarrassed and angry as I felt, I knew that Stewart was just the messenger, forced to tell me about a decision that he did not make.

"It's not my call, guys. Not my decision. Don't shoot the messenger. I'm sorry, Reverend, but I have to ask you to leave."

Steve spoke up. "He can play as my guest. I'll pay the green fee and cart. He's my guest."

Stewart shook his head. "That won't work. Those who lose membership privileges also lose guest privileges. It's a ban from the premises. I'm sorry, but you have to leave now."

There were more protests and angry denouncements from my friends as I stepped aside, pulled out my cell, and called Sally to have her come pick me up.

"You guys might as well get started and play," I said. "Sally will be here soon. Go on now, hit 'em long and straight." I laid my clubs in the grass and sat down on a bench to wait for Sally while the guys finally disappeared down the first fairway.

As I sat there waiting, I envisioned the board meeting and all the discussion at the club. Immoral, indecent conduct. Grounds for dismissal.

Always a price to pay, I guess. I just didn't see this one coming.

***

I stopped by the high school the next week for an appointment with the principal, Mike Decker, who was also one of the deacons at First Baptist. When I called earlier in the week to make the appointment, he seemed hesitant and confused, but we had set a time to meet at his office. He shook my hand as I came in and pointed to a chair. I sat down in an awkward silence, not an occasion for small talk.

"I want you to know, Pastor, I wanted the church to do better for you and your family. You deserved a better severance package than what we gave you. That wasn't fair to your family." He remained standing at his desk, as if unwilling to spend much time with me.

"Well, that's history now, Mike, but I appreciate your thoughts. Speaking of my situation, I wanted to ask about substitute teaching. I would like to be on the list of those you call when you need subs. I enjoy junior high and high school students and I think I could do a good job for you. My Bachelors was in history and social studies. Is there an application I need to fill out?"

Mike was already shaking his head before I could get the words out of my mouth. "I'm sure you would do a fine job, Pastor. You are a wonderful teacher. I used to tell Lori all the time that you were the best Bible teacher we ever had at church. But, the trouble is, we've already got all the subs we can use right now, a longer list than we need. It wouldn't be fair to bump you up the list over the others. Most of those folks need work, too. And besides that, we wouldn't want anyone to get the wrong idea—you know, parents concerned about what kinds of things you might teach their children. In light of the present situation, I really can't use you right now, you understand?" I nodded as he looked at his watch. "Sorry to rush you, Pastor, but I've got another appointment."

I stood and shook his hand. "Thanks for your time, Mike. I appreciate it."

As I walked back to the car, it dawned on me that the explosion at First Baptist set in motion a painful ripple effect, fallout I never anticipated. Where would I find some work?

***

I found a little two-bedroom rental house that we decided would work for us at least temporarily. We wanted to vacate the parsonage as quickly as possible, and after three long days, everything we owned was in our new residence, sold, or in storage.

As we finished unpacking the last few boxes, I noticed the little house seemed overstuffed. "Sally, I'm sorry to move you backwards, having to downsize to such a dinky place. You deserve better than this."

"Oh, Bart, that's nonsense. I was just thinking: this house reminds me of that little place we had that first year of seminary. Remember? We were newlyweds, just kids really. I loved that house."

I shook my head in disbelief. "Sally, that house was a dump. I mean, it was all we could afford, but it was awful. Remember the mice, all the traps I set out? Every morning I had to run the trap line and throw out the dead mice. And what about the plumbing, the toilets and the sink, and the water in the basement every time it sprinkled."

Sally laughed. "I know, Bart, I remember, but we were so happy there. I was learning to cook, and you swallowed whatever I fixed for you. Remember that meatloaf and the eggplant that didn't get cooked? It was awful, but you were a good sport."

"And what about Thursday nights, our date night?" I added, caught up in the nostalgia of the moment. "Popping popcorn and watching Hill Street Blues on that little 19-inch TV, and making love on that squeaky old bed your folks gave us. I'll never forget that."

Sally smiled. "That wasn't just Thursdays, as I recall." She paused and looked around our meager living space. "Bart, let this little house take us back to the beginning, our first year together, our beginning in ministry. Let's try to forget what happened here at First Baptist and start fresh. I'm glad to be here in this little house with you, still with you, always with you." She reached for my hand as I took her in my arms.

"I love you, Sal. I am happy, too, going backwards or forwards, as long as I'm with you." I kissed her, a real kiss like the old days, as she slipped her hands in the back pockets of my jeans and pulled me close.

She opened her eyes with a sly grin and took me by the hand. "C'mon, Bart. Let's go make some noise."

***

As Sally and I discussed my employment options, the hospital seemed like my best bet. There was an opening for a chaplain, working both with the local hospice program and the hospital. It was the same position that George held, and he had recommended me and pushed as much as he could for my consideration. On paper, I was more than qualified, and I already knew most of the hospital staff. I expected to interview soon since they had indicated a desire to fill the position quickly.

A week after I had submitted my application and resume, I was notified that the position had been filled. I called the hospital's CEO, John McCubbin, whom I had served with on several community activities and service projects. He was always friendly and respectful, but I could tell there was more to this story than he wanted to tell.

"I'm sorry, Reverend Sheldon. We decided to go another direction. We had several strong candidates."

"I understand, Mr. McCubbin. Was there some reason why I was not invited to interview for the position?"

He hesitated before contradicting himself. "No, not really. Not sure on that. You were a strong candidate. Well, we have two of our trustees who serve on each of our standing committees, and the trustees that oversee the chaplaincy program decided to go another direction. It was their call, I believe."

Now I was beginning to see how this worked. "Do you happen to know which trustees are responsible for the chaplaincy? I'd like to know."

"Just a moment, Reverend. I've got the trustee assignments right here in my file. Yes, here it is. Roy Miles and Calvin Davis worked with the committee of our staff and the hospice people. It was their decision."

"I understand. Thank you for your trouble. I appreciate it."

Afraid that he had already said too much, Mr. McCubbin was anxious to end the conversation. "I'm sorry it didn't work out, Pastor. We've always appreciated your ministry in our hospital. You always took good care of your people."

"Thank you, Mr. McCubbin. Goodbye."

So much for my optimism. I never had a chance.

***

I wasn't sure how many funerals I had conducted during my sixteen-year tenure at First Baptist Church. With a large, older membership, I averaged about twenty funerals a year, so over three hundred for sure. Joppa had three funeral homes and all three funeral directors did their best to keep up with the competition and market their services. Two of the three had added cremation services, and one, Hopkins Funeral Home, advertised pet cremations and burials. Tom Hopkins had taken over the family business fresh out of mortuary school, and he would soon be ready to turn it over to his nephew, Rick, having no children of his own.

As luck would have it, Tom had put an ad in the paper seeking a man or woman to work at the funeral home. Being familiar with the funeral business, I knew what kind of help he was likely needing — someone to help set up for services, to drive when needed, to go with Tom to pick up the deceased, to wash cars or cut grass, and do whatever else was needed. The job also required some measure of sensitivity in dealing with grieving people. I also appreciated the fact that Tom was a Methodist, not involved in the conflict at First Baptist. So, after checking the paper to make sure Hopkins Funeral Home had no service scheduled for Thursday afternoon, I dropped by to apply for the job.

Like many of the funeral homes in small towns, it was a converted private residence, not originally intended to function as a funeral home. Large homes had to be converted for this purpose, adding an embalming room, a casket display area, an oversized garage or car port. Sometimes walls were removed to increase capacity. Hopkins represented a quality conversion, one of the nicest I had seen, with impressive stonework across the front and beautiful oak woodwork throughout the main floor.

Tom greeted me in his office. Always in a suit and tie, he was prepared for whatever or whoever the next phone call would send his way. After catching up a bit and talking some Braves baseball, I came to the point.

"Tom, as you have probably heard, I'm no longer employed at First Baptist." He nodded as I went on.

"Not sure what you've heard, and that really doesn't matter. I understand you are looking to hire someone to help you out around here. I'd like to throw my hat in the ring. We've worked together on so many services through the years, and I understand and appreciate how you do business, Tom. I'd be happy to work for you. I think I know what you need, and I'd do a good job for you. And, I'm available right now."

Tom leaned back in his chair, choosing his words carefully. "Thank you, Bart. I know you would do a fine job here. In fact, you would bring more to the table than anyone else I could hope to find. No doubt about that. Except for the embalming... you don't do that, do you?" he said with a grin.

"No, I'd have to leave all that mortician stuff to you, Tom, but I can vacuum with the best of them."

"I'm sure you can, Bart. You would be a real asset to me here, but there's a problem, a problem I'm not sure I can get around."

I braced for the worst. "What's that, Tom? I was thinking that I might be able to bring a little business your way as well, people that know me might choose Hopkins over the other funeral homes." I was trying to put his mind at ease, but I could tell it wasn't working.

"That's just it, Bart. I might gain some business because of you, but on the other hand, I might lose some business, too. You have become a highly controversial person in Joppa. You have your friends and supporters for sure, but you also have a large number of people who think you are the devil himself. Now put yourself in my shoes. Last year, Ewing's did a hundred and ten services and Daniels did ninety-three. We did eighty-five, Bart, just right on the edge, barely in the black. If I took you on and it ended up costing me five services, that puts me in trouble. And I might lose more than that, the way people are talking. I'm sorry. I know you would do a great job for me, but I can't use you. I just can't risk losing business because you are here. I am sorry, Bart."

I felt the deep ache of rejection rising from the pit of my stomach, a feeling that was becoming too familiar. "I understand, Tom. I wish it were different. I was hoping you could take a chance on me. Thanks for your time." Rising to go, I extended my hand. "One more thing, Tom. If you have a family with no church or minister, I'd be available to conduct the funeral. I can do that much, I guess."

Tom shook my hand with a sad smile. "I will keep you in mind, Bart, and say hello to Sally. I think David is a brave and courageous person to do what he did that night at the truck stop. I know you are proud of him. Give him my best, Bart, and take care."

As I walked out to my car, it struck me: the unspoken reason why Tom didn't want to hire me. There had been rumors around Joppa for years that Tom was gay, having never married or had children. Tom had a lady friend from out of town who would sometimes accompany him to banquets or ballgames or whatever was going on around town, but the relationship seemed much more platonic than romantic. But in a town like Joppa, it was important to keep up appearances. Tom was likely afraid that hiring me might make people think he had a good reason to be sympathetic to me and my family. That could be bad for business in this town.

But what next? I was running out of options.

***

The next weekend, David and Dinah decided we all needed to get out of the house and out of town for a little while. David found a movie playing at the little four-plex in Edgerton that sounded interesting, something about a young Indian boy who wanted to become a great chef in America, only to end up running a brutal organized crime syndicate. Sounded like the perfect distraction to me. Sally agreed to go, hoping to pick up a recipe or two from the chef in the movie. So, off we went to grab a pizza and a movie in Edgerton, and hopefully not run into too many familiar faces.

What a wonderful diversion. I couldn't remember the last time the four of us had gone to the movies together. Most of our conversation turned back on the past, allowing us a healthy reprieve from the painful present. We laughed and teased and told stories over dinner, and whispered our wisecracks and lame commentary during the movie. It was great fun for all of us.

Then we headed for home.

When we pulled into the driveway, my headlights illuminated a sick display of vandalism, our small rental house smeared with eggs and tomatoes, windows cracked and broken, and there on the garage door, the painted words, "QUEER" and "LIAR."

Sally was the first to find her voice. "Who could do such a thing? Shiloh! Shiloh's inside."

I left the headlights on as we rushed to the door. I could hear Shiloh, our eight-year-old Black Lab, barking frantically as I unlocked the door. The poor old lab was traumatized, still running back and forth and barking wildly. She had messed on the floor in a few places, something she never did. We hadn't crated Shiloh since she was a pup—no need—but she had never been through anything like this.

Sally tried to calm her down while Dinah cleaned up the messes.

David and I went back outside.

The storm door and the plate glass window were both cracked and broken. The smell of eggs and tomatoes, already rancid and pungent, made my stomach turn. I filled two five-gallon buckets with hot, soapy water and a scrub brush, and we went to work. Dinah followed us with the hose. It took us nearly three hours to clean the front of the house. The writing on the garage door was spray paint, and soap wouldn't touch it. Not having any paint thinner, I decided to raise the garage door and leave it up all night, rather than leave the words displayed. Nothing of real value in our garage anyway. It was nearly four in the morning when I came inside.

Only David was still up, sitting at the kitchen table. "I'm sorry, Dad. I started all this mess, and you are the ones paying the price. I should move away, go someplace else to live, far from Joppa. Let things calm down."

I finished washing up at the sink and turned as I dried my hands on a dish towel. "Forget about it. Do you think that would stop the hatred, the ignorance, the violence? You think we should run away? That's what they want, you know, to get us out of town, to drive us out, to make us leave. Then they don't have to think about it. They don't have to face the issue. So, you're the queer and I'm the liar, that's what they think. Well, I'm not going anywhere. We're not going to conveniently disappear. It's one thing to speak the truth on your way out of town. It's something else to speak the truth and stand your ground."

David stood and turned to embrace me, and I held him in my arms for a few lingering moments.

"I'll stand with you, Dad. Thanks for standing with me."

"I love you, Son. Better get some sleep. Good thing I don't have to get up and go to work in the morning, huh? I can sleep in."

***

Weeks went by, and for the life of me, I couldn't find a day's work. The hospital rejected my efforts to volunteer, prohibiting me from delivering flowers and mail. I couldn't believe how thoroughly I was shut out of every opportunity, sometimes out of suspicion or fear, other times out of pure spite, the intention being, I suppose, to force me to leave town. Our tacky rental house provided cheap accommodations while Sally's meager paycheck from the preschool and our dwindling savings kept us afloat. But if something didn't break our way soon, we would have to dip into my meager retirement fund, or move in with my brother, Jerry, in Memphis. Those looked like our only options.

That was the unfortunate reality for lifelong pastors like myself. We were highly trained in a select group of skills that were useful in ministry, but pretty useless in any other line of work. Pastors who changed careers generally had to go back to school and start over in another field. Exceptions to that rule were few, but I tried to remain hopeful. Then, as we were sitting down to dinner, my cell phone rang.

"Hey, preacher, this is Hugh Martin. I got your number from a woman named Donna at the church. She said it was okay to call."

I had never spoken to Mr. Martin outside of his hardware store, and there only a few times. "Yes, Mr.

Martin, what can I do for you?" Perplexed, I wondered what he could possibly want, perhaps to offer more advice.

"It's what I can do for you, preacher. Word is, you can't get a job in this town. Those sons of bitches won't let you work anywhere. Is that the truth?"

"Well, yes, though I wouldn't say it quite that way."

"No, I don't suppose you would, but that's the way it is, isn't it? So, come work for me. I'll hire you. How's that sound to you, preacher?"

Stunned, I struggled to find the words. "That sounds great, Mr. Martin. Should I come by and fill out an application or something? You should know up front, I know next to nothing about hardware and all the things you sell."

"Well, hell, don't talk me out of it. Three questions: First, can you make change?"

"Well, sure, I can."

"Thought so. Can you push a broom?"

"Expert at that, Mr. Martin."

"Great. Now, you're not too old to unload a truck, are you?"

"Certainly not. I can do that, sir. No problem."

"You're hired. Tomorrow morning, nine o'clock. I'll see you then, preacher."

"Thank you, Mr. Martin. I appreciate it very much, more than I can tell you." My words caught in my throat as I choked up.

"No problem, preacher. It's a great day when I can help someone who needs it, and piss off everyone else. See you tomorrow."

I hung up my phone and smiled at Sally. "I guess we won't be moving to Memphis just yet."

Chapter 6 – Hardware Man

"God's grace is ridiculously inclusive.
Apparently, God doesn't care who he loves."
~ Mike Yaconelli

The case was not scheduled to go to trial until January, six long months after the attack at the truck stop. Richie Towns and Mark Hampton were charged with aggravated battery, a felony in Georgia, punishable by one to twenty years in prison. Georgia was one of only a few states that did not have laws against hate crimes on the books, leaving those cases to the federal authorities, who focused more on homicides and lynchings. All indications were that the defendants would plead not guilty and both David and Daniel would need to testify.

Sally and I were filled with dread and anticipation, wishing David did not have to relive such a nightmarish ordeal, and yet anxious to see justice done. We entered the courtroom following David and Dinah, and sat down in the second row of chairs, where Daniel Summers and his parents were already seated. The room was all mahogany and leather and tall windows with plantation shutters open to the winter sun.

A side door opened, and a bailiff led the defendants into the courtroom where their attorney waited for them. Before the judge entered the room, the defense attorney stepped near the prosecutor and the two had a brief exchange.

Then, "All rise!" and Judge Cheney entered the courtroom and took his place.

Richie Towns and Mark Hampton stood up as the charges were read, wearing orange jumpsuits, standard inmate issue, with their hands cuffed behind them.

"You have been charged with two counts of aggravated battery. How do you plead?"

They both glanced at their attorney who nodded affirmatively. "Guilty," they answered together.

"Do you understand that by pleading guilty you are waiving your right to a trial and I will impose a sentence at this time?"

"We do," "Yes, your Honor," they answered in rapid succession.

"Does the prosecution have a recommendation before I pass sentence?" The judge had not been privy to whatever plea agreement had been made.

"Yes, Your Honor, but before we proceed to sentencing, Mr. Summers has prepared a victim's impact statement he would like to read, with the court's permission."

"Very well. Mr. Summers, you may address the defendants."

Daniel stood to his feet, walked to the front, and turned to face his attackers, who remained seated. He pulled his printed statement from his jacket, unfolded it, and cleared his throat.

"I want to thank the court for this opportunity to speak to two men I have never met. Before that night at the truck stop, you were strangers to me, and I to you. We had never had a conversation, let alone a conflict of any kind. I had never wronged you or harmed you in any way. I did not know you and you did not know me. But that didn't stop you, did it? All you saw was someone different, a person who was gay. So, with no provocation and no other reason, you attacked me that night.

"I have spent twenty-two days in the hospital and have had surgery five times. I have limited hearing in my left ear and continued problems with my left eye. I have metal plates in my cheek and in my skull. I have chronic pain and ugly scars that will remind me every day of my life what you did to me. My parents have spent much of their life savings on my medical bills, beyond what insurance would pay. I have only recently been able to return to my job. In spite of all this, I know I am fortunate to be alive, no thanks to you."

Richie Towns kept his head down, focused on the floor, unwilling to look at Daniel.

Mark Hampton sat back slouched in his chair, staring at Daniel as he spoke, sometimes glancing at Towns, and once he turned to look at us with a smirk of sick satisfaction.

Daniel continued. "When I was in high school, after a long personal struggle, I told my parents that I was gay. Though they loved me and still do, it was difficult for them to accept. They thought I was making a bad choice, a huge mistake, going down the wrong path, mixed up about my sexuality. It was a painful time for all of us. For nearly two years, I wasn't welcome in our home, not even for birthdays or holidays. It was hard for my family to accept that I was gay, not by choice but by nature. I was put down and humiliated at school more times than I can say. I was ostracized at my church, and then, on that summer night, I was nearly beaten to death by total strangers, you two, just because I'm gay. You made your motivation very clear. And now I have one question for you to think about while you serve your time. If being gay is simply a choice for people like me, why would anyone choose to be gay? Look what it has cost me, the price I have paid. And if it is not a choice, then what right do you have to hate me for it? Think about that. That's all I have to say." Daniel folded the paper and returned to his seat beside his mother.

"Your Honor, the state recommends a sentence of two years in prison, including time served, and five years' probation."

Hampton and Towns stood up beside their attorney.

The judge looked them over once again. "Do the defendants have anything to say, before I pass sentence?"

Towns declined but Mark Hampton spoke up. "Go easy on us, Judge. We didn't mean nothin' by it. Just some razin' that got out of hand. We over done it."

Judge Cheney shook his head in disgust, raised his gavel, and announced, "As for the state's recommendation, it is so ordered. The defendants will be remanded into custody and transferred to the state prison in Homerville. This court stands adjourned." The sound of the gavel brought the matter to an end.

Richie Towns turned towards David and Daniel with a smirk and a nod.

Mark Hampton remained expressionless as they were led from the room, until he paused at the doorway and glared back at David and Daniel with an angry sneer. It was unnerving to see his face, an expression that chilled the blood.

The deputy closed the door and they were gone.

Sally and I were relieved that David did not have to go through the ordeal of the trial, reliving the pain and brutality of that awful night, but it was an empty, futile kind of relief. Where was the justice? There was no doubt in David's mind that what took place was an attempted murder, convinced that Daniel's attackers thought he was dead when they fled the scene. They wanted to kill him, and they thought they had. Attempted murder. Instead, in eighteen months, they would be free as a bird.

I couldn't help but wonder what had gone on behind the scenes, far removed from the courthouse, to make sure these two good ol' boys didn't get in too much trouble for just 'tuning up a couple of queers.' Attitudes in rural Georgia weren't hard to read, and then to think that I may have reinforced such behavior by my own teaching and preaching all those years before.... The thought stirred a wave of nausea as we walked out into the corridor.

Sally walked out between David and Daniel, taking them each by the arm. "So, that's the end of it. They're going away and we can move on."

David was struggling to put a positive spin on a verdict that he obviously found unsatisfying and unjust. "For a while, I guess, Mom, but it's just not right. If you ask me, they got away with it."

Daniel stopped and hugged Sally. "Thanks, Mrs. Sheldon. You are very kind." Putting his hand on David's shoulder, he said, "Let it go, man. They'll do the time and they have to live with themselves. We've got to move on."

***

I was restocking the battery display rack near the cash register when Stanley Pulliam came in the hardware store. I had not seen Stanley since the night I was fired, but he had that same stern expression, the furrowed brow, and general disdain for me.

"Good afternoon, Stanley. How can I help you?"

He didn't look at me directly, instead scanning around the store in every direction. "I didn't know you were working here. Where's Mr. Martin? Is he here?"

"No, he's not here right now. He's running some errands and getting a sandwich. Something I can get for you, Stanley?"

He shook his head, flustered and embarrassed. "No, thank you. I'll come back later." He turned and pushed open the door, having never looked me in the eye.

I had always known Stanley to be a face-to-face, man-to-man kind of guy, but I guess not anymore. As I watched him walk to his truck, I saw Daniel Summers coming towards the door.

He was looking much better these days. His dark hair was longer which covered some of the scars on his scalp and his new glasses shielded his damaged cheek and eye.

"Hey, Daniel, how are you doing? You're looking well."

He stepped forward with a friendly handshake. "I'm doing fine, Reverend Sheldon. Better all the time, thanks." Always meticulously polite and respectful, Daniel insisted on using my title in all conversations.

"Glad to hear it, Daniel. How can I help you today?" I stepped around the counter.

"Well, I need some camping supplies. Don't know if he told you, but David and I are going camping this weekend up at Black Rock Mountain." He seemed a little embarrassed to tell me, almost blushing.

"Sounds like fun, Daniel. Beautiful place. What do you need?" He pulled a slip of paper from his shirt pocket and glanced at it. "Some tent stakes and twine, mosquito repellent, a twelve-by-twelve plastic mat or tarp, and an extra Coleman propane cannister, the kind for a stove. I think that's it."

We started down the aisle towards the sporting goods section of the store, which was nothing but fishing, hunting, and camping supplies, the only real sports according to Mr. Martin.

"I think we've got you covered," I said.

As I rang up his purchase, he thanked me again for all the support and encouragement during his recovery. "And, I wouldn't have made it without David. You know, I wouldn't be alive." His eyes were moist as he shook my hand.

"You and David will always have that terrible ordeal in common, like soldiers who have been in combat together."

As he scooped up his supplies, he nodded. "He's the best friend I've ever had."

"I hope you guys have a great trip. Be careful up there."

He smiled as he headed out the door. "We will, Reverend Sheldon. Thanks."

***

It took me a moment to recognize the frantic voice on my cell phone. I shook myself awake and glanced at my alarm clock on the nightstand: 12:25 am.

"Pastor, you gotta help me. I really blew it this time, and Kelly says she's done. She's throwing all my shit out in the front yard. You gotta talk to her. She'll listen to you. Remember when you helped us before?" It was Ron Neyland, the deacon at First Baptist that had been so insistent about my termination, even though I had helped him save his marriage a few years before. The issue back then was pornography, and Ron had pledged to get some support and accountability to help him break his addiction, but once Kelly and the kids were back home, he never followed through.

I figured Ron had lapsed and been caught again. "Ron, take a breath and try to calm down. Why is Kelly so upset? Can you tell me what happened?"

"I really screwed up, Pastor. I did something I never thought I'd do. I was with another woman. I was tempted and I did it, a few times, and now Kelly knows and she's leaving. She's so pissed, and she says she's divorcing me and taking the kids. I don't know how she found out. Somebody talked."

"Ron, what have you done? What have you done to your family?"

"I know, Pastor, I know I did wrong, but no one was supposed to know. I didn't want to hurt Kelly. You know I love her, Pastor."

"Do you have any idea how ridiculous that sounds, Ron? How pathetic? Who is this woman that you've been seeing?"

"You know her, Pastor. It's Priss, Priscilla Larson. She's been coming on to me for months. She asked me to come over and fix stuff, her dishwasher and then her ceiling fan. She was lonely, and things have never been the same for me and Kelly after that last blow up. It just happened. I didn't think it was a big deal, just two lonely people having a little fun. And she is so hot. No one was supposed to get hurt. Now Kelly's screaming for a divorce and tossing all my clothes out the front door. Will you come talk to her? She'll listen to you, Pastor."

"Ron, first off, I'm not your pastor, and you made it very clear that you didn't want me to be your pastor. Second, when I was your pastor, you didn't listen to me or keep the promises you made to Kelly. And third, what you have done is unconscionable and inexcusable. You might as well pick up your stuff and get out. Go get the help you needed years ago. You can give Kelly my number, and she can call me if she wants to talk, but my advice to her will be to move on, take care of her kids, and try to make a new life."

I sensed his anger rising as he listened to my rebuff. "I thought you were a pastor. I thought you were supposed to care about people in trouble and help them in a crisis. Well, thanks for nothing. I'm glad we got rid of you when we did, you bastard." He hung up.

I went back to bed and laid awake awhile. Years ago, I would have hurried across town to intervene and try to help in some way, but not tonight, not this time.

Was I just being vindictive, returning evil for evil, humiliating a man who had humiliated me? Or was I practicing tough love towards someone who needed to hear it? After mulling it over, it occurred to me: *I'm not a pastor, anyway. I work at the hardware store. And if you think I'm harsh or tough, go tell your troubles to Hugh Martin.*

***

Sally liked taking long walks in the evening after dinner, but during the week, when I was on my feet all day at the hardware store, I had to pass. So, we made up the lost miles on my days off. Our Black Lab, Shiloh, went with us, and she always had twice the energy we could muster between us.

On that chilly January evening, Sally had plenty on her mind, running back and forth from past to future. "Amy says it happened just like you said it would, Bart. Most of the people who walked out of the church that Sunday came back after you were fired, and most of the ones who had supported you ended up leaving, maybe a fourth of the members. She said that anyone who spoke up for you or for gay people has been asked to leave the church. The deacons have passed a new doctrinal statement, and they want to make it mandatory for all staff and teachers to sign it."

"I guess we shouldn't be surprised, Sally. What's Amy and her family going to do? Are they sticking around?"

"For now, anyway. Amy loves teaching the first- and second-graders, and she doesn't have a backup, but next fall, she'll be done. She has no interest in staying any longer." Sally's friendship with Amy Morrow had been close for years, but this recent crisis had bound them together like sisters.

Shiloh stopped by the Willis's big pine to do her business. Sally always held the leash and I carried the plastic bags, though I was not sure why that job always fell to me.

"Have you talked to Dinah, Bart? I wish you would talk to her. I think she's struggling, bitter about everything that's happened. It's so unlike her. I asked her to go with us to Yvonne's church last week, and she said, 'No, thanks, Mom. I'm done with it, done with church. It's not for me, not anymore.' I know she's been hurt—we've all been hurt—but I hate to see her turn her back on her faith."

"I've tried to talk to her, Sweetie, but she's going to need some time to work through all that's happened. I asked her if she would like to see someone to help her process her feelings, but she's as stubborn as I am. She won't do that either." Sally stopped at the street corner, her anxiety dimming the light in her expression.

Shiloh laid down at our feet and rolled on her back with her tongue sliding side to side from her gaping mouth.

Sally continued. "I can't blame her for feeling the way she does. God knows, the idea of you serving another church terrifies me. I dread the thought of it. I never want to see you in that situation again, at the mercy of such mean and hypocritical people."

I put my arm around her shoulder and kissed her forehead. "Now you're starting to sound like Mr. Martin. Don't worry about me, and don't worry about Dinah, either. She'll work through this, we all will."

"I hope you're right. She's always had a tender heart for God."

I took the leash from Sally's hand, and we crossed Poplar and walked past the furniture store and the old Rexall pharmacy. "Maybe she's waiting, Sal, just waiting."

"Waiting? Waiting for what?"

"It's like this: Dinah says she's done with the church. I don't blame her, but that doesn't mean she's lost her faith. Maybe she's just waiting for whatever's next."

Sally puzzled over that thought for a moment, shaking her head. "What's next, Bart? I don't get it."

"I'm not sure I know just yet, Sal. I've been thinking about it a lot. If the church that we have always known refuses to live up to God's ideal, then the faith will take on new forms. It's happened before in times of reformation, awakening. The old structures falter and fade away, and something new emerges from the rubble, something pure and powerful. I think it's happening again. So, I'm waiting on what's next, God's new thing, whatever that might look like. It has probably already arrived in other places. It will show up here one of these days."

"Maybe you're right." Sally said. "I hope whatever is coming shows up soon. We could all use a whole new thing around here."

***

My first year at Martin's Hardware flew by as the old store became my home away from home. I never would have guessed how much I could learn about the business in such a short span of time. I'd anticipated having the most menial responsibilities, but Mr. Martin soon began to teach me all the ins and outs of the hardware business. Before long I was doing most of the ordering of inventory, managing the store accounts, and running the deposits to the bank. Mr. Martin determined to teach me everything about the business and seemed pleased when I proved to be a quick study.

On Mondays and Tuesdays, Mr. Martin left the store in my hands, giving him a little more time to fish down at the reservoir, or hunt whatever was in season. It was surprising to me how much I enjoyed the store. I never thought of myself as someone who would enjoy retail work, but I liked being able to provide what people needed, helping them solve their problems and finish their projects. It was gratifying to work with customers, many of which I had known for many years, yet in a different context. I noted how many people continued to call me "Pastor," or "Brother Bart," or

"Reverend Sheldon." Only gradually, one by one, folks would leave the past formality behind and just call me "Bart."

It was good that I enjoyed the hardware business, because my past profession was without opportunity. I had hoped I would have a chance to preach from time to time, filling in for vacationing pastors or serving as an interim pastor for churches who were between ministers, but the phone never rang. A few pastors, like Roger Holcomb at Bethany, let me know that I was not welcome to attend their church. Some of the pastors were afraid that I might preach the sermon I used on Gospel Truth Sunday in their church. The only exception was my friend, Yvonne, from the UCC church, who invited me to speak two Sundays in August while she was vacationing down at Jekyll Island. Her congregation was cautiously friendly to me, not sure what to make of a Baptist minister who was too liberal for his own church, but it felt great to preach again, to talk about what was happening in my own heart and mind in a safe, friendly place.

The store was closed on Sundays, so Sally and I could worship anywhere they would let us in the door. We attended Yvonne's church from time to time, but more often we went to the veteran's home, where my friend and former neighbor, George Fletcher, conducted a chapel service every Sunday. Sally and I would arrive early and help George gather his little flock, wheeling the "heroes" to the little chapel with just one stained-glass window, a lectern, and a flag. George always brought his guitar, and would play gospel songs for the old gentlemen, a few of whom could still carry a tune.

Sally was the star of the show, as George and I soon learned, the one the men wanted to see, as she moved among the wheelchairs, flattering and fussing over each one, bringing big smiles to sad faces.

When George spoke each week, he was remarkably simple and direct, no fluff and no bluff, just straight talk about life and faith. I found his words refreshing and encouraging. It seemed to be the only appropriate way to speak to men who had been to war, seen it all and lived long, and for myself, having been through a different kind of war, it was good medicine.

***

Denny's in Joppa was not too busy at six in the morning, with just a few early commuters scattered across the dining room. Margaret poured my coffee, and I caught up on her family while I waited for Michael Peters to join me for an early breakfast. Michael grew up in Joppa, and I baptized him as a boy of ten. His folks raised turkeys for Tyson, and his family had attended First Baptist Church since long before my time, something like three generations. Michael had come to me his senior year to talk about feeling called to be a minister. I couldn't tell at the time whether this was a sincere response to a divine calling or a desperate wish to escape the turkey farm.

It soon became apparent to everyone that Michael was serious about serving God, although he was not sure in what context his ministry might fit. His parents sent him off to Mercer, a major sacrifice on their part, with a ministry scholarship from First Baptist. He did well in college, eventually earning some additional scholarship help. Michael spent two summers back in Joppa working at the church as a youth ministry intern, and did a fine job, displaying remarkable creativity and maturity.

After graduation, Michael began work on his Master of Divinity at McAfee, and he was in his second year. I had not talked to Michael since the blow-up at First Baptist. His parents no doubt filled him in on the happenings at the church while he was away, and I wasn't sure just what perspective they might have shared with their son. Anyway, Michael was back in town for the weekend, and had called to see if we could talk, and an early breakfast was the best I could do on a busy Saturday.

Michael hustled across the parking lot with his jacket over his head against the early morning shower. Margaret filled a fresh cup for Michael as he slid into the booth and said a friendly good morning. We ordered up our Grand Slams and began to catch up on each other. Michael knew all about the happenings at the church and my work at the store. He was also aware that some people had been more than unkind since my termination. He asked about David and seemed pleased to hear that he was doing well.

What an impressive young man, I thought, bright and thoughtful, though he looked more like a seventies rock and roll throwback. His wavy brown hair was almost shoulder-length, parted down the middle, requiring an intermittent shake of the head to keep the hair out of his line of sight. I thought how sore my neck would be after a few hours of that. Michael's clear green eyes revealed his transparent character.

I asked about his future ministry plans, and he still had no definite answer, great desire but no direction. Like most of his generation, Michael was sensitive and inclusive on issues of gender and sexuality, and critical of churches that misused scripture to support their own social biases.

"I don't think I want to be a pastor in the traditional sense. I don't mean to sound critical or judgmental, Pastor, but I don't think churches like First Baptist have much to do with what God is doing in the world today. They're still fighting battles over outdated traditions and issues that should have been settled years ago, beating people up with the Bible. It seems like the church around here is a club dedicated to denouncing the world instead of loving it. They are not really engaging the needs of people on the outside, just fighting over their share of the religious crowd in the area."

I had never heard Michael speak so freely.

Margaret came by to clear the plates and refill our coffee cups.

"You know, Michael," I said, "there was a time not too long ago when I would have argued with you on the issues you've raised. You grew up at First Baptist. I was your pastor for a long time. Much of what you describe was pretty much my approach to ministry, though I sincerely believed that I was following God's will and the teaching of scripture. I know now I was wrong. I was wrong about a lot of things. But it's hard now, painful for me to judge the church that I led for so long. How can I condemn the church for following my leadership? I mean, seriously, five years ago, if I'd had a staff person who preached that sermon on homosexuality, I would have fired him myself."

Michael stirred his coffee as he shook his head. "But you changed, Pastor. You were forced to reconsider the issue, to rethink the meaning of scripture, and you learned, you changed, and that's wonderful. It's a beautiful thing when God opens our eyes to the truth that we've never seen before. I respect you for that, Pastor."

"I appreciate that, and I may be a little wiser, but now my job is working at the hardware store. That's my calling now. You've got to decide what you are going to do about ministry and the future of the church. It's time for your generation to get the church back on track, to help us rediscover what it means to follow Jesus. Are you up for that?"

Michael paused for a thoughtful moment, still stirring his coffee. "I think so, Pastor. I'm up for it. I just don't know what it looks like."

"Me either, Michael. Me either."

***

Most of the deliveries came early on Thursday at the hardware store. I helped the drivers off-load the freight, and spent the rest of the morning breaking it down and getting the merchandise inventoried and ready to stock. Sometimes it would take me all day to get finished, and most Thursdays, Mr. Martin stayed in front running the store while I worked in the back.

It was a Thursday afternoon about three-thirty when I finished and came up front to see how I could help, but the store seemed deserted, not a soul in sight.

"Mr. Martin? Mr. Martin, are you here?" He was not at the cash register or his desk behind the counter. "Mr. Martin?" I checked the bathroom, but he wasn't there either. It was not like him to leave the store unattended, even for a few moments. I walked through the store, aisle by aisle. "Mr. Martin?" I glanced down the back aisle towards the mops and brooms and turned around before what I had seen registered in my mind. I jerked back to look again, and at the far end of the aisle I saw his foot, his black safety shoe pointed toward the light.

"Mr. Martin!" I found him there on the floor unconscious. "Mr. Martin! Can you hear me?"

I dialed 911 for an ambulance, but I feared the worst. His face was ashen and clammy, and his eyes fixed and lifeless.

"Mr. Martin, can you hear me?" I began CPR, but his massive chest seemed frozen solid. I could hear the siren approaching, but there was no pulse, no breath, no chance.

The paramedics did the best they could but I knew before they told me: he was gone.

When they loaded Mr. Martin onto the gurney, they removed his canvas apron and handed it to me.

Before I followed them to the hospital, I quickly closed the store, and before I locked the door, I realized I was still carrying Mr. Martin's apron in my hand. I walked over to his desk and hung it on the wooden coat rack where he always kept it, and from force of habit said, "Goodnight, Mr. Martin. God bless."

***

The funeral service was held at Hopkins Funeral Home over Mr. Martin's protest. He had made it clear that he thought the whole funeral industry was a huge scam, preying on the sentimentalities of grieving people. He'd left instructions for his daughter, Carol Buckner:

> *Burn my body or bury it in the backyard, for all I care. I just don't want to think that I died to make some undertaker a little richer. Screw that.*

But Carol had a family of her own and she wanted to have a real service, like the one for her mother eleven years before. She asked me to conduct the funeral, thinking her dad might tolerate it better in the afterlife if I did the honors.

Carol and I had met over coffee to get better acquainted. She had grown up in Joppa and then finished her pharmacist degree at Mercer. Her husband, Lee, was a real estate broker in Raleigh, North Carolina, where they had made their home. Their two children, Robert and Claire, were in college and grad school.

As Carol talked about her dad, a surprising portrait of his life begin to emerge. It quickly became obvious to me that hardly anybody knew the whole story of Hugh Martin. My respect and appreciation for him grew as Carol had filled in the large gaps in his remarkable story.

As I now stood and moved to the lectern near his flag-draped casket, I was surprised to see a large crowd, nearly a full house, gathered to pay their respects, including local people that I would never have connected with Mr. Martin. Customers at the store, I guessed. I began my eulogy:

> *I might as well say it up front. While Hugh Martin was certainly a good man, he was not a religious person, not a church-going man, at least not in more recent years. In fact, Mr. Martin never had much use for preachers or pastors. But for some reason, he seemed to tolerate me. He even gave me a job when I needed one, and we became friends.*
>
> *I don't know if Mr. Martin had suffered a bad experience way back or what, but he was soured on church, and religion in general. I*

would remind him that the main concern was not how he felt about the church, but what was between him and God. He would nod and say, "Don't worry about that, preacher." I never knew Mr. Martin to come out publicly about his faith, but I had a sense that he and the Lord had worked things out personally, man to man, and that's the way Mr. Martin liked to do things.

It's interesting to me that when we read the Gospels, we see Jesus often in a rage against the most religious types of his day, whose hypocrisy and self-righteous attitudes always offended Christ and drew his sharp rebuke. At the same time, we see Jesus spending His time with those wayward people who were on the outside looking in. He always had great compassion and patience with those for whom faith was a difficult step. People like Hugh Martin.

I thought I knew Mr. Martin well, having worked with him day by day for the past year, but I was wrong. Since her dad's sudden passing, Carol has been filling me in about his life, his story. I must say, I had no idea, and I'm guessing that most of us gathered here today are in the dark as well. Let me hit a few of the highlights.

When Hugh Martin was just a boy of fifteen, the oldest of four children, his father died of a heart attack. For three years, he kept the farm going, raising crops, handling the livestock, and helping his mother keep the family together — a teenager taking care of a large family. His one surviving sister, Elaine, is here to verify the story. Their mother would never have managed the farm or provided for the kids without her oldest. And after young Hugh was called up into the Marine Corps, his income went straight back to the farm and his family.

Mr. Martin never talked much about his years in the service, two tours in Viet Nam. He had the Marine insignia on his arm and that nasty scar across his left hand and forearm. I asked him about it once at the store. His only reply was, "A bayonet, Viet Cong. He started it, but I finished it." Carol showed me her dad's medals and citations, and told me the rest of the story, a Purple Heart and the Navy Cross for heroism. Hugh Martin was credited with rescuing seven fellow marines who were pinned down under heavy enemy fire after their armored personnel carrier was hit during the Tet Offensive. Three of those marines were wounded and were carried to safety by Hugh Martin and the other marines. All this happened under fire in close hand-to-hand combat. He was credited with eleven kills in this action, while sustaining a bullet wound in his leg and the knife wound to his arm and hand. I'd call that heroism.

After the war, Mr. Martin came back home to marry his high school sweetheart, Shirley Hix, and after two heart-breaking miscarriages, they were blessed with a beautiful baby girl, Carol. But, that happy moment nearly ended in tragedy as well. You see, when Carol was born, her mother was sick with diphtheria, and while the doctors worked to save Shirley, Hugh doctored their baby girl, all purple and struggling to breathe, saving her newborn life with his own rough, calloused hands. Who knows? Mr. Martin may have invented CPR for newborn infants.

Carol said that her dad was a wonderful, although overprotective, father. When she was old enough to start dating, Mr. Martin started giving driving tests. When a boy showed up to take Carol out, her dad would insist that the boy take him for a little ride first, so he could make sure the boy was a safe driver. Of course, the real reason for the driving test was to give Mr. Martin a private opportunity to lay down the law as to how his daughter was to be treated. Carol said one boy was so shaken and fearful when they came back that he called off the whole thing.

Hugh and Shirley Martin had thirty-four years of happiness together, and these years since her passing have been difficult for Mr. Martin. Carol said her parents had big plans for retirement, to get a nice RV and travel around the country. They both loved the outdoors. But after her mother died, her dad just kept working, running the hardware store and doing a little hunting and fishing on the side. Mr. Martin said, "Who wants to retire alone? No point to that. I might as well do something useful." And Mr. Martin did make himself useful to our whole community.

I was amazed to hear about Mr. Martin's generous support for higher education, investing in local students for many years, never publicly, always behind the scenes. Carol said that when she was born, her dad set up a savings account for her future college education. Surprisingly, her dad had also set up savings accounts for the two infants that he and Shirley had lost. It was their way to honor their memory and to put their grief to good use. So, for all those years, and continuing after Shirley passed away, Mr. Martin has been sending local students to community colleges, to trade schools, to state universities, sometimes graduate school, whatever was needed. In fact, now his scholarship fund is an ongoing endowment that will continue to bless our local students and open doors of opportunity for generations to come. I would like all of you whose families have been blessed in this way, through Mr. Martin's generosity, to please stand for a moment.

More than half of those in attendance stood to their feet. No one moved or spoke as we looked around and pondered the impact of one man's generosity. Many of the tuition recipients had never dreamed that they were just one among many students so blessed. The magnitude of his contribution left us speechless.

***

Two days later, I was present for the reading of Mr. Martin's will. David Marshbanks, the local attorney serving as executor of the estate, had sent me notification, and Carol had invited me as well. The notification simply indicated that I was named in the will, with no details or specifics. I had no idea what that might mean, since Mr. Martin had never mentioned any intention on his part to me.

As might be expected, the will was clear and direct. All of Mr. Martin's personal bank accounts and personal property, including his home in Joppa, his cabin at the reservoir, his truck and his boat, were bequeathed to his daughter and only child, Carol. Then the attorney continued to read, "I leave my store, Martin's Hardware Store at 601 Maple St., including the building, all the inventory and equipment, and the store's bank accounts, to my recent business partner, Bart Sheldon, with the one condition that he not sell the store for a period of five years."

I couldn't believe my ears. I was stunned, but Carol was smiling and obviously not surprised or upset. "It's true, Bart. Daddy decided several months ago that if anything happened to him, he wanted you to have the store, to keep it going and be part of the community. We talked about it. With my family living in Raleigh, I didn't want to run it, and he didn't want me to sell it off or close it down. So, it's yours free and clear. You've been keeping the books, so you know the score. There's no debt against the business and hardly any overhead. Congratulations, Bart. Daddy just made you a business owner."

"I don't know what to say. Are you sure you're all right with this, Carol? The store really should belong to you. I feel like a usurper."

"Forget about it, Bart. You knew Daddy. This is what he wanted, and it pleases me to be able to honor his wishes. I would make one request that was not in the will, if you don't mind."

"Certainly, Carol. What is it?"

"The name of the store, Bart." She teared up as she spoke. "Would you mind keeping the name, at least for a while?"

"Martin's Hardware it is, and it will remain Martin's Hardware as long as the store belongs to me," I said with a smile. "I wouldn't think of changing it."

"Thanks, Bart," she said as she stepped forward with a hug. "Good luck with the store. I know you'll do great."

As I got in my car, I couldn't help but laugh to myself.

What a crazy, remarkable old man, Hugh Martin, my gruff and grizzled guardian angel. God bless him. Sally is never going to believe this. This morning, I thought I was losing my job, and this afternoon I own the business.

***

Those first few weeks and months running the store on my own were busy, stressful, and exhilarating. I worked twelve to fourteen hours a day trying to get on top of things, and to figure out the aspects of running the business that Mr. Martin had not covered with me. David and Dinah would pitch in with a few hours here and there, and Sally kept me stocked on sandwiches and snacks, and sometimes a warm plate of dinner from home. I wanted to make sure I had a handle on things before bringing on any new help, but after three months of flying solo, I was ready to put the "Help Wanted" sign in the window.

By this time, folks were growing accustomed to seeing me in the hardware store, and few customers called me 'Reverend' or 'Pastor.' I was becoming something of an oddity, an interesting bit of local trivia. People would say, 'Did you know Bart used to be a pastor?' Mercifully, they would usually not go on to recount the saga that drove me from the pulpit to the hardware store. Members of First Baptist Church would do business with me at the store, being courteous and direct, but rarely mentioning any personal connection we may have had before. Even those whom I'd baptized or married or counseled through the years scarcely ever spoke of our past relationship. Some were no doubt still disappointed or bitter. Perhaps others felt regretful or guilty. I don't know, but it saddened me to see so many pretending that our past never happened or didn't matter now. I was troubled to think that I had spent the prime years of my life and ministry serving among people who no longer acknowledged our long history together.

After the sign went in the window, people began to drop by, most interested in part-time work. I decided that I would hire one full-time person and one part-time, perhaps a student who could come in after school and do some stocking and cleaning up. Or, if I couldn't find good full-time help, I would have to find three part-timers, which would likely be an exercise in frustration for me. I needed a dependable full-time person who could do for me what I had been doing for Mr. Martin, but so far, nobody seemed to fill the bill, not even close.

Imagine my surprise when Jim Hinnessy came in the store one afternoon. Jim was the former custodian at First Baptist whom I had terminated years before, and who had spoken out in favor of my termination. Now here he was, standing at my checkout with no merchandise in his hands. He was dressed in canvas painter's pants and a blue work shirt, like Mr. Martin used to wear. He didn't look at me directly, glancing all around the store, obviously nervous and uncomfortable.

"Hello, Jim. Good to see you. Can I help you find something?"

He looked at the floor and shifted his feet. "Well, Reverend, I saw your sign. I've been looking for work, doing odd jobs, some light construction, ever since the shoe factory closed. We been just getting by. Somebody told me you needed a full-time man." Jim lifted his head and looked at me face to face. His eyes were moist as he struggled with the words.

"I know we've got some history, Reverend, and I won't blame you if you run me out of here, but the truth is you need help and I need work. That's why I'm here. I got no place else to go. I've tried everywhere. Nobody's hiring, and I don't have a great history anyway, I know that. But I need a job and I'm ready to work hard. If you took me on, maybe gave me a month or two to prove myself, I'll show you that I can do a good job for you. This is my kind of work, and I'll work hard for you, Reverend, whatever you need." He hesitated, looking down again, waiting in the awkward silence.

Sally would tell you that I didn't often make decisions hastily. I liked to think things through carefully and pray about important decisions before I moved ahead. But this time, as Jim made his request, my decision came with sudden and unmistakable clarity.

"Three questions, Jim: First, can you make change?"

"What? Huh, sure I can, Reverend."

"I thought so. Can you push a broom?"

Jim's expression brightened. "You know I can. That would be fine with me."

"Great. You're not too old to unload a truck, are you?"

His face broke into a wide smile. "No problem for me, Reverend. All day long if necessary."

"Good deal, Jim. You're hired, and you can start tomorrow morning, 9:00. There are two conditions we need to be clear on from the start, okay?"

"Thank you, thank you, Reverend, whatever you say."

I put my hand on his shoulder and looked him in the eye. "First, let's forget about the past, Jim. No need to dredge up all that painful stuff. Let's start fresh, shall we?"

"That sounds good to me," he said.

"Second, you don't work for 'Reverend' anybody. My name is Bart. I run a hardware store. Got it?"

He grinned and nodded. "I get it. Thanks, Bart."

I held out my hand and he took it in a firm grip. "We'll work out the details in the morning, do the paperwork, and work out a schedule. Welcome to Martin's Hardware, Jim. I'll order you a couple of shirts and a work apron. See you in the morning."

He was still shaking my hand, unwilling to turn loose. "Thank you so much, Rever- uh... Bart. Thank you for giving me a chance. I won't let you down."

"I know you won't, Jim. Give Lori my best, and I'll see you tomorrow."

He walked out the door with a spring in his step, and I wouldn't have been surprised if he had started skipping down the sidewalk. I stood there watching him go, wondering if I was being wise or foolish, noble or naive. Time would tell, no doubt, but I couldn't help but smile to myself.

A little bit of grace is a wonderful thing.

Chapter 7 – Knitting Souls

The worst thing about our new neighborhood was the lack of friendly neighbors. Sally and I tried to get acquainted, but even Sally's oatmeal raisin cookies couldn't seem to break the ice. Sally was convinced that we were snubbed because of David and the blow-up at First Baptist, and she was probably right. Most folks in Joppa knew their neighbors and knew how to "neighbor" their neighbors, but we had become the exception to the rule.

I missed George, my friend and former neighbor. I guess I didn't realize how close we had become until the crisis, having to vacate the parsonage and move across town. Sally and I still saw George at the veteran's home on most Sundays, of course, but I missed our evening talks and afternoon lemonade. A couple of times, I had driven by our old place on the way home from the store, though it was several blocks out of the way, just to see if George was around.

One afternoon, I got lucky and saw him washing his car in the driveway. I stopped at the curb and got out. "Hey, George, how are you doing? I think you missed a spot on that fender."

He wiped his hand on his t-shirt, took off his faded 'Navy" ball cap, wiped his face on his shoulder, and stepped toward me with a smile. "Hey, Bart, good to see you. How's the hardware business these days?" He tossed his sponge in the five-gallon bucket beside his Volvo and motioned toward the front steps.

"Don't stop on my account. I would hate to think of you driving a filthy car around town just because I stopped by." Not much chance of that, since everything George owned was meticulously maintained and spit-polished in the best Navy tradition.

"No problem. Sit down, Bart. You doing all right? How's your family?"

"We're hanging in there. Sally puts up a brave front, but this is a painful time for her, and David still feels responsible for everything wrong with the world. I guess you heard what happened to our house?"

"Yeah, I heard. I'm sure that got you off to a great start with your new landlord. Cowardly sons of bitches. If you had still been living here, I would have jumped them, guns blazing."

"Ah, George, you're all talk. I know you have a gun or two, but you couldn't shoot anybody. Remember? You were a chaplain in the Navy, not a SEAL."

He wasn't convinced though. "I'm telling you, I would have made an exception in this case. Damn cowards."

"Yeah, well, we're still here and I'm determined that we are not running away. And, thanks to Hugh Martin, I have a job, a business, so we can eat. And when we get a little money saved up, we'll buy a house of our own. Sally's never lived in a house that didn't belong to somebody else, so I want to get her a place as soon as I can, someplace nice."

"That would be great," he replied. "She'd love that, I'll bet. Might want to find a place with a tall fence and a couple of big Dobermans. No offense to Shiloh, but she's too sweet."

George's wife, Linda, opened the door behind us with two tall glasses of lemonade. "Look at you two. Just like old times," she said, handing me a glass. "Good to see you, Bart. I have some peaches in the kitchen I'll send home to Sally. Give her our love. I miss so much having her next door." She turned to go inside.

"She misses you, too, Linda. I know she does. Thanks."

Linda's lemonade was the real thing, no mix for her—real lemons and plenty of sugar. Wonderful stuff.

George took a drink and set his glass on the step between us. "What about David? What's he doing now?"

"He's keeping busy, I think, still working on his masters and working part-time for me. He had as much trouble as I did finding work around here, so it's great that I could hire him. It's a good deal for both of us. I get great help at the store, and he makes the money he needs."

"That's good. Glad to hear it. Give him my best. What about your daughter? How's Dinah doing?"

"Pretty well," I explained. "After the vandalism at the house, she decided to move out, and now she's living with David, sharing his apartment. I think it's good for them, and our place is so small anyway. She's considering her options after graduation, nothing definite yet."

"She'll make a plan, I'm sure." After finishing off his lemonade, George said, "I never see Dinah over at the veteran's home when you and Sally come over. Does she ever make it to church?"

I shook my head. "No, she's never been back to any church since that awful night at First Baptist, and she says she never will, says she's done for good. I know it's the pain, the hurt that she's expressing, and I can't blame her for feeling that way. I hope she can work through it somehow."

George put his hand on my shoulder. "It's about you, Bart, the way they treated you. Dinah saw her daddy abused and humiliated by church people, and that's not something you can get over easily. That's the deepest kind of scar, when those we love are mistreated. Nobody knows that better than you, my friend. You just hang on to her like you held on to David, hang on like God hangs on to us. She'll come around. She'll come back."

"That's just it, George. Come back to what?"

***

Sally came into the kitchen from the utility room trying to unfold a piece of paper that had been through the washer and dryer. "What's this, Honey? It was in the back pocket of your jeans. It's a little smeared, but still readable. 'A Church for All People.'" She carefully laid the rumpled sheet of notebook paper on the kitchen table as I was finishing a sandwich. "What's this about, Bart?"

"It's some notes I've been working on lately. I've been thinking about the church, not First Baptist, but the church in general and in the future. You know, what's next. I've been pondering what kind of church would be legitimate and authentic today, a church that wouldn't be so institutional and obsessed with its own survival, and not so hypocritical, accepting people instead of judging them. Anyway, I came up with ten core values. Those are my notes."

She studied the list for a moment, but she couldn't make out all of them, the ink washed out where the paper was folded. "Interesting. I can't read them all. Here," she said, and handed me a pen. "Can you fill them in for me? Or better yet, make a new list. Use this." She scooted a note pad across the table.

"Okay, I'll do that." I took the pad and wrote at the top, 'A Church for All People.' Then, numbering to ten, I wrote my brief bullet points. I slid it back to Sally and said, "Here you go, Sweetie. See what you think."

It looked like this:

A Church for All People
1. Christ-centered – focus on the life and teachings of Jesus.

2. Grace-based – a fellowship of love and forgiveness.

3. Inclusive – regardless of status, ethnicity, gender, or sexual orientation.

4. Relational – doing life together, sharing common meals.

5. Local – involved in the neighborhood and community.

6. Compassion – caring for the sick, the poor, those in crisis.

7. Justice – standing for social and racial justice.

8. Worship – diverse expressions, from contemplative to contemporary.

9. Simplicity – shared leadership, using any available space.

10. Missional – encourage and support the birth of new churches.

Sally was thoughtful and reflective for a little while, nodding as she read and underlining some points. Finally, she spoke. "Do you think this kind of church exists? Is there a church like this?"

"I don't know, Sal. I really don't. I hope so. I'm sure other people have pondered these same issues. But I will say I don't know of such a church. I have never seen a church that lived out these values."

She picked up the list and reviewed it once more. "It seems so basic and obvious. I would attend this church you're describing. I think I would love it." She stood up as her enthusiasm grew with each moment. "And you know what else? I'll bet David and Dinah would love a church like this, one that welcomed all kinds of people. It's beautiful, Bart. It's a wonderful picture of what a church could be." She put her arms around my neck and kissed my forehead.

"Thanks, Sweetie. It means a lot to me for you to say that. I appreciate it." I turned to put my arms around her waist as she stood beside my chair.

She leaned down, kissed me, and said with a big smile, "Okay, hardware man, when are you going to start this new church?"

***

David came into the store from the freight dock in back, as I was keeping busy with a few late afternoon customers and a fair amount of paperwork on my desk. David had worked part-time for me for several months and I enjoyed the extra time with him, though I knew he found the work less than stimulating. He never complained.

"It's all done, Dad. This morning's order is all inventoried and put away. You're good to go." He came to my desk, took off his work apron and hung it on the coat rack as Mr. Martin had always done.

"Thanks, Son, I appreciate your help. That was a big order."

"No kidding. Business must be picking up around here. That's great." He didn't seem to be in any rush to leave, sitting down in my one wooden side chair. "Hey, Dad, Mom showed me that list you made the other day, a church for all people. She said you're going to start a new church like that." Just like Sally, leaping to that assumption. "I didn't think you were ever getting back into church work, not after everything you've been through, and now having the store and everything."

"You're right. I doubt I will ever be a pastor again. I was trained to lead the traditional church, old ways and old news, and if you ask me, that kind of church is fading away, having less and less to do with real people's lives."

"So, what about 'A Church for All People'? Who's going to make that happen?"

"I'm not sure, but I think a new kind of church probably needs a new kind of leader," I said. "That seems logical enough, doesn't it?"

"Yeah, I can see your point. So, what does this new kind of leader look like?"

I had been pondering David's question for quite a while. And now I had my answer. "Quite a bit like you, Son."

The expression on his face could not have been more startled or confused if I had said he had been chosen to go the moon. He stood up and bent over my desk as he spoke. "Like me! Are you nuts? Me, a pastor? That's not for me. I've seen it. I grew up in it, and I don't want it, Dad. And I couldn't do the job even if I wanted it."

"Maybe not. I understand your reaction. I know this is a whole new thought for you, but keep in mind what you and I have seen is the old paradigm, the old, traditional church. What we are talking about now is a blank sheet of paper, starting from scratch with those simple core values and nothing else, none of the baggage, none of the rules and restrictions. Now that's kind of exciting, isn't it?"

He sat back in his chair, trying to absorb my words as I continued.

"David, not so long ago, you asked me to consider a different point of view about your sexuality and biblical faith, and I did. I learned and I grew in my faith. Now I'm asking you to consider a whole new possibility about what it means to be the church and what it takes to lead the church, and try to put yourself in the picture. I believe in you, Son, your heart for God and for people, and if you decide you want to do this, I'll help you, I'll support you and work alongside you every step of the way. You won't go it alone. But a new movement of God doesn't need a leader from the old days and the old ways. We can't put new wine in old wineskins. I think you might be the one to do it. Think about it, and we'll talk again."

I thought I was going to have to help David to his car, he was so stunned and bewildered from our conversation.

"But, Dad, I'm gay."

"Yeah, I'm clear on that, Son. So what? Is this a church for all people or not?"

***

It began in our tiny living room with fifteen of us squeezed in, half of us sitting on the floor. Most were in their twenties, friends that David and Daniel had invited. Sally and I felt like old-timers. David began the conversation and Daniel Summers led some songs with his guitar. Everyone had a story to tell. Some had been wounded by past church experiences. Others had witnessed blatant hypocrisy and judgmental attitudes. A few seemed to be more curious than committed, just checking things out. Everyone seemed hungry for friendship and genuine community.

David led the discussion of our core values, highlighting the meaning and significance of each of the ten. Everyone joined in the conversation as people expressed their views and concerns. Enthusiasm seemed to grow as our dream began to take shape.

Daniel mentioned Joppa's Community Cafe, a free nightly meal provided by volunteers for anyone who was hungry. They were always struggling to find willing groups to cover the schedule. Jill Brooks, who I remembered from David's middle school days, talked about the mentoring program at the school where she taught fourth grade. Everyone seemed energized, anxious to do something, more than just talk.

Another item that inspired lots of discussion was what to call this new church. We had no interest in any denominational label, and we did not want to identify with any organization, believing this whole venture to be simply a movement of God. Still, we needed to identify ourselves.

Sally, who had been quiet all evening, spoke up. "The first Christians were simply called followers of the Way. Their faith was a way of life. I like that, the Way. It's simple and clear, and I know we want people to see our faith as a way of life, a Jesus kind of life."

No one said a word for a moment, as we pondered the idea, and then, it was agreed. Our church would be called "The Way."

An African American woman named Jodie read the verses that we had chosen as a theme for this new fellowship:

> *"This is how we know what love is: Jesus Christ laid down his life for us. And we ought to lay down our lives for our brothers and sisters. If anyone has material possessions and sees a brother or sister in need but has no pity on them, how can the love of God be in that person? Dear children, let us not love with word or in speech, but with actions and in truth."*
> *1 John 3:16-18*

David asked me to serve communion to bring the evening to a close. I offered a loaf and a common cup as each person took a piece of bread and dipped it in the wine as we celebrated the Supper together. I looked in each face as they came to me, and I saw the humility and the sincerity in their eyes.

"The bread of life broken for you. The cup of salvation poured out for you."

There was a stirring in the room, a sense of God's presence that was palpable and real. For those brief moments, our shabby living room was transformed into a holy place, a sanctuary. How long since these hands of mine had served the Supper? And how much longer had it been since I knew Christ was in the room, present with us? Too long, indeed.

And so it began, with a stirring of the Spirit and a happy huddle determined to live a Jesus kind of life, and to do it together.

***

We had just finished dinner and I was helping Sally clear the table when I heard a knock at the door. The front door was open so when I glanced across the living room, I could see through the screen door a tall man standing on the porch step. I walked toward the door, and my heart skipped a beat when I recognized his face.

Richie Towns, one of the two men who had attacked and beaten Daniel and David, stood at the door.

I stared at him through the screen, unsure what to say.

"Reverend Sheldon, you know who I am and I'll get outta here right now if you tell me to, but there's somethin' I gotta say, just five minutes. I don't need to come in. We can talk out here if you'll hear me out." He looked as he had in court two years before, the same, yet different — tall and gaunt, the same stringy, ragged hair, and yet something had changed.

Sally stepped to the door beside me.

"Mrs. Sheldon, sorry to surprise you like this, but I come to apologize." His voice broke and he began to weep over his words. "I'm so sorry for what I done to your boy, your family, and Daniel Summers."

Stunned, Sally leaned back against me speechless.

I wasn't fully aware of the lingering bitterness I had buried inside until that moment. My heart pounded and my fist clenched at my side. But his face was changed, and the arrogance, the aggression I had seen in his expression before, was gone, erased.

"I don't mean to upset y'all. I just had to let you know I'm truly sorry, ashamed of what I done. I hope someday maybe you can forgive me." With a nod to us, he wiped his eyes and turned to go.

As we watched him amble off towards his truck, Sally found her voice. "Wait, Richie. Would you like to come in for a minute?" She pushed open the screen door as Richie looked back over his shoulder, surprised and confused. "It's all right, Richie. It's good of you to come."

"Thank you, Ma'am, thank you. I'll only stay a minute." He stepped awkwardly into our living room, and I motioned toward the couch and he sat down. Sally sat in her rocker as I settled into my chair, as he came straight to the point. "While I was away in prison, I had lots of time to think. A chaplain there was a friend to me, and he taught me all about God, what Jesus done for me. I had to face up to what I done, the kind of person I been, a lot of bad stuff. So, I'm tryin' to start over and I'm prayin', askin' God to help me make things right." The shiftiness was gone as Richie looked me in the eye with earnestness and sincerity. "Me and Mark was released on Friday and we're on probation for five years. I knew I had to come see y'all and tell you how sorry and ashamed I am for what I done. Please forgive me. And if they'll let me, I want to apologize to David and Daniel. Would you ask them if they'll see me? I need to tell 'em myself."

The tears flowed freely from all three of us.

I moved from my chair and put my hands on his shoulders. "Richie, kneel here beside me." I pushed aside the coffee table, and the three of us slipped to our knees and leaned forward on the couch. I put my arm around Richie's shoulder as Sally took his arm in hers. Through the tears, I prayed.

"Father, I thank you for your love. We are all sinners in need of your grace. I thank you for loving Richie so much that you sent your Son so that he could be forgiven and make a new start. Help us to forgive and love each other as you have loved us. In Jesus' name, amen."

As we stood to our feet, Sally put her arms around the man who had beaten and humiliated her son, and held him while he sobbed. After a long moment, Richie collected himself and Sally went to pour some coffee.

"Sit down, Richie," I said. "How can we help you get started? Have you got some job prospects?"

Settling back on the couch, Richie nodded. "Yes, sir, I think so. My uncle has the tire shop there with the Shell station. He's needin' help and said I can work there for now, and if it works out, I can run the tire shop for him. That would be great."

Sally brought us two mugs of coffee keeping up with our conversation. "That's wonderful, Richie," she said smiling. "I'm happy for you."

I nodded in agreement. "Glad you've got work, Richie. What about your friend, Mark Hampton?"

Richie's hopeful expression clouded as he thought about his friend and fellow inmate. "Mark's a different story. He's still real bitter, angry 'bout doin' time. He won't listen to me, won't even take my calls. Wish you would pray for him, Pastor. Mark's so filled with hatred. I know 'cause that was me before, but he won't let it go."

"I'm sorry to hear that, Richie. I will pray for Mark. Is there anything else you need?"

"Well, like I said, I want to talk to David and Daniel, if they'll let me. Will you ask them and let me know what they say? I'll understand if they say no."

"I'll do that, and I'll tell them about you coming here and our conversation today." Richie nodded appreciatively, but I could tell there was something else on his mind.

"Yes, sir, that's great. Just let me know. There's one more thing, Pastor, something personal, if you don't mind me askin'."

"What is it, Richie? What can I do for you?"

He seemed hesitant, embarrassed to make his request. "Would you be willin' to baptize me? They don't do that at the prison. The chaplain told me all about it, being raised up from the dead like Jesus, startin' a whole new life. I heard you don't have a church no more, but can you baptize me?"

"Richie, I would be honored to baptize you. What a wonderful way to mark this new beginning in your life. Let me work on that, find a place and figure out all the details. We'll make that happen for you."

His face lit up, and it occurred to me: *This is not the same person who attacked our son.* I thought of the words of scripture: *"If anyone is in Christ, he is a new creation. The old is gone. The new has come."*

***

In just a few weeks, "The Way" had outgrown our little house and we were looking for a larger, more permanent location. This proved to be far more challenging than we'd anticipated. We had hoped to rent space from one of the other churches in town, but it soon became apparent that none of the existing churches were anxious to see a new church get started, competing for the same customers. The lone exception, Yvonne Meadows' Lutheran Church, was already sharing their limited space with a Hispanic congregation and several community organizations. The African American churches declined to help, fearing that allowing us to meet in their church would be viewed as an endorsement of our views on homosexuality.

Our next option was the school district, which also declined to allow us to use space on Sundays, even though several other groups and organizations used the schools regularly. We might have been able to litigate our way on to the premises, but we didn't have that kind of time, since we were hoping to begin worshipping together on Easter Sunday, just three weeks away. When we were also turned down by the YMCA and the local theater, it became apparent that there was some behind-the-scenes conspiracy working against our new church, if not against me personally. The only option left to us seemed to be to meet in a shelter house at the park, but the large shelter was already reserved for more than half of the summer Sundays for family reunions and such.

That same week, Brian Ward, my associate pastor at First Baptist, stopped by the hardware store.

Brian and I had little contact after my termination. Though we had worked together almost daily for eight years, we hadn't had a conversation for several months. I missed the friendship we enjoyed during my tenure at the church, and I grieved that loss.

"Hey, Bart, how are you doing today?" Brian had added a few pounds and lost a little hair since my dismissal. Must have been the stress of everything at church.

"I'm fine, Brian. Good to see you. I hope your family is well." He didn't seem anxious to shop, so I motioned to the chair beside my desk.

"Doing well, thanks. Hey, Bart, I've been hearing the talk about this new church starting up. I guess you and David are behind it. Is that right?"

I braced myself for another speech on why this town doesn't need any more churches because the ones we have are barely half full. "That's right. We want to launch on Easter Sunday. It's a new approach, or I should say it's an old approach, hopefully more like the church in the beginning."

Brian nodded. "That's what I'm hearing. I ran into Daniel Summers the other day and he showed me your core values. Interesting stuff, Bart. You certainly got my attention. I've been doing a lot of thinking, real soul-searching since you preached that sermon and everything blew up. I guess in takes longer for some of us hard-headed types to come around."

"Thanks, Brian. Don't feel too bad about that. It took me thirty years to begin to figure things out. Frankly, we haven't been getting much encouragement from anyone. I think we're being stone-walled, trying to find a place to meet, some space to rent."

Again, Brian seemed to already be aware of our problems. "Well, I'm pretty sure First Baptist would say no, too."

We both laughed at that prospect.

"Nope," I said. "I didn't bother to ask you guys. I didn't want to cause you more trouble or controversy. But we are up against it. I'm not sure what we'll do for space."

"That's why I'm here, Bart, not from First Baptist, but as your friend and someone who believes in what you are doing. Daniel explained your dilemma and your needs, and I might have a solution, but it's complicated. Do you know the old Jenson factory down on Missouri, next to the tracks? It's been out of business for over twenty years and the place is a mess. It was storage for a while, and then a recycling drop-off. Fred Watson owns it now. I hope you don't mind, but I talked to him this morning about the building and your situation, and he said, if you will clean it up and do the building repairs and maintenance, and pay the taxes, you can lease the whole building for three years for no additional cost. And, you'll have an option to buy after that."

"Are you kidding me?" I asked. "That place is big, I mean huge, maybe fifty thousand square feet."

"Fred says, with the offices and the rail dock, it's a hundred and ten thousand."

"Wow. We would have room for all kinds of ministry. That would be incredible. I have to call David. When can we see it?" I couldn't believe the possibilities exploding in my mind.

"Take it easy, friend. Keep in mind, right now it's a dump. Fred says the roof leaks, lots of windows are broken, the plumbing's no good, not sure about the electricity. Tons of work to do, Bart."

But my mind was already racing miles ahead. "No problem, Brian. Don't sweat it. Just so happens I know a guy that has his own hardware store."

***

I had not been this excited about an Easter Sunday in my thirty years as a pastor. The past three weeks had been a whirlwind of activity as we worked on the old Jensen factory. Fortunately, the old machinery had been removed and sold off years before. What remained was enough junk and debris and trash to fill a thirty-foot dumpster eight times. Our volunteers had focused on one corner of the huge building for our services, saving the rest for future work days and projects. The roof had been repaired and the plumbing on the north end was clean and functioning. We replaced broken glass and changed the locks, so the building was secure.

The factory offices had been converted into a spotless and inviting nursery, thanks to Sally's creativity and tireless efforts. Most exciting to me was the large display of a new floorplan, depicting what future ministries might be housed in our huge facility: a service center, food pantry, clothing, furniture, a homeless shelter, even a medical clinic.

Our local newspaper editor, Oliver Woodson, interviewed David and myself for an article about The Way. I think he was hoping to fan the controversy, but it gave us an opportunity to talk about our core values and our reasons for including all kinds of people.

David and Daniel planned the Easter service along with some help from Michael Peters, who was also enthusiastic about this new beginning. We brought in a large water tank, the kind used to haul water for cattle, to use as our makeshift baptistry. My part in the worship was to serve communion and to immerse the two men who desired to be baptized.

When we drove to the factory-turned-church on Easter morning, we were not the first to arrive. Protestors stood all along the sidewalk carrying signs and holding posters, perhaps a hundred people or more. Most of the people, I didn't recognize, but I did see a few familiar faces. Roger Holcomb, the pastor from Bethany Baptist, held up a sign with the words, "HOMOSEXUALITY IS SIN." Another sign was more blunt: "GOD HATES FAGS." Stanley Pulliam of First Baptist carried the words: "GOD WILL JUDGE THE UNRIGHTEOUS."

We went inside, and I winced at the thought of everyone having to walk past that gauntlet of protestors to come to worship this morning. It struck me as sadly ironic that so many church people would spend Easter morning judging other Christians, rather than celebrating the resurrection of Jesus in their own church. But somehow, the condemnation of protestors could not quench our enthusiasm as we worshipped that first Easter morning. Nearly as many came to worship as came to protest, a diverse collection of seekers and saints, some I knew, many I did not. Some were probably drawn by the novelty of a new church in an old factory. Others approached cautious and hopeful, unfamiliar with church but looking for the love and acceptance we had promised.

As Daniel played his guitar and sang, the cavernous space played with the sound sending back a distant echo, like an answering voice from beyond, as if Heaven was singing along with us. The old factory had never heard such a sound. Prayers were offered, including a prayer of grace and blessing for our brothers and sisters holding the angry signs across the street.

David spoke about the words of Jesus, "I am the way, the truth, and the life." He challenged the people not to join a church but to live a life in Christ following his way, his truth.

When it was time to baptize, I stepped behind the water tank in the front. Everyone stood and gathered around close. The first person to be baptized, Daniel Summers, laid aside his guitar, took off his shoes, and climbed into the tank. Daniel had grown up Methodist and had never been immersed as an adult. He had asked if he could be baptized to mark his new beginning, having been so close to death. So, here he stood before me, almost waist deep in the water.

Then came Richie Towns wearing a Metallica t-shirt and jeans. He tossed a towel on the front row of chairs. Some of the people gasped, not knowing that Richie was out of prison, and certainly unaware of his change of heart. Being so tall, Richie just stepped over the side of the tank and stood beside Daniel.

I put the question to the two of them. "Daniel, Richie, do you believe that Christ died on the cross for your sins, that he was buried, and that he rose again on the third day, according to the scripture?"

Richie paused for Daniel to answer. "I believe," Daniel answered, and looked to Richie.

"Me, too," Richie replied, as smiles and laughter rippled around us.

I asked the second question. "Then what is your confession today?"

They answered together this time. "Jesus is Lord."

Then, they stepped forward, each in turn, Daniel first.

I baptized them with these words: "In obedience to our Lord and Savior, Jesus Christ, and upon your profession of faith in Him, I baptize you, Daniel Summers (Richie Towns), in the name of the Father, and of the Son, and of the Holy Spirit. Amen."

There they stood before me, with big wet smiles, and when they embraced, a spontaneous shout of joy went up from an old factory in Joppa, Georgia, all the way to the halls of Heaven. It was Easter morning, the miracle of resurrection all around us.

***

As the crowd around the water tank began to disperse, I took a towel from Sally and dried my hands and arms. No one seemed anxious to go, staying, meeting new friends, getting acquainted. Daniel and Richie were showered with encouragement, hugs and prayers, before departing to change into dry clothes.

As people moved aside, I spotted our daughter, Dinah, standing behind the back row of chairs, smiling. What an Easter surprise, a wonderful bonus on an already blessed day.

Dinah smiled and moved toward the front, but before she could get to me, she was intercepted by her mother.

I knew she wouldn't make it to me for a little while. It had been nearly two years since that ugly night at First Baptist, and this was Dinah's first time to come back to church — any church.

Wiping her eyes and pulling aside, Dinah started my direction once again, only to be waylaid by her brother.

"You came! I didn't see you back there," David nearly shouted, so pleased to see his sister there for this beginning. They hugged and laughed and teased each other. David turned and introduced Dinah to Richie, who had just returned from his wardrobe change.

Dinah seemed startled, hesitant at first, but shook Richie's hand and left him with a smile.

Finally, I got to hug my baby girl. "Welcome back, Dinah. I'm so pleased to see you here."

Dinah looked up into my eyes with a grin. "This is it, isn't it, Dad? This is what's next, church without all the baggage. It's wonderful, Dad, and I have to hand it to you. Your church is bigger than the Georgia Dome."

***

If I had known how much it would please Sally to finally move into a house that she could call her own, I would have found a way to buy a house years ago. She was giddy with excitement. She wore out the realtors with her questions. We looked at every house on the market in our price range. The hardware store provided a level of income that we had never enjoyed before, and I was determined to find a comfortable home for Sally, small compensation for a lifetime of modest and sometimes pitiful parsonages. Also, we were both anxious to get out of our little rental house. After all the recent vandalism and controversy, our landlord shared our sentiments.

We settled on an old Victorian, nearly a hundred years old, on the north end of Gulf Street. A previous owner had done the major restoration and modernizing of the house, which was great, since I didn't have the time or expertise to do it myself. The large, two-story house was painted a pleasant shade of blue with white trim, and had a broad porch across the front, which we loved. The front door opened to a hall with a broad staircase ahead and large rooms on either side. The oak woodwork was spectacular, with hardwood floors, panel doors, and two marble fireplaces with oak mantles. It was love at first sight, and we were thrilled when our first offer for "Old Blue" was accepted.

Moving day brought some pleasant surprises. I had picked up a U-Haul for the day, and when I pulled up at the rental house to begin loading, people had gathered and stood all over the place. Everyone in our little church was already there to lend a hand. I was touched to see so many friends pitching in. I came into the house and Sally's kitchen was almost completely packed up and ready to go.

Mavis Brown and Amy Morrow were carefully wrapping Sally's china. "Good morning, Pastor," Mavis said with a smile. "I'd give you a hug, but my hands are full. I brought you some of my plum jam, but I'll take it over to your new place first."

"Thank you, Mavis. That's sweet of you. And thanks for your help today."

She stood there holding a plate in her hand shaking her head. "No, Pastor, this is my thank you for your good help to me, the least I could do."

I looked out the window over the kitchen sink and saw Daniel and Richie clearing out the little lawn shed in back. Shiloh was running back and forth playing with anyone who would pay her attention. In two hours, the truck was full, and what few items would not fit were placed in two pickups to bring along. Shiloh climbed up in the cab with me, and Sally rode across town in Amy's Subaru.

When I pulled up in front of "Old Blue," I was amazed to find a cleaning crew—more friends— washing windows, trimming the shrubs, and polishing the woodwork. Brian Ward stood up on a ladder cleaning out the gutters.

"What are you doing, Brian? Wouldn't you rather be the one watching me do that? Don't fall off that ladder! I'd never hear the end of it."

He looked down and tossed some wet, leafy debris towards me. "Nope," he said. "This is my job. I love this stuff. And after all that work on the factory, this is a piece of cake."

"Amen to that, Brian."

The rest of the day passed as a blur, a flurry of activity. At about five, George and Linda showed up with dinner, enough barbeque for everyone, and after we had all eaten and reflected on the day, our friends went on their way, leaving us to ourselves in our new home.

Sally and I immediately understood what it was like to have a basement, two floors with high ceilings, and a large attic, after living in a small house on one level. Those beautiful stairs had worn us out.

"Well, Bart, we're going to get our exercise. Tell me we won't always have to go up and down a hundred times like today." She was sitting in our upstairs bedroom with her shoes off and her feet propped up on a cardboard box.

I sat down beside her on the bed. "Yep. This is going to be like boot camp, Sal. Think what great shape we'll be in, back in our skinny clothes."

"I gave away your skinny clothes years ago. Never thought you'd need them again."

I figured she was serious. "Thanks a lot. Way to motivate your chubby husband."

She reached over and pinched my love handle with a grin. "You'll do just fine, hardware man. You know, I don't think I ever told you, but I've always felt a little uncomfortable making love in a parsonage, kind of like God's watching, you know. Always seemed kind of inappropriate, like making love in a convent or something."

I leaned back on my elbows and smiled at my exhausted, sweaty, sexy wife. "You never told me that before. I didn't know you felt that way."

She leaned back against my shoulder.

"Well, this is our place now, your home, and nobody else's. How's that make you feel?"

She kissed me and kissed me again. "I feel like I need a long, hot shower. Care to join me?"

"That would be wonderful, Mrs. Sheldon. Welcome home."

***

Soon after we moved into Old Blue, Sally started a new family tradition: Friday night dinners together. Having a big dining room made it feel like a special occasion every time we were together around the table. David and Dinah did their best to adjust their schedule to join us every week. Sometimes I cooked out, other times Sally prepared the meal, and once a month or so, David and Dinah would cook for us. But we all agreed that the most wonderful meals came from our most frequent guest, Daniel, who made himself at home and enjoyed cooking for us from time to time.

In fact, we often had guests with us for Friday dinner. Jim would come home with me from the store, or Richie would drop by, and when Michael Peters was in town, he would often eat with us. Whoever put their feet under our table was treated like family, eating their fill, enjoying the conversation, and helping with the dishes.

One Friday evening in October, Daniel cooked a Mexican dish — I think he called it green enchilada pie — that was terrific. We were still talking about it after we had cleaned up the kitchen and moved to the family room.

"Pastor," Daniel said, "I put the leftovers in the refrigerator for you. David says you have a microwave at the store. You can take it for your lunch, if you like."

"Thanks, Daniel, I'll do that. And you can call me Bart, if you're comfortable with that. There's no need to stand on formality around here."

I had encouraged Daniel a few times before to call me Bart, but he insisted on "Pastor." He said it was a matter of respect for my calling. Hard to argue with that.

After dinner, David and Daniel sat with me in the den without checking their phones or the TV. It made me wonder what was on their minds.

After an awkward silence, Daniel came to the point. "Pastor.. Bart... uh, David and I have been talking about something really important, and we would like to know how you feel about it. Is this a good time to talk?"

There seemed to be growing tension in the room. I could see the anxiety on David's face, though Daniel seemed more at ease.

"Sure, guys. What's on your mind?"

They looked at each other, David nodded, and Daniel pushed ahead. "David and I have been friends for a long time, even before he saved my life at the truck stop. You remember how David was with me at the hospital and through my long recovery. We've grown to be very close, and now working together at the new church is wonderful. We care about each other very much. I think you know that, Pastor."

"Yes, Daniel, I do know."

"Well, Pastor, what we want to know is... what we are wondering... what we want to ask you is, ah... how would you feel about... us, I mean David and I... getting married?"

The words hung in the air for a long moment, and I don't think either one of them was breathing. I had been pondering and anticipating this moment for months, at least since the day Daniel came by the store for camping supplies. Seeing how close David and Daniel had become, and their obvious love for each other, forced me to take the next step. It was one thing to tolerate gay people, and it was something else to allow them to live out their lives and their love in public, God-honoring ways.

David jumped in and broke the silence. "Dad, I know this may still be hard for you, but it's important to us for you to understand, to have your blessing. What do you think, Dad?"

I turned to Daniel with a firm expression. "Daniel, from now on, please stop calling me "Pastor." I won't hear of it any longer. And for that matter, don't call me Bart, because that's not appropriate either. Do you understand what I'm saying?"

Daniel sat back in his chair, confused, bewildered.

"From now on, Daniel, you will call me Dad. Understand? I know you have a father of your own, but I'm going to be your dad, too. I would be honored to welcome you into our family. Of course, you have my blessing."

The two of them came out of their chairs and embraced me, a two-man tackle on the couch.

"Thank you, thank you, Dad. That means so much to us," David said. "Will you do the ceremony, Dad? Will you marry us?"

"It would be my privilege."

Sally and Dinah came in and joined the commotion.

David reached for Dinah and hugged her.

I wanted to share the news. "David, tell your mother what we just talked about."

Sally just smiled and put her arms around my neck. "Are you kidding? You were the last one to know. We were all waiting to hear what you would say, and you didn't let us down, hardware man. Looks like we've got a wedding to plan."

***

It was a long way from Washington, D.C. to Joppa, Georgia. The Supreme Court's controversial decision in favor of gay marriage was not widely applauded in the rural South. On the contrary, the decision was viewed as a liberal, immoral intrusion into the affairs of respectable, God-fearing Americans. Some county officials refused to grant licenses to same sex couples, or they simply added requirements that delayed or otherwise hindered couples from getting state sanction for their marriage.

David and Daniel had anticipated the worst, and so were prepared to request a federal court order, if necessary, to get their marriage license. The county recorder of deeds, Melody Miles, was the wife of Roy Miles, a deacon at First Baptist, and no supporter of me or gay rights — two strikes against us.

The first time David and Daniel went to the courthouse to apply for a license, Mrs. Miles told them that she had not yet received the proper forms for a same sex marriage, and therefore they would have to wait until she received the proper forms from the state capitol. When asked if she could have the proper forms emailed or faxed to her, she grudgingly complied. When the new forms were printed out, David and Daniel could see that it was the exact same form, except someone had blacked out the male/female gender blanks. Anyway, with the legal obstacle overcome, the boys had a license in hand.

Where to have the wedding? We considered several options. Local church buildings would not be available, no doubt about that. We talked about having the wedding at our home, converting Old Blue into a wedding chapel. An outdoor ceremony at the state park was an option, but the December weather could be dicey in Georgia.

"What about the church, our church at the factory?" Daniel asked as we sat around the table drinking coffee.

Dinah responded, "The old factory works pretty well for a church service, but it's not exactly a wedding venue, is it?" She voiced what we were all thinking.

"That's just it," Daniel went on. "If the old building is good enough for God, it's good enough for me. We worship there, we baptize there, we take the Supper there. It's a house of God, and it's where David and I worship and serve together. And, it's the only place where we are accepted and blessed." It seemed so obvious as Daniel explained it.

David smiled and nodded. "It's the church then. We're going to have our ceremony in the biggest wedding chapel in the state of Georgia."

We all laughed and I said, "That's the truth, David, but you'll have to limit your guest list to two or three thousand."

Dinah added, "How cool would that be? You could leave the wedding on a train, get on right off the rail dock." More laughter.

Sally summed up the plan for us. "We'll make it a day to remember, that's for sure. We'll make it special, and we'll make the old factory beautiful."

***

The weekend before Christmas, we completed the old factory's transformation into a wedding venue. The big, metal-framed, rust-stained windows were draped with white sheers, and the massive steel girders were hung with crepe and ribbons of silver and purple. The fragrance of fresh flowers offered a welcome reprieve from the stale smell of the old building.

After helping Sally with the last-minute preparations, we hurried home to change for the ceremony. I put on my usual wedding attire, a black "marrying and burying" suit that every pastor requires, with one change: a silver tie David had given me for the occasion. I was happy to wear it, an obvious reminder that this was not just another wedding to conduct and enter in my pastoral record. This was family.

Sally looked stunning in her purple gown, her amber hair up and set in curls like I hadn't seen since our own wedding day, twenty-eight years before.

I helped her with her zipper and stood behind her before the mirror. "Wow. What a knockout you are, Sweetie. You look terrific." I kissed her shoulder.

She smiled and turned towards me. "You're not so bad yourself." Fixing my collar, she said, "I like your Lone Ranger tie."

"As I recall, the last time you wore your hair that way, I messed it up badly by the end of the evening."

"Play your cards right, and you might get a chance to try that again," she said with a sly grin. "We better get going, Honey. Will you check on Shiloh? She probably needs some water before we go. And, don't forget to unplug the Christmas tree."

"I'm on it," I said as I headed down the stairs.

In five minutes, we were locked-up and on our way to a wedding.

***

When we pulled into the factory parking lot an hour before the ceremony was to begin, the protestors had already arrived. My heart sank to see dozens of people standing on the sidewalk across the street, holding those awful signs again: "Adam and Eve, not Adam and Steve," "Turn or Burn," and "Remember Sodom and Gomorrah." Another one said, "Gay Marriage is an ABOMINATION to God."

We had talked about trying to have a small private ceremony, but David and Daniel felt strongly about sharing their wedding with all their friends and those who were part of our new church. Once the invitations were sent, word got out and spread all over town. I hated the thought of this protest marring what should be such a joyous occasion.

About a hundred friends and family gathered for the ceremony as the winter sun was setting, and the candlelight illuminated just one corner of the huge room. David and Daniel were wearing gray cutaway tuxes, the old-fashioned style with striped pants, tails, and silver ascots. A string quartet from the university played for the ceremony. Daniel had asked Richie Towns to be his Best Man. and it surprised me how a haircut and a tux made Richie look downright debonair.

David had asked his sister, Dinah, to stand up with him, calling her his Best Sister, and she was pleased to participate.

David escorted his mother to her seat, and soon we were all in place, ready to begin the ceremony. David and Daniel stood before me, the candlelight catching the joy and the anticipation on their faces.

And so it began.

> *Dearly beloved, we have come together in the presence of God to give our blessing to Daniel and David as they covenant together in marriage. The scripture gives us this instruction:*

"Beloved, let us love one another for love is of God and God is love. Love is patient and kind; love is not jealous or rude. Love does not insist on its own way; it is not irritable or resentful; it does not rejoice at wrong, but rejoices in the right. Love bears all things, believes all things, hopes all things, endures all things. Love never ends."

Love is the reason that God put us here on this planet. It is the gift that God has given us, and any expression of that love is truly a blessing that God can smile down upon. For his wish for us is to love and be loved, that is all. There are no rules for love, no restrictions or boundaries. There are no laws for love, no limits. Our love and the capacity to love another human being are endless. Marriage has always been about family and community. To stand before all those we love most in the world, and promise to love another person openly and trustingly, without limits for a lifetime, is perhaps the bravest thing two people will ever do.

David and Daniel had memorized their vows, and it was a precious moment watching the two of them, face to face, promising their love: *"...for better or for worse, for richer or poorer, in sickness and in health, to love and to cherish, till death shall part us."*

Their rings were identical gold bands, simple, but significant, given with a purpose and a pledge.

I put my hand upon theirs as I prayed.

Most loving God, you have called Daniel and David to a lifetime of loving and giving and forgiving. As they grow in the life you have granted them, shelter their hopes and dreams within your own perfect will. Give them power and wisdom to fulfill your purpose in their lives. Light their way by the flame of your most holy, passionate love. By your Spirit of truth, strengthen them in faithfulness to you and to each other. Bless with joy the home they make together, that its love and laughter may refresh all whom they welcome within it. In Jesus' name, we pray. Amen.

Forasmuch as Daniel and David have covenanted together before God and this company, I pronounce that they are united in marriage, one life together, in the name of the Father, and of the Son, and of the Holy Spirit. Amen. Those whom God has joined together, let no man put asunder. Let these words of a Native American blessing be your benediction:

Now you will feel no rain for each of you will be shelter for the other;

Now you will feel no cold for each of you will be warmth for the other;

Now you will have no more loneliness for each of you will be companion for the other;

Now you are two bodies but only one life is before you;

Go now to your dwelling place to enter into the days of your togetherness,

And may your days be good and long upon the earth. Amen.

The music for the recessional began, but no one recessed. Daniel turned to hug his mother seated near him, and David hugged Sally as she wiped the tears from her cheek. Then Dinah hugged me, Richie hugged

Daniel, and a love fest at the altar broke out, family and friends coming forward, embracing, laughing, celebrating. The string quartet, recognizing that we were off the script, changed their tune to music for a celebration. We were all caught up in the joy of the moment and the music.

Sally squeezed my hand and whispered, "Dance with me, Bart."

I knew better than to protest, took her hand and drew her close, and we started dancing across the front of the altar.

Dinah saw us, aghast and pointing, until Richie stepped forward and grabbed her hand. In a second they were gliding across the floor, the Best Man at six-foot-five and the Best Sister at four-foot-eleven, quite a sight to see.

Daniel and David began to dance, and then everyone in the old factory danced and sang and celebrated, with spontaneous and contagious joy.

***

Eventually, we danced our way over to the reception, set up in what was once the lunch room for the factory, with a small kitchen attached. Daniel's parents had insisted on providing the food for the reception, and it was wonderful, a seafood buffet with beef rounds for the landlubbers. The cake was triple chocolate in the shape of a guitar, Daniel's request.

George found me going back for more stuffed shrimp. "What a wedding, Bart, and what a party. Never seen anything like it." George had watched the ceremony from the main door, wanting to make sure that no protestors came in to disrupt the wedding.

"Me, either, George, a first for me. It was also the first time I've ever had such a mean-looking bouncer watching the door. Thanks for your help."

"Well, that wasn't your usual crowd of church people outside there, Bart, some tough customers. I thought they might try something, since they weren't able to scare anybody off."

"I guess they're gone by now. Too cold to stand out there all evening." I grabbed the tongs and scooped up three more shrimp.

"Yeah, they gave it up. I still don't understand why people think they have to interfere in other people's lives, when it's none of their damn business." He grabbed one of my shrimps with his fingers. "Great stuff, Bart, thanks." He dropped the shrimp tail back on my plate and chewed as he spoke. "The boys going away? Are they taking a trip?"

"Just a short one, two days in Atlanta. They want to be back here for the Christmas Eve service. Why don't you and Linda plan to join us?"

"We may do that. Thanks, Bart. I think we are going to head for home now. Goodnight."

I shook his hand and squeezed his shoulder. "Goodnight, George. Thanks."

In another thirty minutes, the place was nearly empty. We stayed and helped with the cleanup. With Christmas Eve coming, we wanted to leave everything just right. I set up the ladder and we began to take down the decorations in the worship area. Richie took off his coat and tie and climbed the ladder, able to reach much farther than the rest of us.

It was nearly eleven when Sally and I walked out to get in the car. "What a night, Bart. It was everything I dreamed it would be."

I laughed. "When did you dream that our son would marry a man named Daniel?"

"You know what I mean. I never dreamed that David was gay, but now I'm so happy he's with Daniel, the perfect pair."

"I think so too. It was a wonderful evening, wasn't it?"

She leaned over from her seat and gave me a kiss. "Really wonderful. You did a great job, too, for a hardware man. Take me home. My feet are killing me."

Chapter 8 – Burning Love

"So comes snow after fire,
and even dragons have their ending."
~ *J. R. R. Tolkien*

I started the car and pulled my phone from my coat pocket while the engine warmed. I had put it on silent during the wedding and had not checked it since before the ceremony. There were eight missed calls, five from a number I did not recognize. I listened to the first voicemail as I put the car in gear.

I immediately turned to Sally. "There's a fire at the house, Sal. They've been trying to reach us."

Her face wrenched like she was in pain. "Our house? A fire?" I was already speeding down Missouri and across town as she grabbed her phone from her purse. More missed calls and messages.

"No details. They didn't give any details. Just fire," I said.

We could see flashing lights as we turned on Gulf Street. I drove up behind two fire trucks and jumped from my car. The night air was heavy with smoke and ash. The sight of our house sickened me. The whole structure was engulfed in flames against the night sky, fire roaring out of every window. I turned to see Sally starting toward the house and collapsing in shock. I rushed to catch her.

"Shiloh!" she said. "Shiloh's in the house, Bart. Did they get her out? Is she out here? Where's Shiloh?"

I held Sally in my arms and shouted to the closest fire fighter. "Our dog was in the house, a black lab. Have you seen her? Did you get her out?"

The fireman shook his head. "I'm sorry, sir. By the time we got here, the fire was advanced, widespread. We've not been able to get anyone inside. These old houses can go up like a torch. I'm sorry."

Sally sat on the ground in my arms and cried like I'd never heard her cry. "Our house, Bart. Our own house and now it's gone. Poor Shiloh. Why did we leave her in the house? What have we done?"

I tried to comfort her, but she would not be comforted as we watched our home blaze against the black sky, collapse, and burn to the ground. The fire chief offered to call someone, to help us make some arrangements, but I just shook my head.

"Chief, do you know yet what caused the fire? Can you tell where it started? Was it electrical? We had all the wiring inspected."

He took off his hat and wiped his face with his sleeve. "It's too early to say for certain, but we think the fire started in the cellar in back. It looks like the latch was broken and the cellar doors left open."

I shook my head, bewildered. "Ah, the cellar doors were closed and locked when we left about four o'clock."

The chief nodded and made a note on a small pad. "Reverend, it looks like there's a gasoline can in the cellar. Could that be yours, or maybe left by the previous owner?"

"No, sir, I don't keep anything flammable in the house. My mower and gas can were in the garage."

The chief shook his head. "Actually, there is no gas can in the garage. It appears that someone broke into your garage and your cellar, spilled your gas can in the cellar and started the fire, leaving the doors open to feed the flames."

Sally's blank expression turned incredulous. "You mean somebody did this on purpose? Someone broke in and burned our house down? Who would do such a thing?"

"I don't know, ma'am, but I called Sheriff Wade. I'll finish my investigation as soon as possible, in the next day or two, and then the sheriff will decide what to do with it."

Sally couldn't get her mind around the thought that someone would do such a thing to us.

My mind was running in a different direction. Somebody had to know that we were gone and would be gone for a while. They would have to know about the wedding. Was this someone's protest? Who would be so angry and vindictive, to burn down our home?

Only one name came to mind.

***

When George and Linda heard the news, they insisted that we spend what was left of the night in their home. Dinah stayed at her apartment.

We were back at the house by nine, wearing some clothes and sweats that our hosts gave to us, since Sally's entire wardrobe consisted of one muddy purple gown.

What was left of "Old Blue" was still smoldering. Three of the first-floor walls were still standing, but the rest was gone, just piles of ash and debris. I asked Sally to stay in the car until I came to get her. A fireman who was still on sight monitoring the fire loaned me some boots and gloves, and I waded carefully into the back of the house. The floor plan was barely recognizable, and most of the furniture had been consumed by the fire. I found the charred remains of our dog, Shiloh, in what was left of our utility room. I had to use a shovel to pick up her body and carry her to the back yard.

Once at the garage, I got a spade and a large leaf bag. I chose a spot near the back fence in the shade of a big maple tree, dug a little grave for Shiloh, placed her remains in the leaf bag, sealed it up, and laid it in the hole. Then I went to get Sally.

"Did you find her, Bart? I don't think I want to see her."

"It's okay, Sally. I wrapped her up and I'm going to bury her now. Come and see." I put my arm around her and led her to the little grave near the fence.

"This is a good place, Bart." She began to weep again. "Do you think she suffered?"

For the first time in twenty-eight years, I lied to my wife. "I don't think so, Sally. It was probably just the smoke that got her." Sally watched me as I picked up the spade and filled in the soil. "There, it's done." I put the spade away, and Sally and I spent the rest of the day picking through the debris, finding almost nothing recognizable, let alone usable.

In the front room, our Christmas tree, a real one this year, had been burned to oblivion, leaving just a tree stand melted and bent. Blackened pieces of Sally's china and crystal lay strewn about, and one charred piece of shelf in the dining room, all that was left of her mother's china cabinet. In the den, my library was a total loss. What few books were still recognizable had been soaked down with water. Two laptops and all my files were destroyed as well.

I didn't realize how much the old house had come to mean to us in just a few months, until it was so suddenly gone. I never thought I would grieve over brick and boards, but I did. "Old Blue" represented a new beginning for us, a new season of our lives, leaving behind the painful past. But the past determined to land one more devastating blow, a real haymaker that we didn't see coming.

Sally looked so forlorn and pitiful, wearing George's big Wake Forest sweatshirt and rolling up Linda's jeans so they wouldn't drag in the mess. By the afternoon, she had quit crying, having run out of tears and getting past the initial shock.

The news had spread all over town by now, and many friends came by, some who had been celebrating with us at the wedding just hours before. Dinah came, of course, and Jim, and Brian. We had decided not to call David last night, knowing that he and Daniel would scrap their plans and come back to Joppa. When we talked to them late in the afternoon, they immediately headed back home.

Then, there were the curious and the nosey, the gawkers and the gossips, who would slowly drive by without stopping—no offer of help or sympathy or anything—just checking it out like a wreck on the highway. Oliver came by to take some pictures for the newspaper. Somehow that didn't feel right to me, but news was news in Joppa, Georgia.

Our insurance agent, Julie Hadley, came by to survey the damage. She said an adjuster would be coming by soon, but it looked like a total loss. The only difficulty would be determining the value of the contents. "You don't by chance have pictures of the interior of the house, so we can verify the contents?" she asked.

Sally shook her head. "Sure, I do, but they were all on my laptop, which is now burned to a crisp."

Then Dinah spoke up. "Plus, all of your Christmas stuff, Mom, the gifts you had purchased, the decorations."

Sally was suddenly reminded of the day. "I had forgotten. Tomorrow is Christmas Eve. What will we do for Christmas?" Dinah hugged her mother, both of them in tears.

I tried to reassure them. "We'll figure something out, Sweetie. We'll be just fine." I surely sounded more confident than I felt.

***

Monday morning, Christmas Eve, I sat in Sheriff Wade's office at the same table where David had given his statement about the attack at the truck stop nearly two and a half years before. Strangely enough, the same names came up in this interview. Sheriff Wade was anxious to solve this crime that was so blatant and obvious. He summarized his preliminary thoughts on the case.

"I read the Fire Marshall's report. There's no doubt about what happened. Someone who likely knew that you and Sally would be gone for a while, broke into the cellar and used your gas can to start the fire. I've interviewed all the neighbors, and nobody saw any vehicles come and go, nothing suspicious around your house. We're going to widen out and canvas a larger area. Someone had to see something. Knowing what happened before, I called Richie Towns. I know he's made some changes. In fact, I bought a set of tires from him last week. I understand he's become a friend of yours."

I nodded and smiled. "Richie has made some changes. He is a friend, a friend of David's, all of us. And, he was with us at the wedding Saturday night. He even stayed to clean up."

The sheriff agreed. "No, Towns is not a suspect, but I wanted to ask him about Mark Hampton, the other boy involved in the attack. He was released several months ago, back in the spring. Richie says Hampton still bears you and David a grudge, a bad one, and that he promised to get even for having to go to jail. Have you had any contact with the Hampton boy since he got out of prison?"

"None, Sheriff. I've never had a conversation with him, before or after. I remember his face that day in court when he went to jail. He looked angry, vengeful. It was frightening. Then, someone said they saw Mark among the protesters on Easter when we launched our new church, but I didn't see him myself."

"Well, I'm going to bring him in for an interview. I'd like to know what he was doing Saturday night. But even if he doesn't have an alibi, it will be a tough thing to prove unless we can find a witness, or whoever he might have bragged to afterwards. If he did it and we can prove it, he'll go away for a long time."

"Sheriff, what if we can't prove it and he doesn't go away? What will we do then? Will he keep coming after us? What if he burns down our house while we're asleep inside?"

"Reverend, you'll have to trust me on this. Whether he did this or not, we'll do our best to convince him to forget the past and move on."

"Well, I'm not sure what that means, Sheriff, but let me know what you find out." I stood and offered my hand. "Thanks for your efforts."

He shook my hand and nodded. "No problem. It's my job. Sorry for what happened. I hope you folks can get back on your feet real soon. And Merry Christmas, Reverend."

"Thanks, Sheriff. You too."

***

While I'd been meeting with Sheriff Wade, Sally and Dinah were doing some frantic last-minute shopping—not our usual approach to Christmas, but we were desperate for something to wear. Our insurance agent was ready to settle us into temporary accommodations at the Ramada, but George and Linda wouldn't hear of it. We arrived at their place in time to shower and get dressed.

Sally laid out some khakis, a plaid button-down, and a burgundy sweater on the bed for me. "I think I got all the tags off, but make sure when you put these on," she said.

It felt strange to be dressing for a Christmas Eve service without putting on a suit, but this time I would not be leading, just attending, merciful in my bewildered state of mind.

I knew perfectly well that life was more than just stuff, the things we possessed. How many times had I preached about the dangers of materialism, and yet, when everything we had was suddenly swept away, gone in an instant, my world was shaken. And this was no accident, no unfortunate set of circumstances beyond anyone's control. My family was deliberately attacked, violated, abused once more, and I wanted to scream, to lash out, to punish those who seemed bent on hurting us.

We left for the service and drove down Maple Street past the hardware store. Mr. Martin's big plastic wreath was blinking faint Christmas cheer in the window. Jim was just closing the store, having put in a long day for me, which I greatly appreciated.

We passed First Baptist Church as folks were going in for their candlelight service, eliciting a flood of memories for me, waves of nostalgia and regret, after so many years in that church, sixteen Christmas Eves. This year, a different pastor was doing the honors, and I was okay with that reality. I didn't regret the choices I'd made or the words I had spoken on that fateful "Gospel Truth" Sunday. What did cause me deep and painful regret were all the years before, when I preached a narrow, judgmental gospel, leading a church that was self-centered and spiritually lifeless, out of touch with the community. After more than two years, I still felt the sting and regret.

We arrived at the old factory for the first Christmas Eve service in a most unlikely place. As we entered, people gathered around us as if drawn by a magnet, anxious to give hugs and encouragement, and offering all kinds of practical help. We were overwhelmed by their gracious welcome. I couldn't find the words, and Sally was in tears, so touched by the love extended to us. The heaviness and hurt that had settled on my heart were lifted and carried away, and before long, Sally was smiling and laughing for the first time since the wedding.

The worship area had been transformed from the purple and silver wedding decorations to the green and red of Christmas. One advantage to the old building was that we didn't have to worry about damaging the place with our decorations. It was impervious to our efforts. So, the girders were hung with fresh greenery, poinsettias were everywhere, and the tree must have been all of twenty-five feet tall, illuminated with white lights and hung with gold ornaments and Chrismons, the symbols of the Christ Child. Extra chairs were carried in for the large crowd, all kinds of people, many who had been outsiders to church.

David and Daniel led the worship time as usual.

The children were invited to the front for an impromptu nativity around a makeshift manger. The Myers baby, just two months old, got the starring role, and the rest of the kids formed a miniature mob of bathrobes and wings and crowns, even a couple of woolly sheep. Together they sang for us.

> *What can I give him, poor as I am,*
> *If I were a shepherd, I'd bring a lamb.*
> *If I were a wise man, I'd do my part.*
> *Yet what can I give him, give him my heart.*

Then it was time for communion. On Christmas Eve, the Supper is not so much about Christ's death but more about his arrival, the miracle of incarnation, "the Word made flesh." After the bread and the cup, we shared one more sacred moment, the lighting of the Christ Candle in the Advent Wreath. All the other lights were dimmed, and the overhead lights turned off.

Tori Aker, a single mom, came forward with her daughter, who lighted the white candle in the center of the wreath.

It shone in that cavernous room as we sang together:

> *Silent night, holy night, all is calm, all is*
> *bright.*

The light was passed, candle to candle, person to person, reflecting the soft glow of joy on each face. It was an unforgettable moment as the old factory was transformed into a cathedral of light. No one wanted the moment to end and, as Daniel continued to play his guitar, we sang one carol after another.

As I turned my head and saw the expressions in the candlelight, the smiles and the tears, I knew that if Christ was anywhere, he was with us on that Christmas Eve. Immanuel. God with us.

As the lights came on, we blew out our candles and prepared to depart, but Daniel had other ideas. He took the mic from the stand and invited everyone to be seated, and said, "Pastor Bart and Sally — I mean Mom and Dad — would you please come here to the Christmas Tree?"

I looked at Sally, who was obviously as confused as I was. We stood and walked to the front, and Daniel pointed us to two chairs just placed beside the tree. Sally and I sat down, still with no clue what was happening.

Daniel filled us in. "Pastor Bart, Sally, we are all sorry for what has happened to you, the loss of your home and all of your possessions, and we decided that since we are all family here, we want to bless you tonight. After all, it's Christmas. So, this is your Christmas Tree, and right here are your Christmas stockings." He pointed to two large red stockings being hung on the wall behind us, for 'Bart' and 'Sally.' "So, you two just sit back, and we're going to have a little carol sing and bless you with some gifts that we hope will help you have a home again."

The music began, and just about everyone stood up and started towards us. Many were carrying gifts, all wrapped and bright, to place under the tree. Some of the gifts were not wrapped, but with bows or ribbons attached. Others brought gift cards to drop in our stockings. There were piles of gifts, blankets and sheets and towels, pots and pans and dinnerware, a coffeemaker, a blender, and a food processor. A stack of boxes all the same size sat beside the tree, and I recognized them as place settings of china, Sally's pattern, box after box, stacked there for her.

I had never seen such thoughtful generosity or felt so loved. We had no words, no way to express our thanks to this new fellowship, our brothers and sisters who loved us like their own family, God's kind of family.

***

Early Christmas morning, Sally and I had a cup of coffee with George and Linda. We felt like we needed to clear out of the way early to make room for their kids and grandkids, who would soon be arriving in droves.

Linda was gracious as always. "You know you are more than welcome to stay and spend the day with our crew. We'd love to have you meet the family, Bart."

"We appreciate the invitation, Linda, but you are going to have a houseful. We're going over to the factory to sort through all the wonderful gifts we received last night, and then our kids insisted on bringing dinner, so we'll have a great day, too. Thanks for all your kindness."

A heavy frost crunched under my feet as we walked across the lawn, about the closest Georgia ever gets to a white Christmas. The sunshine made our frosted windshield glisten in patterns of crystallized ice, and we could see our breath in the car as we waited for my Honda to warm up.

What a strange and wonderful Christmas morning, just the two of us in that massive old building. Sally put on some coffee in the breakroom, and I managed to get some Christmas music on the sound system. The sun through the oversized east windows gave the concrete floor a warm glow and caught the tinsel and glitter on the tree. We took turns unwrapping gifts and marveling at all the love lavished on us.

Sally went back to the kitchen area to refill our cups and called out in surprise, "Bart, come in here. I think somebody's been in the building." I hurried into the breakroom as Sally stood with the refrigerator door wide open. "Someone has been in here and helped themselves to some of the leftover food and some of the items in the food pantry. Look here, see?"

"Yeah, I see, but who could've been in here since last night? No one was eating in here on Christmas Eve, just preparing the communion. That's strange."

Sally closed the refrigerator door and opened the dishwasher which was empty. Then she reached for a dish towel hanging on the oven handle. "Bart, this towel is wet. It's still damp. Someone has used it this morning. Do you think there's someone in the building right now? What if there is? Who could it be?"

I shrugged and glanced around the breakroom. "Stay calm, Sally. Nothing has been disturbed except some food, and whoever it was even cleaned up after themselves. Let's look around a little, do our own walkthrough. I don't want to call the police on Christmas Day unless we must. C'mon, let's check it out."

She nodded, and we headed down to the far end of the old factory, towards the freight dock. As we walked along, I called out in as calm a voice as I could muster.

"Come on out, wherever you are hiding. You are not in trouble. Just come on out. Maybe we can help."

Sally kept a close grip on my arm, pinning my elbow to her side with both hands. She had her cell phone all ready to dial 911 if needed.

"Come on out, please. No need to hide from us. You are not in trouble. Come out."

The door to the freight office opened and a timid voice answered. "Here we are. Don't shoot. We don't mean no harm, just took some food and someplace warm to sleep." A young woman in jeans and a ragged wool sweater stepped through the door pulling along a frightened little girl, perhaps six years old, in a dirty pink jacket.

"We're not police, just part of the church that meets here. I'm Bart and this is Sally."

My wife had already turned loose of me and stepped toward our uninvited guests with a relieved smile. "What's your name?" she asked. "Did you find something to eat? This drafty old building is no place to sleep."

The little girl smiled at Sally, but her mother held firmly to her hand. "My name's Molly and my daughter here is Laura. We got no place to go. My boyfriend left us when they turned the gas off, just took off and left us with nothing. Somebody said this church here helps people, so we came last night. We had nowhere to go after, so we just slipped in that back room and stayed so we wouldn't be in the cold. I got nobody in this town, only been here three months. Sorry for trespassing." She stood there quivering as she spoke, and the tears began to flow.

Sally moved to embrace her, and little Laura wrapped her arm around Sally's leg.

Molly sobbed on her shoulder as I tried to reassure her. "It's all right, Molly. We're glad you're here. Come on in with us, have some coffee, be our guests today. We don't have any place else to go, either. Our house burned down a couple days ago. You are welcome to spend Christmas here with us."

I reached out my hand to Laura as her mother released her grip and she put her little hand in mine. Her dimpled face was smudged and dirty, and her brown hair was pulled back in a ponytail secured with a rubber band. She looked up at me through sad brown eyes that would melt the coldest heart.

"Let's go see what we can find. Would you like a cup of hot chocolate?"

A faint smile came across her face, and we all headed to the kitchen.

***

The kids came in about four-thirty with a smoked turkey, three kinds of pie, and all the groceries needed to complete a Christmas feast. Sally handled the introductions, and Dinah quickly made a new friend of Laura. Soon David was peeling potatoes and Daniel was helping Sally with the stuffing and baked pineapple, an old family favorite.

Molly noticed the green beans, soup, and onion rings, and volunteered, "I can fix them green beans if you want me to."

Sally nodded and smiled. "Of course, Molly. That would be fine."

Soon the rolls were in the oven and the aroma of Christmas dinner filled the old factory. Dinah and Laura set the table for our family and guests, with two long tables side by side.

Sally called from the kitchen, "Save room for one extra place, girls. I think Richie is coming for dinner."

"Are you kidding, Mom? Save room? We could seat a thousand people in this place. Plenty of room for Richie."

By six-thirty, dinner was ready.

Sally was lighting two candles on the table when Richie came in the door. "Merry Christmas, everybody!" he said with a friendly smile, though Laura was frightened, clinging to Dinah, as she gazed up at this man towering over her.

"It's okay, Laura," Dinah assured her. "This jolly giant is our friend, Richie. He is like family to us."

Richie beamed. "Is that right? That's nice of you to say. Thanks. You all are family to me, too."

Sally looked at me with that "knowing" smile, then to Richie, who was carrying a big cardboard box with a red bow.

"You're pretty skinny to be Santa Claus," I said. "What did you bring, Richie?"

Richie put his present beside the tree. "It's just something I found that I knew you all would like to have. You'll see." He smiled and looked at the steaming dishes spread across the table. "But, it's fine with me if we eat first."

Everyone laughed as we moved to the table.

Sally reached for Molly's hand, beginning a circle around the table.

"Dinah, would you like to ask the blessing?"

"Sure, Dad. Let's pray. Thank you, God, for this Christmas Day, for this food, and for each person around this table. Bless each one. And thank you for sending Jesus to be with us, to make his home with us, even when we don't have a home of our own. Thank you, God. Amen."

After dinner, we gathered around the tree and looked through all the gifts we had been given, and setting aside lots of things for Molly and Laura.

Dinah laid out the plan for all of us. "Molly, you and Laura can come to my apartment tonight. I have an extra bedroom since David moved out. You can stay with me until you get situated again."

Molly nodded with a grateful smile. "If I could get the heat on and find some work, I know we would be all right. I've got a car, a little Nissan, but it's broken down, won't run. My boyfriend took his truck when he left."

Richie spoke up. "Well, that's my business. I'll get your car in the shop first thing tomorrow and see what we can do to get it running."

"Thanks, but I can't pay for that right now. I need to find work. I applied to clean rooms at the Super 8, but they're not hiring until January." She pulled Laura up on her lap as she talked about her circumstances.

Now it was my turn. "Let me worry about the money for now, Molly. We'll get your car fixed and your bills paid just to get you back on your feet. If you want to work a few hours at the hardware store, I can use some extra help with inventory until another job opens up. How about that?"

Molly nodded as she fought back the tears. "I don't know what to say. Nobody ever helped me. Thank you, all of you. I went to a couple of churches two days ago. One offered me a turkey, which I couldn't cook, and the other one sent me to county services, which paid a hundred towards my rent, but nothing for the heat. Then a woman at the county office said to come here, so I'm glad I did. Didn't know there were people like you. And you just lost your own home. You should be worrying about yourselves, not my problems. You lost everything you have."

Richie interrupted. "Well, not quite everything." He scooted the big cardboard box he had brought in front of Sally's chair. "Go ahead, Sally. See what's inside."

Sally pulled off the large red bow and saw the label underneath, a sticker bearing her own handwriting. Her expression was incredulous. It was marked, "Family Albums."

"Where did you get this?" Sally asked as Bart moved to cut away the packing tape. "Is this what I think it is? But it can't be. Everything was lost in the fire."

"Almost everything," Richie said. "Remember when you moved in? Nobody knew where to put stuff except you. Once, when you weren't around, somebody told us to put a load of boxes in the garage until we knew what to do with them. Most of them made it to the basement and got burned up. I got to thinking about it last night, and wondered if any of them boxes might have been put up in that little loft in the rafters of the garage. So, after church last night, I drove over and looked in the loft, and sure enough, there were three boxes still up there. Two were just odds and ends, flower pots and cleaning stuff, but then, I found this box."

"Look, Bart. Our pictures, the kids, our scrapbooks, they're all here," Sally said through her tears. "Our wedding album. It's all here. I thought we lost everything, but it's all here."

Then we all got to our knees around that cardboard box, pulling out one album after another, laughing and telling stories, feeling like a family again after all.

Sally stood up, wiped her eyes, and put her arms around Richie. "You are my hero, Richie. You have made me happier than you could ever know. Thank you. Thank you so much."

Richie smiled, a little embarrassed but pleased. "Merry Christmas, Miss Sally."

Chapter 9 – From the Ashes

"To forgive is to set a prisoner free and
discover that the prisoner was you."
~ *Lewis B. Smedes*

Before New Years, Sally and I had moved into a cozy, if cramped, apartment. We spent most of January and February following a local realtor, John Davis, all around town to see what houses were available. We must have walked through thirty houses, but Sally had no enthusiasm for buying a new place, even my favorite, a nearly new brick ranch on a quiet cul-de-sac. It looked great to me, but Sally couldn't turn loose of Old Blue.

"Why can't we just build it back, Bart, put it back like it was? Isn't that possible?" This wasn't the first time we had traveled this road.

"I guess we could rebuild it, but it would cost a lot more than what we paid the first time. And it wouldn't be the same. It wouldn't have the same charm and character as the old house."

"Well, it could, if we do it right. People are building houses today and bringing in all kinds of stuff from old houses and buildings and barns. People track down woodwork, cabinets, mantles, bannisters, even panel doors like we had, and build them right into the new house. I've seen lots of pictures, and you can hardly tell a new house from an old Victorian like Old Blue, if it's done well. Why can't we do that?"

I could tell from the eager intensity on her face that I might as well get on board this train now, because it was definitely leaving the station. "Okay, Sweetie. If that's what you want, and if you don't mind the extra months and the additional money it will take, we'll do it. We'll build a 'New Blue' that matches 'Old Blue.'"

Sally put her arms around me and pulled me close. "It'll be wonderful, you'll see. I can't wait to get started. Let's make a list tonight of what we need to be looking for and where we might find it."

Fortunately for us, Mr. Davis had listed our house for the previous owner, and still had all the figures and measurements, so new building plans could be drawn up easily enough. Doug Evers, the most sought-after builder in Joppa, was excited about our unique rebuilding project and hoped to begin work in May. So, Sally spent most of the spring looking at old homes, attending estate sales and auctions, trying to find just what we needed for our old-look new home. We figured it might take a year or more to finish the job, but we had never built a house and were game for the adventure.

In the meantime, our apartment was comfortable enough and an easy walk from the hardware store, so we didn't mind the wait. Sally would have her home once again, and it pleased me to see the excitement on her face.

While Sally tracked down all those old treasures, I kept busy at the hardware store. Jim Hinnessey had worked out well, quickly becoming a trusted friend and a hard worker. This job was truly his niche, and he seemed to enjoy the work, never anxious to leave, never slow to come in.

I stopped him one winter evening as he was hanging up his canvas apron. "Jim, I don't think I ever told you how much I appreciate you stepping up and handling things around here after the fire. It was a nightmare for us, and I'm not sure what I would have done here at the store without you. I appreciate all the extra hours and covering the year-end inventory. You were a godsend, and I appreciate it. I'd like to give you an extra week of vacation, Jim, so you and Lori can take the kids and go do something fun." I handed him an envelope, which he reached out hesitantly to take. "This is just our way of saying thanks, a little something extra to help pay for your getaway."

Jim nodded as he folded the envelope and poked it in his shirt pocket. He was looking down and struggling to get the words out. "Thanks, but you don't owe me anything. It's me should be thanking you. I wish I could send you and Sally on a trip after all you've done for me and my family." The words stuck in his throat as he stammered on. "You took a chance on me, Bart, when no one else would. I won't forget that. You've treated me more than fair, and Lori and I are finally able to get ahead a little bit and save for Julie's college. Never happen without this job. So, thank you. I appreciate all you've done for me."

"Well, Jim, it's a good partnership when we need each other. The blessing goes both ways."

***

I came home to our apartment one evening in February to find Sally gone and a note on the table.

> *Amy and I are at an auction in Edgerton, home by seven or eight, chops and potatoes in the frig.*

I had just got my plate out of the microwave when the doorbell rang. Not sure who I was expecting, but the last person I might have anticipated was standing there holding a puppy in his arms as I opened the door.

Stanley Pulliam, my primary persecutor at First Baptist Church, gave me a half smile and nodded. "Pastor Bart, I haven't seen you for a long time now, and I know we didn't leave things between us on good terms. I regret that. I heard about your fire. That was an awful thing, terrible to think somebody would burn down your house."

I was so surprised to see Stanley that I forgot my manners, just standing there holding the door. "Thank you, Stanley. That's kind of you to say. I appreciate it." Realizing the awkwardness of the moment, I added, "Would you like to come in?" I stepped back and Stanley came in, still holding a large puppy in his arms, not quite black, but black and tan together, a beautiful brindle color. "Have a seat, Stanley. What a great dog. What breed is it?"

He put the dog on the floor between his feet and held a leash in his hand. The pup sat there dutifully, and I could see his large round paws. This was no lap dog.

"You might remember my son, Travis," he said. "He lives in North Carolina now. He's a conservation agent, and he raises and trains hunting dogs as a hobby and a little extra income. This pup is a new breed, a Plott Hound, bred to hunt bears and wild boars in the mountains, but they're not mean or anything, just protective. They make great pets, really good dogs."

By now the pup had moved just far enough from Stanley that I could scratch him behind his ears. "Wow. Bears and wild boars. Not many of those around here, I guess."

We both smiled at the thought.

"I know, Pastor, but I'm thinking no one is likely to sneak into your place with a dog like this around. I brought this pup back for you and Sally. I know you lost your Lab in the fire. Someone should be horse-whipped for that. Anyway, I thought you might need a good dog, so if you want him, he's yours." Stanley's eyes were wet as he offered the leash to me. "It's a gift, Pastor, and my way of saying I'm sorry for what happened, for all of it, not just the fire. I was out of line at church. I was wrong about some of those things. Didn't know it then, but I know it now. I have a grandson, Michael, he's like your boy, David, so I've had a lot to think about, and I've got a lot to learn."

I took the leash in my hand as the pup stretched out on the floor. "Stanley, I don't know what to say. That's very kind of you. Thank you for your words and for this beautiful pup. Sally will be thrilled. Does he have a name?"

"Well, you know everyone in North Carolina is a basketball fan, my son Travis included, so they named him Duke. But I'm sure you can call him whatever you like." Stanley was getting to his feet, preparing to depart.

"No, that'll do just fine. We'll call him Duke, a great addition to our family. Thank you, Stanley. It's very thoughtful. I appreciate it."

As we shook hands, I noticed that Stanley was smiling like I'd never seen him smile before. Gone was the furrowed brow, the stern manner, the stone face. His smile was warm, his eyes still moist, as if the weight of the world had been lifted from his shoulders. Maybe it had.

As I watched Stanley drive away, my new companion and I headed out for the first of many walks together. "C'mon, Duke, let me show you around the neighborhood."

***

On one of the first warm evenings in April, George and Linda came over to play cards and catch up. After enjoying Sally's lasagna and Linda's apple pie, George and I were clearing away the dishes and planning our strategy for the evening.

"Let's stick with Spades tonight. They always kill us when we play Pitch," George said just above a whisper. The four of us had played cards together for years, and sometime back, we made the mistake of suggesting that we should play men against the women. Since that fateful night, we had a long record of humiliation and defeat, a losing streak for which we had no explanation.

"They beat us at Spades, too, George. I don't get it. You'd think that just the law of averages would let us win occasionally." I was loading the dishwasher as George rinsed off the plates.

"I still think they have some secret code, some signal that we can't pick up on. Maybe we ought to switch games again, try something different. How about Poker? Is Sally any good at Poker?"

"Gosh, I don't know. I can't remember her ever playing Poker. We are not really casino types, you know."

George smiled at that unlikely prospect. We finished up in the kitchen and brought the coffee to the dining room table.

"Thanks for cleaning up in there," Linda said. "So, what's it going to be, guys? What are we playing tonight?" She was already taking the deck from the box and shuffling the cards.

"We were wondering how you guys would feel about playing Poker tonight?" George asked nonchalantly.

"Poker?" Sally said in surprise. "I've never played Poker in my life. I don't even know the rules."

"Perfect," George replied with a smile. "A couple of rookies. Maybe we can win tonight."

But Linda was shaking her head and cutting the cards. "Nice try, guys, but Spades it is."

George looked at me with a shrug of resignation as Linda began to deal. And yes, we took yet another beating.

After the game, we moved to the comfort of our cozy living room.

"Well," Sally said. "You guys are taking it better than you used to, our lovable losers." She curled up beside me on the couch.

George settled into my recliner. "This calm and gracious demeanor masks our inner rage and frustration," he said with his typical dramatic flair.

"You certainly hide it well, that's all I can say. You take it like a man," Sally replied as we all laughed together.

It wasn't long until the conversation came around to family matters.

"How are David and Daniel doing by now? I haven't seen them since right after Christmas," George asked.

"Real well. Things are calming down for them in the community," I said. "And both are working hard at The Way. I was a pastor for thirty years, but I've never seen anyone more committed or invested in a church. It's a beautiful thing."

"What impresses me is how David and Daniel live out their faith. It's a real testimony to the whole community, that a same sex couple can serve the Lord and lead the church," Linda added thoughtfully. "Those who would condemn them can't find much to criticize."

George shook his head. "Oh, they'll find something. They'll ignore the boy's ministry, disqualifying all of it because of their "gay agenda." In their minds, The Way cannot be an authentic church because they tolerate those perversions. They would rather deny the good being done than acknowledge that perhaps God uses gay people in his work."

"What matters to me," Sally said, "is that the protests and the threats of violence seem to be over since the fire. I hope and pray that's the end of it."

George agreed. "I think it's over, at least the worst of it. That fire cost you your home, but I think it jolted this whole town. People knew it was wrong, terribly wrong, no matter what your views, unacceptable in any circumstance. That's why even a guy like Stanley Pulliam shows up to give you a puppy."

"Well, he's not a puppy anymore," I said. "He's closer to a horse and still growing." On cue, Duke got up from his rug and looked at me, eye level on the couch. "We are feeling safer by the day. I may start taking him to work with me, put him in charge of security. I won't have to worry about shoplifting, that's for sure."

But Sally was reliving the ordeal of the fire once more. "It was a horrifying thing, so frightening to think that anyone would do such a thing. I still think of Shiloh. I can't help it, and I still wonder if it will happen again. It scares me."

I pulled her close and kissed her forehead. "It was a terrible night, but it's over. It's done and we're still here. Our family is safe and sound. And maybe, just maybe, like George said, something good can come of it. Maybe the beginning of real change. God knows we need it."

***

The next few months flew by in a flurry of activity. Construction had begun on our new home and Sally was scouring the countryside to find vintage materials that we could work into our house. Amy often went along for the ride while I was tied up at the store. Sometimes Dinah joined the search.

The store kept me busy, and when I wasn't working, I was helping with the new ministries getting started at The Way. A team of volunteers converted the freight dock into a warehouse for used furniture, and a thrift store for used clothing and household items. On the north end, our children's area needed to be expanded for the daycare program we hoped to provide for single parents. The west side annex was refitted with shelves and cabinets and a large storage area. Here food would be collected and distributed to our hungry neighbors. No telling how many trips I made to the hardware store, picking up whatever was needed for these projects. So much to do, but everyone jumped in, finding ways to be helpful. I was moved and inspired to see the whole church at work, side-by-side and shoulder-to-shoulder, to meet the needs of our town.

Week by week, the old factory was being transformed from industrial manufacturing into a ministry center for the whole community. By the first of June, we were ready to launch the food, clothing, and furniture ministry. We planned to start the daycare in the fall. And those were just the first steps. David was working hard to secure volunteer professionals to staff onsite free dental and medical clinics and a pharmacy. After that, we had plans in the works to convert the south side of the factory into a shelter for homeless people, and maybe a few low-cost apartments. Plenty of room for everything under that one enormous roof, but tons of work to make it happen.

The Way was gathering a growing and diverse fellowship, people not content to sit and listen but determined to put their faith to good use. Kelly Neyland, recently divorced from her husband, Ron, volunteered to lead our daycare efforts. One of my golf buddies, Cory Moss, agreed to oversee the furniture ministry. Lori Hinnessy offered to run our food pantry and keep the schedule of volunteers. And without being asked, Luther Gray landscaped around the main entrance on Missouri with roses and azaleas. One by one, people stepped forward wanting to make a difference.

Incredibly, the only real opposition to our efforts came from a group of local business people, retailers who were afraid that our efforts would be bad for business, cutting into their sales. Some were people I knew well from my years at First Baptist, fine upstanding citizens who never let their religious devotion interfere with their profit motive. It was "just good business," from their perspective, even if it flatly contradicted what they claimed to believe on Sunday. But despite the naysayers, the plans went forward, there being no law against collecting donations and giving things away.

I marveled at the strange collection of volunteers that converged on the old factory on Saturdays and weekday evenings. In addition to those who were part of The Way, people, young and old, from all over Joppa came to help. Many of the churches were represented — Catholics, Lutherans, Disciples of Christ, Baptists, Methodists, and Pentecostals. I recognized a few Jehovah's Witnesses and Adventists working right alongside the rest. It was a remarkable display of unity, coming together to bless our community. Most of the "Bible-believing" churches, including Bethany Baptist, refused to get involved, afraid that their participation would be viewed as an endorsement of our inclusiveness. Defying Pastor Holcomb's prohibition, a few of his folks dropped off donations anyway.

Our local civic groups and clubs brought generous donations and volunteered their time. The local Harley Davidson club came to volunteer two Saturdays each month. The Rotarians, the Elks, and the Optimists took their turns. I couldn't help but contrast their selfless generosity with the indifference or opposition of some of those who claimed to follow Jesus.

***

Sally's Friday night dinners were a little cramped and crowded in our small apartment, but we kept the tradition alive. More than half the time, we could gather David and Daniel, Dinah and Richie, sometimes George and Linda or Molly and Laura, and occasional guests like Michael or Brian. We always looked forward to the conversation, the good food and fun.

Friday night before Father's Day, we had a full house. I grilled all the burgers and brats I could find, and Sally made a huge bowl of pasta salad and a pan of her baked beans. Everything else arrived courtesy of our guests. When all the food was ready, we made a standing circle around the room.

Sally had recently reinstituted an old Wesleyan blessing from her childhood, always offered in unison:

"Be present at our table, Lord. Be here and everywhere adored. These morsels bless and grant that we may feast in paradise with thee. Amen."

George was the first to break the post-blessing silence. "And be present at our TV trays also, lest the dog get our morsels."

In the laughter, Sally spoke up. "That's a good reminder. Please don't feed Duke. He's growing fast enough as it is. And you'll have to guard your plate, too. He's pretty quick."

"That's an understatement," I said. "Duke got two brats off the hot grill, and probably would've got them all if I hadn't come back outside. I can't leave it open at all. Not sure how he did it."

"I'll bet you just dropped a couple for him," David chimed in. "You feed him all the time, Dad. No dog ever had it so good. No wonder he's so big."

All the nods and laughter indicated they were buying David's version of events as much more believable than my story, but I refused to confess. "I'm telling you, I don't know how he did it. Duke's the wonder dog." I pleaded my case to a skeptical jury.

All the while, Duke stood there next to the table with a big slobbery grin on his face, telling no tales.

Later that evening, Dinah and Richie stayed to help us clean up the kitchen after everyone else had gone. Sally brewed a pot of decaf and we sat down for some unexpected bonus time, the four of us. I soon got the impression that Richie had some unspoken agenda for us to discuss.

Sure enough, he soon got to the point. "Bart, you and Sally have been good to me, really kind when I had no right to expect it. You could've run me off, but you didn't. You forgave me and helped me make a new start. You've been a real mom and dad to me, and I appreciate it, even if you say no to what I'm about to ask."

I could read the earnestness on his face. "What's on your mind, Richie?"

He paused, glanced at Dinah, and cleared his throat. "It's about Dinah. I love her. I love her more than I ever loved anyone, more than everyone else put together." He hesitated, his voice choked with emotion. "We want to get married, but only if it's okay with you. I won't go against you, but I promise you I will do right by your daughter. I'll love her and take care of her all my life."

Dinah reached up to touch Richie's cheek, and her blue eyes betrayed the depth of love she had come to feel for this rangy, ragged young man who had so frightened her in the beginning.

I felt Sally take my hand as she gave me a smile and a nod.

She spoke for both of us. "Richie, we feel like you've been part of our family for a long time now, and we've seen how happy you and Dinah are together. Right, Bart?"

"We might as well make it official, Richie. We would be pleased and proud to welcome you to our family. Of course, you have our blessing." I got to my feet to give him a hug, but he wasn't finished.

He turned towards Dinah and slipped out of his chair, down on one knee, though he was still eye to eye with her sitting in her chair. He reached inside his jacket and presented a blue velvet box.

Dinah gasped, not anticipating this moment, at least not here, not now, with her parents at the table.

"Dinah, will you marry me? I love you and I wanna be with you all my life." He opened the box and offered the ring, hopeful and yet vulnerable.

I had never seen Dinah's face so radiant, glowing with anticipation, her eyes wet with tears. She reached past Richie's extended hand, wrapped her arms around his neck, and pulled him close. "Yes, Richie. Of course, I'll marry you. You know I love you!" Dinah leaned back and held out her hand as Richie slipped the ring on her finger. It was a modest solitaire, but Dinah held it up like the crown jewels.

***

Cory Moss had quit the country club soon after I was kicked out. He went to a board meeting demanding an explanation, but he never got any satisfaction. So, the next month, he sold his stock and quit. Then Greg Phillips had followed him out the door in the spring, deciding his money could be better spent elsewhere, in places where his friends were allowed to play. My other golf buddy, Steve Dudley, stayed on at the country club, needing to keep his membership for his business connections, but he played most of his golf away from the club.

I felt bad for them, but strangely affirmed by their decision to walk away from the club—that's what friends do.

I met my friendly trio at the Wal Mart parking lot early on a warm Friday morning. As I opened the trunk of my Honda, I asked, "So, who's driving today?" It was a running joke since Steve had a big Escalade and the rest of us drove little two doors. "Don't worry, Dud. I'll buy you a hot dog at the golf course, and after all, you get like eight miles to the gallon in that thing, don't you?"

"You guys just keep me around to haul your butts to the golf course in my Cadillac," Steve bellowed as he opened the rear door. He kept his vehicle spotlessly clean and only complained on muddy days, when our golf shoes and bags mucked up the carpet.

I was the third to arrive, Cory always running late. We had our own theories as to why he never could make it on time, but he never seemed bothered by our teasing.

When he finally pulled up, Greg let him hear about it. "Cory, either you need to start taking care of business the night before, or tell Janell that she's just going to have wait until you get back in the afternoon. She can't be jumping your bones when it's time to go play golf."

Cory shook his head, having heard the same advice on many golf days. "How about you come over and tell her that, Flips. I think she would take it much better coming from you."

"Oh, c'mon, Cory. Be a man. Let her know who's boss."

"I think she already knows who's the boss," Cory concluded as he climbed in the back seat.

We drove about thirty minutes to the old public course in Marshfield. Along the way the conversation shifted to more serious subjects.

Greg said, "Bart, I hear your daughter is engaged. Somebody said it was that Towns boy, the one who went to jail for David's attack. Is that right?"

"Well, yeah, Flips. Dinah is engaged to Richie Towns, but he's not the same man he used to be. Big changes in his life. He came back from jail a different person."

Steve spoke up. "I bought some tires from him a couple of months ago, and I was impressed. In fact, I thought it must be a different guy, a twin or something. He's nothing like I remember him."

Greg was a tougher sell. "I hope he's not just playing along and coming to church to get on your good side, just to get to Dinah. She's a peach, I know, and he wouldn't be the first guy to put on an act to get a woman."

I just smiled at Greg's natural skepticism. "I know, Flips, but this is the real deal. Richie is the genuine article, living proof that people really can change. I'm telling you, it's a God thing."

Cory had been listening to our conversation. "I believe you, but how do you and Sally do it? How do you forgive a man that tried to kill your own son? How do you take him into your family, let him marry your daughter, maybe father your grandkids? I mean, I know we are supposed to forgive people, but isn't there some limit to that? I mean, forgive them, but you don't have to let them into your family, do you?"

"I guess not, but it's not so hard to forgive when I see the change, the transformation. To see God work in Richie's life in such beautiful ways makes it easy to forgive. He's not the same person he used to be. I'm telling you, he's a new man." I paused for a moment, wondering how much I should say, and then decided to push on. "The hard part for me is trying to forgive those who are not sorry, who never apologize, and have no intention of changing. That's the struggle, forgiving those who would still do me harm, me or my family. That pushes me right to the limits. It's a hard step for me."

Cory nodded. "Me, too. I respect you for that, for being honest. I know I couldn't do it."

Greg was more pragmatic. "Well, forgive him or don't forgive him, but if that Hampton guy comes after you again, we are going after him. We already talked about it, Bart. You can be the man of God if you want to, but I'll go after him with my three iron, and he won't be walking away next time."

Steve grinned at Greg's bluster. "Not your three iron, Flips. You can't swing that club worth shit. Probably miss him altogether. Might as well use your umbrella."

Cory and I laughed at Steve's advice.

As we pulled into the parking lot, Cory wrapped up our conversation. "Here's praying that there is no next time. Whether that guy ever wises up or not, I hope he has the good sense to steer clear of you and your family."

"Amen to that, Cory. Amen to that."

***

Like most little girls, Dinah had been dreaming about her wedding since childhood. She wanted to be married on a mountain, one we had visited years before: Pine Mountain, Georgia. Nestled in the woods beside a clear mountain lake, Callaway Memorial Chapel was sacred and surreal, a breathtaking blend of stone and timber and stained glass, a majestic setting for a wedding.

We gathered there on a clear, crisp Saturday in October, with the autumn colors adding their splendor to our mountain venue. Only eighteen of us made the three-hour drive to Pine Mountain, Richie and Dinah limiting their guest list to family and the closest of friends. Richie had lost his dad when he was just ten years old, but his mother and stepfather made the trip, along with his uncle, who also happened to be his boss at the tire store and car repair shop.

Dinah had asked David to conduct the ceremony so that I could give my full attention to my duties as the father of the bride. Daniel was Richie's Best Man, and Molly was the Maid of Honor. Laura made a cute flower girl with her hair up in curls.

As the ceremony began, I stood in the chapel foyer waiting to escort my daughter down the aisle and watched as David seated his mother, Sally beaming and beautiful as she found her place. I could see David facing back towards me, Richie standing tall beside him, and then Daniel, who was also going to sing later in the ceremony. I felt Dinah take my arm.

"Are you ready, Daddy? It's almost time. Doesn't Richie look handsome?"

I turned to see my baby girl transformed into a striking young woman. "Yes, he does, Dinah, and what a beautiful bride you are. I am the proudest father on Earth."

She squeezed my arm and reached up to kiss my cheek, and quickly wiped away the lipstick as we waited for our special moment.

I couldn't help but marvel at the unlikely family beside me and before me. Had I any inclination of who our children would grow up to marry or how in the world they would find their one true love, I could never have imagined a more unlikely scenario. I realized in that moment what a gift we had been given, what a work of grace we had witnessed. I walked my daughter down the aisle giving silent thanks for the startling, surprising ways of God.

Daniel sang the words that Richie had requested, words from Rascal Flatts that told his story better than he could say:

I set out on a narrow way many years ago
Hoping I would find true love along the
broken road
But I got lost a time or two....
~~~
*I think about the years I spent just passing*
through
*I'd like to have the time I lost and give it*
back to you
*But you just smile and take my hand*
*You've been there, you understand*
*It's all part of a grander plan that is coming*
true.
~~~
Now I'm just rolling home
Into my lover's arms
This much I know is true
That God blessed the broken road
That led me straight to you.

***

"Good morning, Bart. This is Tom Hopkins over at the funeral home. We've got a situation here. Did you hear about the accident last night out on 45?"

It was nearly noon and several customers at the store had been talking about the news.

"Yes, Tom, I did hear about that. A motorcycle, I guess, out of control. Someone said it was Mark Hampton. Is that right?"

"That's right, Mark Hampton, and I know you have some history with him."

"Well, yes, I do. Plenty of history, all of it bad."

"Yes, I know all that, and I know how you must feel about him. Well, I just talked with his brother, Jack, and they're going to have a little graveside service for Mark on Thursday afternoon. He wanted me to ask you to have the service."

I almost dropped the phone. I could hardly process his words. "Are you kidding me, Tom? There must be some mistake. They would never ask me." All I knew from Mark Hampton was bitterness and violence. "I'm pretty sure Mark Hampton hated my guts."

"Jack said they would understand if you said no, but they don't have anyone else, and he said you had shown kindness to Mark's family last Christmas, his girlfriend and his little girl, Laura."

"Wait a minute. Are you kidding me? Molly and Laura are Mark Hampton's family? I never dreamed there could be any connection." Molly hadn't said a word about it, but then again, we never asked for any details about her boyfriend.

Tom continued to fill me in. "I guess Mark took off last year, kind of left them to fend for themselves. Don't think they were officially married or anything. Jack said Mark was working up north and would blow through town once a month or so. Sometimes that was a good thing, but once or twice it got ugly. Mark was an angry, violent man, we all know that. Anyway, he's gone now, and it looks like you're the man to lay him to rest. What do you think, Bart? Will you do it?"

"All right, Tom. I'll have the graveside for Mark. I'll do the best I can, just get me the details."

"Thanks, Bart. I didn't really have a plan B if you said no. I appreciate you doing this. I'll be back in touch real soon. Thanks again."

***

Did you ever wonder how ministers find appropriate words to mark the passing of people who seemed to have no redeeming qualities or positive legacy? What does one say over the grave of a bitter, violent, abusive man like Mark Hampton?

It was certainly a fair question and a real challenge at times, but I always tried to keep two things in mind. First, every grieving family deserved some words of comfort, no matter the circumstances. And secondly, judgment was God's business, not mine or anyone else's.

On a blustery December afternoon, we gathered in Joppa Community Cemetery for Mark Hampton's service. Old Bishop, the cemetery caretaker, had made certain to get the green tent set firmly against the cold wind. It flapped in the breeze but stood solidly in place. About twenty people gathered, including Mark's mother, two brothers, some other family, and of course, Molly and little Laura. Several of Mark's drinking buddies came out, and some of those apparently had a few before they arrived. Richie and Dinah also attended, staying close to Laura.

The casket was already in place and remained closed despite a request from one of Mark's inebriated buddies. Tom Hopkins kept things in good order and managed to get everyone under the tent and out of the wind.

So I began:

> *Through Mark's sudden passing, God has caught our attention for a little while to focus us on the things that matter most. We realize how precious and fleeting are the moments we have in this life. For most of our lives, death seems so*

remote, so far removed from us. Death comes only to others, not to us, not to our son, our brother, not to one we love, not to our friend.

Death comes to all, you see. It is our common experience. George Bernard Shaw once noted that death's statistics are very impressive: "One out of every one dies." Whether our years are few or many, whether our lives are well-lived or wasted, whether we are ready or not, death comes to all.

The Gospel of Luke records these words: "Now the tax collectors and sinners were all gathering around to hear Jesus. But the Pharisees and the teachers of the law muttered, 'This man welcomes sinners and eats with them.'"

This accusation from Jesus' enemies was the only truthful charge they could bring against him. Jesus does welcome sinners. He is the sinner's friend. The Pharisees and religious leaders thought that Heaven rejoiced when a sinner was destroyed. Jesus taught that Heaven rejoices when a sinner repents and comes home.

Jesus is the sinner's friend. I'm glad he is, aren't you? I'm grateful, because I'm a sinner. What hope would any of us have if Christ were not the sinner's friend? We are all signing on Jesus' credit card. None of us deserve eternal life and all that God has promised. The scripture says that all have sinned and come short of the glory of God. None of us deserve it. None of us can earn it.

We all have our share of regrets, things we would have done differently, choices we made, words we spoke. We all bear the burden of our *sin, our guilt and regret. Thank God, Jesus is the sinner's friend.*

One man left behind a one-word epitaph carved on his headstone. The word was "Forgiven." And that's the word we all need, isn't it? Where would we be without the grace and love of God for broken, fallen people like us?

As Jesus was dying, suspended on the cross between heaven and earth, do you remember what he did? A convicted criminal dying beside Jesus made his pathetic plea, "Lord, remember me when you come into your kingdom." Jesus said, "Friend, today you will be with me in Paradise."

***

"How do we lose to a team like Vandy? I just don't get it," George said with disgust. "We can't shoot the ball. I think we went seven minutes without a bucket."

We were grabbing some dinner at a steakhouse in Athens on a Saturday evening after watching the Georgia Bulldogs blow a fifteen-point second half lead.

"You know, George, games like that one make me glad I didn't go to UGA. That was sad," I said, trying to be sympathetic. "And by the way, you didn't go to Georgia, either."

"I know, but by God, I bought a ticket. I'd like to see the team play ball, put out a decent product."

"Yeah, I get that." George and I usually made it over to Athens for a football game and at least one basketball game each year. We had both adopted the Bulldogs, since they were the closest major university and had such a loyal following. Mostly, we enjoyed the time and the conversation, another good outlet for our friendship. One thing I had learned about George: no matter how upset he might be after a ballgame, a cold beer and a thick ribeye always improved his mood.

"Bart, did you have a chance to read the paper this morning before I picked you up?"

I nodded in the affirmative.

"You did, huh. Did you see the letter to the editor from our friend Roger Holcomb?"

"Yes, I did. I guess I shouldn't be too surprised, although you would think that at some point, he could just let it go. I guess not."

Roger Holcomb, the pastor of Bethany Church, had written about certain unnamed local churches that were condoning immorality, preaching a false gospel, and trying to cover it up with lots of social ministry.

George shook his head. "He's a real peach, that guy is. Where does he get off being God's one true spokesman? It makes me sick."

"Yeah, me too. I wonder if he knows how many of his own members have come to The Way for assistance of some kind."

"I'll go you one better. I wonder if he ever noticed just how much "social ministry" is in the Gospels. Jesus always focused on the sick, the hungry, the poor, the suffering. And the only people he gave holy hell were the self-righteous blowhards who didn't give a damn about the people."

"I know, I know, but I think in Roger's case, it's not that he objects to the ministry we are doing, though his church never helps out. It's the gay thing, of course. That's what drives him. Some of these pastors see that one issue as the linchpin of orthodoxy. If they are wrong about that... well, they just can't be wrong, or their whole world crumbles."

It's the Bible, Bart. They've been reading the scripture with the same blinders all their lives, and they can't accept the reality that the Bible doesn't speak directly to every contemporary issue. All we can do is apply the ethic of Christ and go from there." With that thought, George polished off his last bite of steak.

"I can't be too hard on him, George. After all, I used to agree with him. We were on the same page. I grouped all homosexuals together, certain that same sex attraction led only to perversion and sin. I never imagined that there might be sincere, devout Christians who had God-honoring same sex relationships."

"I know. It makes me wonder if these guys ever had a conversation with a gay person. It's easy to condemn and pontificate when it's just an abstraction, but it's a little tougher writing off a real person, face to face."

"Yes, or your own son."

Chapter 10 – All Good Things

"As in nature, as in art, so in grace;
it is rough treatment that gives souls, as well as stones,
their luster.
~ *Thomas Guthrie*

"Bart, you didn't touch your breakfast. Aren't you hungry? You've got a long day ahead."

I looked at the scrambled eggs and toast and felt that same sour ache in my stomach. "Sorry, Sweetie, just not hungry this morning."

Sally picked up my plate and laid her hand on my shoulder.

There's no fooling her.

"Seems like lately you are never hungry. You've lost quite a bit of weight and you're not even trying. Your work clothes just hang on you, all big and baggy. What's going on?"

"I don't know. Just never seem to have much appetite. I feel like I'm wearing down. It's like I run out of gas sometimes and have to take a break. Maybe I should get a checkup. I haven't seen Dr. Bowman for quite a while."

Sally looked at the calendar stuck on the refrigerator door. "I'll call and see when he can get you in, and I'll try to get Tuesday, when you are not at the store. But we need to get you checked out." She kissed me on my forehead. "In the meantime, I'm going to order you some new pants before you lose yours altogether. Don't want you embarrassing yourself." She left the kitchen as I finished my coffee.

Funny how people could live with annoying physical symptoms and never seem to connect them. Sally was right about my weight loss, and the fatigue had become a real problem. A few weeks before, I was climbing into the back of a truck and winced with a sharp pain, deep in my abdomen, too high to be my appendix. I passed it off as indigestion or maybe the beginnings of an ulcer. It passed, and I thought no more about it. Then, from time to time, the pain would strike again, sudden and excruciating, and then vanish again. I told myself I'd get it checked out if it didn't stop. So, maybe this appointment was a good idea for lots of reasons.

***

Dr. Bowman had been in family practice in Joppa for twenty-seven years, the only doctor for our family since we moved to town. I appreciated his thoroughness, and his determination to find his patients the care they needed beyond Joppa when necessary. He was a fine small-town doctor who always seemed to know when to send his patients on to the big city specialists.

"Bart, I can't say with real certainty, but I think there may be a serious issue here. It's a hard thing to spot, difficult to diagnose, but I think it's your pancreas, and if it is, we need to get you to the right people right away. If it's cancer in the pancreas, it's serious, as you probably know. Pancreatic cancer can be advanced before people begin to have symptoms. We need to send you to Emory, to make sure we know what we're up against, and determine the best plan for your care. I'm sorry to give you such news, Bart, and I hope to God I'm wrong about this."

Sally clung to my arm more tightly with each word. We sat there, attentive and appreciative, yet stunned, dazed to find ourselves facing a hard, new reality.

We waited through the longest two weeks of our lives before heading to Emory University Hospital in Atlanta to get the final word on my condition and treatment, though I had already prepared myself for the worst. Having spent far too much time on the internet reading about the signs and symptoms of pancreatic cancer, I was all but certain that this was my particular illness. Sally had gone on to investigate the treatment options and the dreadful survival statistics.

It's the deadliest form of cancer, not a helpful bit of research for those trying to keep a positive mental outlook.

The doctors at Emory confirmed Dr. Bowman's suspicions and painted a grim picture of my treatment options. As was often the case, my cancer was significantly advanced before producing noticeable symptoms. The MRI indicated that the tumor involved the entire pancreas and had spread to the liver. Chemotherapy and radiation had a record of minimal effectiveness against pancreatic cancer at my advanced stage. The only real surgical option presented was a pancreatectomy, removing the entire pancreas, the gall bladder, the spleen, part of the stomach and small intestines, and the lymph nodes in the neighborhood. Even with the surgery, though, the doctors were still not overly hopeful. The statistics were sad and sobering: only twenty-three percent of those who have pancreatic cancer are alive one year after diagnosis, only four percent live five years.

Sally absorbed the news in stoic silence. We didn't talk much on the drive back to Joppa—too much to process, in such a short time.

When we were nearly home, she reached over to take my hand. "I love you, you know, and I'll be here for you, no matter what. Don't forget that, hardware man."

I lifted her hand to my lips and kissed it. "I won't forget. Your love is my treasure. Try not to let your worry run ahead. Let's just go a step at a time. God knows where we are and what's going on here."

"That's good," Sally whispered. "'Cause I sure don't."

***

That Friday night, we told the kids. David and Daniel, Dinah and Richie, came over to the apartment for dinner. It was David and Daniel's turn to cook, and they brought pizza dough and all the toppings for us to build our own individual pizzas. Everyone wanted to contribute some strange topping to my pizza, affectionately dubbed "the kitchen sink pizza." I'm certain no human being had ever tasted such a pie—cheddar brats, anchovies, red onion, banana peppers, portabellas, pineapple, walnuts, artichokes, and bacon. Surprisingly, it was not as bad as it sounded—confused, but tasty.

After dinner, we sat around the table finishing our coffee and chocolate cake. Sally wasn't anxious to do the talking, so I began.

"We need to talk with you all about something that's come up, a serious health issue that I have." The relaxed levity of the evening vanished as I tried to look each one in the eye.

"What's wrong, Dad? What's going on?" David asked.

I breathed a deep sigh and began. "I've been having some symptoms: fatigue, losing weight, some abdominal pain. I went to Dr. Bowman for a checkup and he sent me on to Emory. They ran some tests and did a scan and told me that I have cancer, advanced-stage pancreatic cancer."

Dinah leapt up from her chair and hugged her mother and reached for me at the same time. The tears began to flow.

"What's your prognosis, Dad?" David asked. "What are they going to do? Is surgery an option? There must be some kind of treatment for you. The people at Emory are supposed to be the best."

"I think they are, David. The problem is that this kind of cancer doesn't show up until it is advanced, and in my case, it has spread to the liver and abdomen. The doctors want to do surgery to remove as much as possible, but they can't stop it or remove it all. With surgery, the doctors said I could expect to live six months to a year, maybe longer."

Those words hung in the air and were swallowed up in tears and hugs all around. Richie's long arms reached around Sally and Dinah and myself, as David and Daniel burrowed in from the other side. Not many words were spoken — not much to say, as they struggled to process the news.

We eventually sat back down for an impromptu family meeting. Each one asked their questions and voiced their feelings, except Daniel. He was obviously concerned, upset, but he didn't say a word.

"Daniel," I said, "are you okay? I know this is tough to hear, hard to accept."

He stared down at his hands, then finally looked my way. The words came slowly, as he was still forming his thoughts. "I don't get it. I don't understand why these things happen. Why should you be sick with cancer? I mean, all you do for people, what you've done for me." He paused to gather his emotions. "Your whole life is serving God, and this is what you get, six months to a year? I'm sorry, but that's bullshit, Dad. It's just wrong. It's not fair." David moved to put his arm around him, but Daniel pulled away.

I knew he was baring his soul and wanted answers, if there were any answers to be had.

"Those are fair questions, Daniel, questions that people have been asking for centuries, including me. And you're right, it's not fair. Life's not fair. It rains on the good and the bad, the just and the unjust. This world is broken, fallen, and bad things happen to all kinds of people. Nobody is immune. Nobody gets a free pass. We all roll the dice, take our turn, and pay our dues. You know that's true, don't you?"

Daniel nodded as I continued. "It's not what happens to people of faith that makes us different or unique. It's how we respond to hardship. It's how we react to all that is unjust and unfair. It's how we play whatever cards are dealt to us. That's the difference. I know you understand that truth, Daniel, because I learned it from you."

He turned his head, puzzling over my words. "You learned it from me?"

"Of course, I did. You taught all of us. When Mark and Richie went after you, nearly beat you to death, you were innocent. You did nothing to deserve their abuse. But God wasn't punishing you. It just happened. And how did you handle it? How did you meet such a cruel injustice? With faith and with grace, didn't you? You forgave Mark and Richie, and now Richie is your brother, right here beside you. A terrible thing happened to you and you responded in a beautiful, godly way. So now,

I've got cancer, a bad thing, something I never signed up for, but it's here. Now I've got to find some of that same faith and grace, Daniel. I know I am loved by God. I am his child, and I will live my life to please him, even if it's just six months to a year."

Daniel nodded slowly. "I guess it was easier when it was me. I just hate for you to go through this. I hate it."

"I know," I said. "It's easier to suffer hardship ourselves than to watch those we love go through painful experiences. Thanks for caring so much, Daniel. Thanks for being such a good son to me." I moved to embrace him as he rose from his chair and buried his face in my shoulder, sobbing like a child.

"I don't want to lose you," he said through his tears. "I don't want you to go."

"That makes two of us, Daniel." Our embrace suddenly became a huddle as Sally and David, Dinah and Richie, wrapped us in love.

David whispered. "No, Dad, that makes six of us."

***

I lay in bed reading a novel, thinking that Sally was already asleep. I read to the end of the chapter, marked my place, laid my book and my glasses on the headboard, and reached for the lamp.

Sally turned toward me. "Don't turn it off yet. Can we talk a minute?"

"Sure. What's on your mind?"

She scooted over close to me and took my arm in hers as she liked to do. "I was thinking about the house. They're making good progress and it should be done by the end of next month. We've got everything we need to finish, except just a few odds and ends, fixtures and such, and a mirror for the front hall."

"It's going to be beautiful, Sal. You did such a great job. It's going to be a brand-new house with all the style and character of an old classic, Old Blue. I can't believe you found all that stuff."

"Well, I did run around the countryside for months, and I know I spent more than we planned to spend on some of those things, but when you find what you are looking for, the perfect thing, you have to get it. No second chances."

"I know. I got a little snippy a time or two. I'm sorry for that. You found all the right stuff and I'm proud of you." I pulled her close, her head resting on my shoulder.

"Bart, I'm excited about the house, I really am, but I'm scared, too. I'm scared that we're building a big, beautiful house for an old widow lady to live in. I'm frightened at the thought of living in my dream house without the man of my dreams, growing old without you. I mean, I love Duke, he's good company, but I'd rather have you around, too." Her warm tears dampened my shoulder.

"I don't know what to say, Sal. You know I love you, and I want nothing more than to grow old with you, to be by your side for the whole journey, but we both know that's not my call, it's not our decision. We'll fight this battle and do the best we can. We'll play every card in our hand and let the chips fall where they will. And if I must go, then I trust God will take care of me. And if you have to stay, then I trust God will take care of you. That's all I know, Sweetie."

She reached up to kiss my cheek, and then lay there beside me in the quiet for a while. "You know, for a hardware man, you sure have a way with words. Reach up there and turn off that light," she said, wiping a tear from her cheek. "Then, come here a minute. I'm wondering just how much of your basic equipment is still in working order. Mind if I check it out?"

I switched off the lamp with a grin on my face. "Fine with me, lady, just go easy. Everything still works, but won't tolerate excessive wear and tear."

She giggled as if we were back in college. What a woman I married.

***

I felt as if stranded in a crowded parking lot, lying there on a gurney in the pre-surgery holding area at Emory, with other patients on either side, each of us waiting our turn for surgery. The countless questions finally ended, and I was tagged and marked and ready to go under. Only Sally remained with me, only one being allowed in the holding area. All the kids and George and Linda, Amy, and Brian had settled into the waiting area. My pastor friend, Yvonne, had come by earlier and prayed with me, a comfort that I had given to countless others but had rarely received. It meant more than I could tell her.

It's not the knife, you see. It's not the actual surgery. It's not even being rolled away from my family that was the worst part. It's the loss of control. It's that totally helpless feeling, knowing that I was completely at the mercy of others, trusting strangers with my life. The outcome would be determined by the hands of others, human hands, divine hands.

One last kiss from my teary-eyed Sally, and they rolled me into a bright and freezing operating room. I shuddered at the chill. A few more questions to answer, and then the light faded — shadows, sleep.

***

"Mr. Sheldon, can you hear me? Are you awake? Mr. Sheldon?"

The recovery room buzzed with staff around my bed, and I heard the incessant beeping of whatever monitors or machines they'd attached to me. I could only open my eyes and manage a slight nod, my mouth and throat occupied by a respirator tube — like someone was sitting on my chest shoving a bathroom plunger down my throat.

"On a scale of one to ten, how is your pain? I'll say the numbers and you just nod when I say the number you choose. One means not much pain and ten is the most."

When she got to eight, I blinked my eyes.

"All right, we'll get you some relief."

I just wanted to go back to sleep, hoping that waking up next time would be better than this.

"You are doing fine, Mr. Sheldon. We're going to move you into intensive care in a little while, and then you can see your family, two at a time, I think. The doctor will come talk with you there. Do you understand?"

I nodded again, as I realized I had made it through the easy part. It would be a rough road from here.

***

My family and friends had been notified when I was out of surgery, and later when I was moved to ICU, but no other details had been shared with them. Sally and David were with me in the ICU when my doctors came in to share their appraisal.

Their mood seemed grim, not many smiles. "Mr. Sheldon, you did well, you came through just fine, as we anticipated you would. What we found was also what we expected. We removed the pancreas, the gall bladder, spleen, a portion of the small intestine, as we had planned, but the cancer is widespread in your abdomen. The liver and the lymph nodes are malignant, advanced, and more than we can deal with surgically. We'll know more when the lab work comes back, but I will tell you it does not look good. The oncologist will talk to you about your options, but none of them are promising. Nothing is very effective in this situation."

Sally stood beside my bed, trying to be strong, softly weeping, her hand on my shoulder.

David held my hand firmly, hanging on the doctor's words. He spoke for me. "So, Doctor, what is your prognosis? What should we anticipate? Can you tell us what to expect?"

The doctor nodded and continued with what must have been the worst part of his job. "What we were able to do today may buy you some time, Mr. Sheldon—time with your family, time to get your things in order. It's always difficult to say how much time you may have, but if you do well, I would hope you can have several months, maybe six months. Beyond that would be unlikely. I'm sorry. I wish there was more that we could do for you. We will get you resources, we will put you in touch with Hospice there in Joppa. I guess you already know about them. We'll help you with pain management. There's no reason for you to suffer. We can guarantee you that. Hopefully, you can recuperate from this surgery and enjoy to some extent the time you have left. I'm afraid that's the best we can do for you. Again, I'm sorry."

***

Eight days in the hospital felt like a month, as each day seemed to drag along, highlighted by burps and bowel movements, bland meals, and lengthening walks down the hall. The pain began to let up day by day, and I slept a little better each night when the staff would leave me alone. I did watch quite a bit of basketball, accidentally timing my recuperation during the NCAA tournament. Our family did our brackets, as usual, which perhaps gave us some sense of normalcy in this crisis. I found myself picking more and more upsets and longshots round by round. Feeling like the biggest underdog myself, I wanted to beat the odds. Despite my high hopes for the lower seeds, three of my final four picks went down the first weekend.

Blind optimism can only carry you so far.

A steady stream of visitors came during my last few days in the hospital, which surprised me, given the distance to Decatur from Joppa. Sally stayed with me the whole time, and the kids were great, at least one of the four at the hospital each day over my insistence that they didn't need to come so often. David and Daniel were keeping Duke at their place with reluctant and temporary permission from their landlord. My little brother Jerry made a fast trip from Memphis to see me, a big surprise. He didn't take the news any better than the rest of us.

"What about getting a second opinion, Bart? They could be wrong. What about those places that are doing all the cutting-edge research, like M. D. Anderson or Mayo's or Johns Hopkins?" Jerry said, never one to give up without a fight.

"I understand how you feel, but we've been all through that, and the doctors all say the same thing. In my condition, my stage, I'm not a candidate for their trials or even their experimental treatments. They won't accept me as a patient, and I guess I can't blame them.

The people here have been great. They've done everything for me that can be done medically."

"I feel so damn helpless. I hate seeing you go through this, Bart. It's not supposed to be this way."

"I know how you feel. Thanks for caring. Now, if you want to be helpful, go get me some decent food. How about some barbeque? Go get me some ribs from that Community Q place that's supposed to be so great, maybe some slaw and beans, too. That sounds really good today."

"I'm on it, big brother. I'll bring it in for you, and if they won't let you eat it, I'll just eat it in front of you." Jerry was out the door, just glad to have something he could do for me.

My partner at work, Jim, drove up one evening after closing and caught me up on store business. I knew he had all kinds of questions, and things we would need to discuss about what my condition might mean for the future of the store, but this was not the time. I just wasn't ready for that conversation, and had no idea what we needed to do. I assured him that I'd be back at work in a couple of weeks, and we would have plenty of time to talk and make some plans. He seemed reassured.

The next morning, while taking my morning walk around the floor, I heard a familiar voice behind me.

"Man, Bart, you should tie up in back, buddy. Too much of a view, I'm telling you. You're putting on a show back here."

I turned around to see my golf buddies coming down the hall. I grabbed for my gown and was relieved to find that I had indeed covered up my backside. "I'm trying to leave just a little bit to the imagination, Dud. Good to see you guys. Aren't you supposed to be at the golf course today?"

"Yeah, we are, but one of our foursome didn't show up, gave some lame excuse about having a date with a bunch of young nurses," Steve said.

We all laughed, including my nurse, Lucinda, a large African American woman who could probably whip any two of us. We walked down to a waiting area, and Lucinda let us have a little while to talk.

"How are you doing, Bart? Everything we hear is bad news. How are you and Sally holding up?" Cory asked.

"We're all right, doing pretty well. I guess the reality of our situation takes a while to soak in. Sally and the kids are taking it hard."

Greg shook his head. "Well, we've got to get you through this. You've got to beat the odds, Bart. Some people do, you know. There's always some percent, even just a few, who make it, who beat this stuff. You've got to be the one to get through this. And we're with you, man, with you all the way."

Steve nodded in agreement. "You know me. I don't make it to church too often. I'm not the praying kind, but since I heard the news, I've been praying for you every night. I haven't been down on my knees since I was a little boy, but I've been on my knees for you, Bart, and I'll keep on praying until you are well again." His eyes were wet as he spoke.

I put my hand on his shoulder. "Guys, I appreciate your friendship and support during this time and the days ahead, however this plays out. I'm going to do my best, take care of my family, and trust God for the rest. That's all I can do. Maybe I will be the one who beats the odds, but just wanting it won't make it happen. I have to be ready for whichever way it goes."

Greg sighed and said, "Well, maybe God should get off his butt and do something. You're one of his players, you know. You're on his team. What's God thinking about anyway? He's dumping on the wrong man."

"To be honest, Greg, I've had some of those same thoughts, not so much about me, but about my family, leaving Sally, our kids. It sucks, doesn't it?"

We paused for a thoughtful moment pondering that reality.

Cory broke the silence. "When you get out of here and you get your strength back, are you going to feel like playing some golf? Even nine holes? We'll use a cart and drive right up to the green. I don't care what they say. We'll work it out. If you feel like it, whenever you want, just holler, and we'll make it happen. I'd really like to play again."

"Sure, guys. Just give me a couple of weeks. I'll be ready to go, well enough to beat you guys, anyway."

We stood to our feet as Lucinda rounded the corner to finish our walk.

"Thanks for coming to see me, guys. It means a lot. Just... thanks."

***

Well past regular visiting hours, Sally was making some phone calls in the waiting room down the hall. I was just drifting off when I saw a man standing in the doorway.

"Brother Bart, it's me, Luther Gray. Are you still awake?"

"Come on in, Luther. It's good of you to come see me. How did you get here? It's a long way from Joppa." I remembered that Luther had no car or driver's license.

"Oh, I hitchhiked up to Atlanta and took the bus out here. It comes right to the door of the hospital. I can always get a ride." He stood at the foot of my bed with his cap in his hands.

"Luther, I appreciate you going to all of that trouble."

"No trouble at all. I heard you was bad, the doctors sayin' you ain't gonna make it. Cancer's gonna take ya. That's bad news, all right." No one ever came to the point quite like Luther.

"That's the bottom line. I might have six months, but no more than that unless God intervenes."

Luther shuffled up closer beside me and reached for my hand. "Well, I want to tell you something, Brother Bart. You're gonna be just fine, not the gettin' well kind of fine, but the dead or alive kind of fine. Either way it goes, whenever it happens, you're gonna be all right. You know that, don't cha?"

"Yes, Luther, I do."

"I was thinkin' bout it while I was waiting on the bus today. I got to the station too late for the bus I wanted, but they said just wait for the next one. They said it don't matter whether you're early or late, just catch the next one. So, I'm thinkin', Brother Bart, we're all at the bus station, lined up, waiting on the bus to go home, all the way to heaven. And it don't really matter whether we're on the early bus or the next bus or even the last bus, just so long as we get home."

None of my many visitors had expressed our hope so clearly.

"That's right, Luther."

A tear rolled down his brown cheek, lost in his grey beard. "And if you got to take the early bus, that's a real blessing, Brother Bart. It's a rare privilege to go first, to sit in the front of the bus, and to finally get there and step out and be the first to see Jesus. And then you get to greet the rest of us and be the welcomin' committee."

My own tears began to flow as he squeezed my hand.

"So, if you got to go, then go on home, and don't think a thing about it. The rest of us will be along directly. And someday, when I get off that bus, you will be there to shake my hand again and show me around. Okay?"

"I'll do that, Luther. You can count on it. I'll be waiting for your bus. Thanks for coming all this way, my friend. God bless you."

***

We couldn't have had a more beautiful spring day to move into our house, the "New Blue." The azaleas and dogwoods were in full bloom and a warm breeze carried the scent of blossoms and fresh-cut grass. The move itself was not such a big job this time, since we had lost most everything in the fire. Many of the furnishings had been ordered for delivery at our new place, so we didn't need much of a truck. Three or four trips in Richie's pickup did the job.

The house turned out far beyond our expectations. Solid as a rock, over-engineered, it was built to stand as long as Old Blue had lasted. And yet, if one didn't know better, they might swear that our new house was a well-maintained or refurbished Victorian. All the antique cabinetry, woodwork, fixtures, doors, stairs, and mantles were smoothly and seamlessly incorporated into the construction and finish work.

The view from the front lawn was startling, as if our old house had been miraculously resurrected, raised up from the ashes. Sally was walking on air as she helped set up the new furnishings, many of them antiques as well. Seeing her joy made the whole ordeal worthwhile. This would be her home, her dream home, and hopefully our home together, at least for a while.

Duke, our big Plott Hound, spent most of our moving day running up and down the stairs, thrilled to have a house big enough to fit his muscular dimensions. Sally insisted that we have a door installed for Duke in the utility room, so he would always be able to come in or go out. Our house would be his castle as much as our own, and that gave us both an added sense of security.

Dinah laughed about the pet door and remarked that it worked for her as well, plenty big enough for her petite frame.

As for me, I couldn't do much of anything, having just come home from the hospital a month before. I was still under strict orders not to pick up anything more than five pounds, and I wasn't sure I could even carry that much. The surgery had weakened me more than I had anticipated or ever experienced. I felt like a rag doll, lifeless and listless, with little strength and no stamina. The doctors assured me that I was making normal progress after such a major operation, and that, in time, I would regain some strength, though for how long they did not say.

On this day, I sat in a green canvas lawn chair under the maple tree in our front yard. Sally had given me orders to sit still and resist any temptation to be helpful. Fortunately, we had a steady stream of friends come by who would spend a few minutes visiting with me, either while coming or going.

My friend, Brian Ward, who had served with me at First Baptist, stopped by on his lunch hour. He unfolded another lawn chair and sat down for a while. "Bart, the house is gorgeous, really amazing. I've never seen anything like it. I better not let Karen come over here, or she'll be wanting to build an old house like yours."

"Thanks. Sally deserves all the credit. It was her idea to try to rebuild Old Blue, and she did all the legwork, finding all the old things we needed. She did a wonderful job."

"Yes, she did, and with all that your family is dealing with right now, this is a good thing, good timing, it seems to me."

I nodded in agreement.

Brian went on. "Bart, I wanted to tell you about what happened the other night over at the church, at First Baptist. You know the Wednesday schedule, dinner and then a prayer time before we break up into all the classes and rehearsals."

"Yes, I know the drill all right," I said.

"Well, Brother Ted, the new pastor, asked for prayer requests the other night and we went over our usual list, the sick, the homebound, our missionaries, and such. That's when it happened. Mavis Brown stood up and requested prayer for you since you have been diagnosed with cancer, and your name was added to the prayer ministry list. I may be wrong, Bart, but I think that is the first time your name has been mentioned publicly at First Baptist since you were fired."

"Wow, I guess that's nice, but kind of sad, too. I mean, I appreciate the prayers for sure."

But Brian wasn't finished. "Let me tell you the rest. After Mavis spoke, Stanley Pulliam raised his hand. Brother Ted called on him, and you know what he said? He said, 'I think we should also remember Pastor Bart's family at this time and pray for Bart and Sally, David and Daniel, and Dinah and Richie.' He said, 'Let's keep them all in our prayers at this difficult time.' I couldn't believe it. The good folks at First Baptist, at least a few of them, are praying for your whole family, Bart, including your gay son and his husband. Imagine that."

"That is a stunner. Not sure what to do with that, but it touches me to think that Stanley's heart has changed. You might not know it, but Stanley gave us our new dog, Duke—a gift—and an apology."

"No, I didn't know that. Hearts can change. You always said so. You preached it all those years. It's nice to see it actually happen once in a while." Brian was getting to his feet as he glanced at his watch. "I've gotta run, Bart. Don't get up. You take it easy and don't overdo it. Holler if you need anything."

"I'll see you, Brian. Thanks for coming by."

As Brian got in his car, I saw Molly's old Nissan pulling up behind him. Molly helped Laura out of her booster seat and held her hand as they crossed the street. Molly had come a long way since we met her on that Christmas morning after the fire. She was a beautiful young woman, not so terribly thin anymore, and a different spirit altogether. Gone was that frightened, harried, desperate expression, her face smiling freely now. She was dressed for work, part of the cleaning staff at the Super 8. Laura was skipping as her mother tried to hang on to her hand, her long brown curls dancing around her shoulders.

"Good afternoon, ladies. How are you today?"

Laura gave me a hug and started to climb on my lap, but I gently held her back. "I'm sorry, Sweetie, I can't hold you today."

Molly kept hold of her hand.

I motioned to the chair that Brian had just vacated.

"Good afternoon, Mr. Bart. How are you feeling? Are you doing better, getting your strength back?" She sat down, and Laura stood between us, her little hand on my arm. "Laura has been praying for you at bedtime."

I pulled Laura closer to me and kissed her forehead. "Thank you, Miss Laura, for praying for me. That's wonderful. It's good of you guys to come by. I know you've already been through the house, but Sally will be thrilled to see you."

"Well, Mr. Bart, actually, I came to see you. I wanted to tell you about college. I did what you suggested... remember, when we talked about me taking some classes and getting started towards a degree? I told you I wanted to go, and I've been saving what I could. Anyway, you said to go ahead and get enrolled, so I did. I went by JCC yesterday and talked to the admissions lady. She was really nice and I filled out the application. I asked her about the cost, and she said there would be no charge for tuition, and I would only be responsible for my books. I asked her why and she said I had a scholarship, but I didn't sign up for any scholarship. So how is that possible? I don't understand."

"I'm pleased you got enrolled, Molly. That's terrific. You will do great. I know you will. It's like this: a special friend of mine set up a scholarship fund a long time ago, and it helps students who otherwise would not have an opportunity to go to college. My friend is gone now — he died — but it's my job to keep it going, to keep using his fund to help students like you. So, even though you never met my friend, he has given you a wonderful, generous gift."

Molly was listening intently and dabbing a tear from the corner of her eye. "Thank you, Mr. Bart, and thank God for your friend. I never thought I'd go to college, never even dreamed about it. Nobody in my family ever did, and now I'm going. I'm going to college. I can't believe it." She stood and reached down to gently hug my neck, her tear falling on my cheek.

"I'm happy for you, Molly, happy and proud of you. I know you'll make the most of this chance you've been given. I know the books are expensive. You holler if you need some help."

Molly smiled and shook her head. "I'll get my books, so help me God, I will. I've been saving, and I'll make it work. That's the least I can do, buy my own books. Thank you, thank you, Mr. Bart."

"And, one more thing, Molly. When the time comes, down the road someday, we can share that same gift with Laura. Even if I'm not around, my friend's scholarship will help you send Laura to college. You can count on that."

The tears came freely as Molly struggled for words. "Are you kidding me? I don't know what to say?" She leaned down and kissed my forehead. "I can send Laura to college," she said, letting the reality soak in. "You mean somebody I never met, who isn't even alive now, is going to pay for my daughter's college, years from now?"

"That's the truth of it, Molly. You can count on it."

As she and Laura headed toward the house, now both of them skipping along, I thought about gruff, old Mr. Martin, who as a young man about Molly's age turned his own grief into a gift, transforming his tears into countless smiles.

God bless him.

***

The next week, while I was still trying to get my strength back after surgery, David and I met Michael Peters for breakfast at Denny's. Michael had been wanting to get together for several weeks, and had graciously put it on hold until I had my operation and had begun to recuperate. He was waiting for us in the corner booth when we walked in.

I waved at Margaret and she grabbed the coffee pot and headed our way.

Michael greeted us warmly. "Good morning, Pastor Bart, David. How are you doing? Starting to feel better, I hope." Michael gave us a friendly smile as we sat down.

Even sliding around the corner table was a delicate and painful proposition for me. It took me a minute. "Doing a little better each day, Michael," I said. "I'm still taking it easy, following the doctor's orders."

"And Mom's orders. That's where he gets into real trouble," David added.

"How are you doing, Michael? David tells me that you've been doing some scouting for The Way. Is that right?" I asked as Margaret poured our coffee.

"That's right, Pastor Bart. That's what I've been wanting to talk about with both of you, before discussing it with the whole church."

We ordered our breakfast, made some small talk until it came, and I listened to Michael and David as I finished my scrambled eggs.

Michael's eyes were bright with enthusiasm as he shared his vision. "What I want to do is take the core values that were the beginning of The Way here in Joppa, and start new churches like ours, or maybe not just like ours, but still based on those ten values. I don't think it's enough to have a new fellowship here in town, which God is blessing in amazing ways, but not share what we have learned about being the church today."

David followed every word, encouraging Michael at each point of the conversation. "Dad, Michael's not the only one, either. You know we've been talking about this—Daniel, Bruce, Annie, Kim, a bunch of us. What has happened here needs to spread. It needs to happen everywhere. Every town and city needs The Way."

Michael responded, so alive in the moment, he hadn't touched his breakfast. "David's right, and we can help make that happen. I believe this is just the beginning of a movement of God, like the book of Acts happening all over again."

We let those words hang in the air for a moment, recognizing the enormity and significance of what we were discussing. I sensed they were pausing now, waiting for me to reply, wondering if I would try to rein them in or turn them loose.

I was anxious to reassure them. "I'm with you, guys. I'm in. It's been on my mind, too, especially since I've learned that I may not be around to help much longer. From the first day we met over two years ago in our little rental house, I could see that God has been doing a new thing, or maybe an old thing, like you said, an Acts thing. Those core values didn't come from me. They were around in the beginning."

Michael seemed to inhale his eggs and bacon without taking his eyes off me.

"I knew you would feel that way, Dad," David said. "I knew you could see it, too, a bigger picture of what is happening here."

"My only concern is that we stay in step with the Spirit and not get ahead of ourselves," I said.

Michael and David both nodded in agreement.

Michael went on as Margaret refilled our cups. "Exactly, Pastor Bart, that's right, in step with the Spirit. Several people at The Way here in Joppa have connections in other towns and cities, family or friends or work. Some of those people have been here and seen firsthand what is happening, and they want to be a part of it. You might be surprised how widely your core values have been distributed, shared person-to-person. It just captures people. It stirs them to see what being the church is all about, and they want in, too."

"If that's the case, I'm glad Sally pulled them out of the washing machine," I said, smiling at the thought. "They might have been lost forever."

Michael gave a puzzled shrug to David, who just waved it off and moved on. "Dad, we've been thinking about Athens. We've got some connections at UGA and some extended family there, and Ron and Julie Durbin just moved there two months ago, and they're interested in helping to start a new The Way. There's also a chance of getting something started in Macon and Lawrenceville, maybe Statesboro, but we've been praying about it these past few months, and we think Athens is the place, the next place for The Way."

It all made sense to me.

Then, Michael made his request. "Pastor Bart, I want to go to Athens. You and I have talked before and you know my heart. I've been praying about it, and I want to go. I can hardly describe it. I feel compelled, sent to go. I'm not sure how I'll support myself to begin with, but I want to help start a new The Way in Athens. What do you think?"

At that moment, I was pretty sure I couldn't stop Michael even if I wanted to, but such was not the case. "Go, Michael. Go do it. go with God. I'll pray for you, I'll help you all I can, and I'll support you until you can find a job, get you an apartment, whatever you need. Go do it."

Michael came out of his seat, nearly knocking over our coffee, and reached around to hug my neck. "I will, Pastor Bart. I will. Thank you so much, for your prayers and support. Just knowing that you believe in me and believe in what we're doing means so much."

He and David went into a flurry of nonstop conversation, making plans and discussing details.

I couldn't help but wonder how my simple words of encouragement could have such power to release and inspire this young man. After all my years as a pastor, this was a novelty to me.

Why should my opinion or approval change the course of a person's life? Do people believe that I have some special insight into the mind of God?

I smiled at the thought, and felt sure God was amused as well. Yet, never was I more certain that I was speaking for God than that day in the corner booth at Denny's.

***

It took a full month to get back to work at the hardware store, and even then, I couldn't do much. A half day at my desk and the cash register was all I could handle. Jim had done well managing the store in my prolonged absence, but much of the paperwork and inventory had fallen behind. I knew we would need to be hiring additional help soon.

My third week back, I found that if I went home at noon and laid down for a couple of hours, I could come back around three and finish the day.

Folks would stop by the store just to say hello, to see how I was doing, to let me know of their thoughts and encouragement. Those who have lived their whole lives in a big city wouldn't know what to make of such concern expressed so openly and often, but I can say it was nice to be on the receiving end of such care.

Sally called me two or three times each day, and sometimes would come by to check on me or bring me something to eat. My weight gain had become her primary life goal, either feeding me or weighing me all the time.

At seven weeks, I was working full days again, though still restricted from picking up anything more than ten pounds. My incision was healing well, but I still moved about gingerly and took the stairs with caution.

Jim and I had the same basic conversation over and over.

"Bart, I'll be in the back. If you need anything, just buzz me. Don't pick up something or move anything. Don't come all the way downstairs to find something or to tell me something. Just buzz me and I'll be right there." He tried not to nag, but he was persistent and uncompromising.

"Thanks, Jim, but I'm doing well. I'm fine. I will holler if I need something, but for the most part, I'm good. Don't worry about me."

Jim nodded, though not believing a word of it. "Look, I'm under orders, Sally's orders, to make sure you don't do anything to hurt yourself. So, don't get me in trouble. You have to be careful and take care of yourself. Let me help you, okay? Don't push it."

"I got it. I will do my best to remain a virtual invalid while I try to run a hardware store. Should be easy enough."

He would walk away still shaking his head.

I did my best to be true to my word. I really did try to be careful in every way, but....

What can I say? Accidents happen.

I was carrying a few boxes of furnace filters downstairs, 24x16x1's that hardly weighed anything. I didn't know how it happened, but I was a little dizzy, unsteady, and I missed a step. I started to fall, tried to catch myself, and then hit my head on the handrail and again on the stairs. Anyway, I made some noise and Jim came running. My scalp was cut and there was lots of blood on me, and everywhere around me. Jim called 911 over my protest and got some pressure on my bloody scalp. I knew something wasn't right in my side, my ribs or my incision, but I wasn't thinking clearly, still a little dazed.

The paramedics took me to the ER, where I faced my family, their concern, and their frustration.

Sally was beside herself. "Bart, what are you doing trying to carry stuff down the stairs? Your head is a bloody mess and the doctors are afraid you've torn something internally, in your abdomen. Your wrist is so swollen, it may be broken." She was crying and yelling at the same time.

"Just a sprain, they say, Sal, and my head looks worse than it is. You know how scalp wounds bleed. It's just a little cut, a few stitches." I wanted to ask her if she had brought some of my pain pills, but I knew that would upset her more.

"They think you have a concussion, too. Jim said he heard your head hit the stairs. You could have killed yourself right there in your own store."

I was still foggy-headed, but I knew this was not an argument I wanted to have right now. I just nodded. "But I didn't, Sal. I'm right here, and I'm going to be fine. They'll patch me right up. I'll be more careful next time, I promise."

Dinah and David both arrived at the hospital before I was dismissed, giving Sally two more opportunities to recount my fall and describe my injuries. The x-rays revealed two broken ribs, but no other internal damage. The doctors allowed me to go home as long as we followed the concussion protocol, and Sally assured them we would.

It was nearly 8:00 when we got home. Sally ordered some pizza for all of us, but I had no appetite. After the kids left, I laid on the couch with my bandaged head on a pillow in Sally's lap. We watched part of a movie, but the pain medicine was making me sleepy. Her anger and frustration with me were gone by then, as she stroked my hair and touched my cheek.

"I'm sorry to upset you, Sweetie. I'm sorry. It shouldn't have happened, my mistake."

Sally gently gathered her arms around me and kissed my forehead. "It's all right. It was an accident, a bad accident, and it could've been worse. But I'm telling you, hardware man, it's time for you to come home."

***

Two weeks later, Sally and I were sitting in the office of our attorney, David Marshbanks, along with David, Jim Hinnessey, and his wife, Lori. I had called the meeting to discuss the future of Martin's Hardware in light of my health crisis and terminal prognosis. Mr. Marshbanks reminded us that Hugh Martin's will had prohibited me from selling the business during my first five years of ownership. That was not quite three years ago, so an outright sale of the store was not on the table. I knew we needed to find a workable solution that would keep the store going and provide Sally with some financial security.

Jim was understandably concerned that his job might be in jeopardy, but he didn't need to worry. He had worked for me for just over two years and proved to be a hard-working and reliable employee. What made Jim even more valuable was the way he had stepped up during my illness, assuming more responsibility and learning the financial side of the business. He was always self-motivated, and I hadn't found Jim's ceiling at this point. Nothing about the store seemed beyond his capacity to learn and manage.

"Thanks, Mr. Marshbanks, for filling us in on the legal aspects of the business and reminding us of Mr. Martin's intentions. Here's what Sally and I have discussed and would like to consider for the future of the store. In the event that I am incapacitated, or if I should die, Martin's Hardware will remain in our family with Sally as the primary owner of all property and assets. If something should happen to Sally, David and his sister Dinah are next in line to inherit the business. Is all that clear?"

Everyone nodded in agreement.

I continued. "Now, the big question is who will run the business and manage it when I am gone? Here's my plan: I would like to name Jim to be the general manager of Martin's Hardware and to take responsibility, after some additional training on my part, for running the whole business. Jim would be a salaried employee, but would eventually have the opportunity to become a part owner of the store and share in its profits."

Jim turned and looked at Lori, who had a proud smile on her face.

"Jim, here's what we would like to ask you to do: if you will learn what you need to know and manage the store, run the business, we'll give you five percent ownership after five years, or really three years since you have already worked for us two.

After another five years, an additional five percent of the business, and so on, up to twenty-five percent of the store. And if anything happens to you, your ownership share passes to Lori or your daughter, Julie, whatever you decide. Sally remains the principal owner but part of the business will be yours. How does that sound?"

Jim was incredulous, shaking his head. "You don't have to do that. I just need a job and you gave me one. I'll work hard for you, and I think I can run the store and find some new help, but you don't have to give me part of the business. I'll run it for Sally."

"I know you would," Sally said, "but if you are going to carry the load, you should share in the benefit, beyond your regular salary. As the business thrives, you should thrive, too. That's only fair, isn't it?"

"I guess so, Sally. That's more than fair. It's very kind of you," Jim said as he breathed a deep sigh and smiled at Lori. "What a relief. I thought I might lose my job, and instead I got a promotion. Thank you again, Bart."

I reached out and shook his hand. "What a relief indeed. I can quit worrying about what happens to Sally when I'm gone. Thanks to you, I know the store will keep right on going and Sally will be fine. Thank you, my friend."

Chapter 11 – Angels

"The meaning of life.
The wasted years of life.
The poor choices of life.
God answers the mess of life
with one word: 'grace.'"
~ Max Lucado

Eating out was Sally's strategy when she couldn't get me to eat enough at home. Even though I was feeling better, less pain and a little more strength, I couldn't seem to maintain my already reduced weight. My favorite dishes at my favorite restaurants with my favorite people was her strategy to beef me up again. I did my best and enjoyed the food, but I could no longer clean my plate. A few bites and I was done, despite her and Dinah's "good cop, bad cop" approach. Coaxing and scolding had the same effect. Full means full; it was all I could do.

The kids joined us on a warm summer evening at Dolce's Country Inn, a big farmhouse converted into a kitchen homestead, with red-checked tablecloths, and pan-fried chicken served family style. Mashed potatoes with gravy, green beans, and cinnamon sticky buns completed the short but tasty menu. The whole house smelled like heaven as we settled into our usual round table for six near the bay window.

David carried a bud vase with a single pink rose as he came to the table. He set the rose in the center without any explanation.

Dinah was the first to ask. "Beautiful rose, David. What's the occasion? I don't think it's anybody's birthday. What's up?"

David just smiled. "I'll tell you later, Sis. Let's eat. I'm starved."

We didn't have to wait for long, as our table quickly filled up with a bounty of country cooking. My least favorite part of the evening was Sally's uncompromising efforts to fill my plate for me, as if the quantity piled before me would automatically be transferred to my smaller stomach. Every time I turned my head, another piece of chicken or a heaping pile of green beans appeared on my plate. I could hardly make a dent.

The choice for dessert was simple: peach or blackberry cobbler, with or without ice cream. Honestly, if I could have finished any food on Earth, I would have consumed every bite of that peach cobbler, too good to describe, but after a few luscious spoonfuls, all I could do was watch the vanilla ice cream melt.

"Richie," I said, "finish this up for me. I hate to waste it."

Richie looked at his empty bowl and nodded as I passed my bowl toward him. "Well, I ate the blackberry. I might as well try the peach to see which is better."

We all laughed as Dinah shook her head. "He never quits, I'm telling you. He could eat all day and stay skinny as a flagpole."

Richie offered a familiar reply. "Hey, it takes a lot of food to fill all the way to the top." He went to work on my hardly touched cobbler.

By now, Dinah was getting anxious for an explanation. "So, what's with the rose, guys? Are you going to tell us now?"

David looked at Daniel and smiled. "Sure, we can tell you about that. The rose is actually for Mom and Dad in honor of their new granddaughter."

A breathless moment of confusion ensued, with glances back and forth, as we puzzled over those words.

Sally reached for my arm and asked the question. "What granddaughter, David? What are you saying?"

David put his hand on Daniel's shoulder as he answered his mother. "You know Daniel and I have talked about becoming parents someday. We've been looking into adoption for several months. It's not so easy for a same sex couple, especially domestically, but there are some opportunities internationally. Since Russia stopped allowing adoptions, and with the conflict in Ukraine, there are many children needing homes and healthcare in parts of eastern Europe. We checked it out and made an application. We didn't want to say anything until we knew something definite. We made a fast trip to Kiev last month, and we've paid the fees, money we had been saving up for quite a while."

Daniel picked up the story, unable to keep still any longer. "We found this little girl, five years old. She's beautiful. Her name is Zoya. In Ukraine, the children must be five years old to be eligible for adoption. She turned five on June 21. We just got word yesterday. She's ours. We get to bring her home next weekend. It's like a dream."

"So that's it, Mom," David said. "You're going to have your first grandchild. What do you say?"

Sally was speechless, her mouth open, her eyes tearing up as David moved behind me to hug his mother. "How wonderful," she finally stammered. "How wonderful. I don't know what to say."

Dinah joined in with a hug from the other side. "I'll say little Zoya is one lucky girl." She reached up to kiss David's cheek. "What a great dad you will be."

I felt Daniel's hand on my shoulder. "Dad, do you know what Zoya means? Our daughter's name means 'life.' It's the Ukrainian word for life. I love that."

"Me too, Daniel. Do you have a picture?"

"Just a little one for now." Daniel handed me his phone with a picture of our newest family member. Little Zoya was smiling through crooked teeth and straggly blonde hair, but her blue eyes were bright and beaming. She looked very thin and perhaps undersized for five years old, to be expected coming from an overcrowded, underfunded orphanage.

"She's precious, just precious," Sally said, her eyes glued on the photo. "When will we meet her?"

David kissed his mother's forehead. "Soon, Mom. Real soon."

***

Sally was beside herself and couldn't sit still. She'd hiked the full length of the long connecting corridor at Hartsfield-Jackson Airport at least four times while I sat at the gate and waited. At her insistence, we had arrived at the airport a full two hours ahead of the scheduled arrival time for the Delta flight from Amsterdam, there being no direct flights from Kiev.

David and Daniel had called to say things had gone according to plan, just a few more fees to pay. Zoya had to be transported from the war-torn region of Donetsk, where she had been living in an orphanage, to Kiev, where her new parents would meet her and process the necessary paperwork. The orphanage had put five-year-old Zoya on a bus with a packet of documents, a small bag, and a note to the driver as to her destination. An immigration official had met her bus and brought her to meet her new family. David had then called a second time to say that they had made it on time to their plane and were preparing to board.

Our nervous anticipation seemed to grow with each passing moment. We never thought we would become grandparents at an airport rather than a hospital, but this was every bit as exciting to us. Sally stood gazing out at the afternoon sky, trying to telepathically guide that jumbo jet into Atlanta and right up to the terminal gate. The arrival monitor indicated that the plane would arrive thirty minutes later than scheduled.

"Bart, if they left on time, how can they be running late? Was there bad weather or something?"

I tried to reassure her. "No big deal, Sally. Flights going east to west usually fly into a headwind, and strong winds slow them down. Flights going west to east often arrive early with a tailwind. Just part of it." I might as well have saved my breath, as Sally wasn't hearing me at all, her gaze still locked on the runway.

The flight arrived forty-five excruciating minutes late, not bad for a long international flight, but nerve-wracking for us. We stood at the checkpoint watching for our first glimpse of this new little family, as unlikely a combination of parents and child as we could have ever imagined. And there they were, David and Daniel, with their new daughter walking between them holding their hands. David and Daniel were scarcely touching the floor, filled with a new kind of love and pride, the kind only our own children can stir up in us.

Zoya was wearing a pink jumper over a white shirt, with a sweater tied around her waist. Her hair was pulled back in a big blonde ponytail. She was smiling a cautious smile, holding tightly to her new parents, and taking in her strange surroundings as they walked towards us.

Sally knelt down to welcome her. She had been rehearsing her words all the way to Atlanta. "*Zoya, ty takaya krasivaya.*" (You are so beautiful.) Sally put her hand on her own heart and said, "*Babushka.*" (Grandmother.)

Zoya smiled, stepped into her arms, and hugged her neck.

Sally didn't want to let go as Zoya turned to me.

I bent down and said, "*Dedushka.*" (Grandfather.)

Without turning loose of Sally, Zoya reached with one hand to add me to their welcome hug.

I looked up to see David and Daniel in tears.

After a moment, she turned back to her new dads and said, "Papa, Papa," as David and Daniel smiled and nodded. It was a wonderful beginning.

Life changed at that moment for the Sheldon clan. A gift from God, she was, bringing joy into our lives when we had been living on tears. Zoey, as we began to call her, was picking up English much faster than we were learning Ukrainian. Her spirit seemed to brighten with each passing day and week, as she sensed that this dramatic change in her life was real and permanent. One by one, she captured our hearts, Dinah and Richie savoring their new aunt and uncle roles. Even Duke took a shine to this little one as Zoey played and petted and sometimes fell asleep beside the big hound, and God help anyone or anything that frightened her, as Duke became her guardian angel.

Sally and Dinah took turns shopping for Zoey, who had come to us with just one change of clothes. As they shopped, they were also teaching David and Daniel the finer points of dressing a little girl. Dinah focused on Zoey's hair, and Daniel caught on quickly, what to do and what not to do.

My job was to read to Zoey, a task I treasured. Even when she didn't understand, I could say the words and point to the pictures and she would sound out each word. Her recall was remarkable, rarely needing more than one or two reminders. I wasn't sure how long she would sit and read with me, because I always gave out before she did. When I'd get sleepy and start to fade out, I'd feel her little hand on my cheek and hear her say "Dedushka, Gwam-pa," the sweetest words I had ever heard.

***

Summer did not end well for me. Whatever I had gained by my surgery, I had quickly lost. What looked like the beginnings of a little beer gut was my enlarged and distended liver. I also suffered the shortness of breath and difficulty swallowing, all signs the doctors had warned us about. The rest of my body seemed to be dissolving or evaporating day by day, my weight dipping below high school days. The pain was deep and excruciating, but only occasional, not constant—at least not yet. The hospice doctor had prescribed some heavy-duty pain meds, but they made me feel like a zombie, so out of it that I couldn't function. I took them only as a last resort.

David and Daniel soon began to talk about needing more space. Their two-bedroom apartment was more crowded than they anticipated since Zoey moved in, and they wanted a yard and room for a swing set or a trampoline. Daniel brought the latest real estate listings when the three of them came to dinner on Friday. We were sitting in the den after dinner discussing their options and looking at listings on David's tablet. Their big obstacle in this process was their lack of savings for a down payment, since they had spent just about everything they had on the adoption, nearly twenty thousand dollars.

Sally was in the front room with Dinah and Zoey, so I decided to make my case. "Guys, here's the deal. You need more space, but you also need more time to save up a down payment. Move in here with us. We've got all kinds of room, a big yard, and Duke's here for Zoey. We would love to have you here and spend the extra time with you and our granddaughter."

David said, "Dad, are you sure you want us to do that? I mean, you and Mom have a full plate, plenty to deal with right now. We wouldn't want to be an extra burden on you."

I could tell such an offer was a surprise to them. "Well, I guess it works both ways," I said. "I mean, maybe we can help each other. That's what we always do anyway. We can help you and you can help us and be here for your mother. What I'm saying is, it looks like my time may be short, and I would like to have as much time as I can with you guys and Zoey. And, I would like for you to be here for a while when I'm not around. I don't want your mother to be here alone when I'm gone, at least not for a while. Do you understand, guys?"

They both nodded, acknowledging the coming reality. "Okay, Dad, we get it. We want to be with you, too, and Zoey. We'd be happy to move in, assuming Mom's all right with that."

I smiled at that condition. "Are you kidding? This will be the easiest sale I've ever closed. Now forget about real estate and use that tablet to find a trampoline and a swing set for my granddaughter. Let's make a plan, boys—no time to waste."

***

Something told me this might be my last day, my final opportunity to attend worship at The Way. I noticed the calendar in the kitchen while Sally tried to coax me into a bite or two of scrambled eggs that morning: September 20, the third Sunday of the month. It was just four years ago on this day that all hell broke loose—Gospel Truth Sunday at First Baptist Church. What a day that had been, and what a journey, a path I could never have imagined. I wondered for a moment how different my life might have been if I had never preached that sermon, but I had no regrets. There was no going back, and even if I could, I wouldn't change a word of it.

Let that one sermon stand.

The cancer continued to advance with a vengeance, and I scarcely recognized myself in the mirror. Yellow patchy skin, jaundice eyes, and my protruding gut, like those old black and white pictures of prisoners of war or Holocaust survivors, only I knew I was not going to survive my battle. It took David and Sally longer to get me in the car than it did for Daniel to load up Zoey in her booster seat. No one spoke of it, of course, but I think we all suspected that this might be my last ride to church.

I had never considered myself a vain person, but I admit I was embarrassed by my appearance, and by everyone's reaction to my decimated and distorted body—stunned expressions, such sad faces. No one knew what to say. Some just smiled and nodded. Others expressed their love and prayers, while a few gave me gentle hugs. And there were tears, plenty of tears, including my own, as we stood in the bright morning light of the old factory and sang and prayed and worshipped. It bothered me to think that my presence might be a distraction, making others uncomfortable, but I knew that was more just me. People were very gracious and loving, on this day, as they had always been. I might not have put myself through it, except for the occasion, a parent-child dedication service today for David and Daniel and Zoey.

These brief two months since Zoey's arrival had been transformative for her. Her health had improved and her shy and cautious demeanor had been dramatically transformed. She moved like a bird set free from its cage, flitting about, curious and carefree. She ran to David and Daniel with loving abandon, already trusting and teasing, constantly talking in her own Ukrainian and English mix of language. What a heart this little one possessed, and what an enormous capacity to love. I honestly couldn't tell which little Zoey delighted in most: being loved, or finally having a family to love. What a gift from God.

The worship service was crowded, more people than I had expected. Richie and Dinah had saved some seats for us near the front, and I struggled to find my chair and catch my breath. I was already exhausted, but determined to lead in this sacred moment. Daniel and David led the people in praise and prayers, and friends reached to lay their hand on me as they prayed. When the time came, Sally helped me to my feet and walked beside me a few steps to the front of the worship area. When I turned to face the people there was silence for a moment and then several people stood to their feet. There was no music or instruction, as others, and then everyone in the building was standing quietly. I was surprised and confused.

Sally squeezed my hand and whispered, "It's for you, Bart. They're standing for you."

I had no idea what to do or say, just nodding my thanks and appreciation, finally waving them back to their seats.

David and Daniel and Zoey came before me, flanked by Richie and Dinah. Sally was holding my Bible and the brief words of a dedication service.

I tried to clear my throat but I couldn't get enough breath. I whispered to Sally. "Please start for me, the first part."

Holding me steady with her arm, Sally shifted my notes toward her and began:

> *"What a joyous, happy occasion it is, when we can ask a blessing and offer our love and encouragement to our little ones and their parents as they begin their long journey together.*
>
> *"We are told in 1 Samuel that Hannah presented her son, Samuel, to the Lord. In Luke, we read that Mary and Joseph brought their baby, Jesus, to the temple in Jerusalem to present him before the Lord. In the same way, David and Daniel today bring their daughter, Zoya, before the Lord. Beside them are Zoya's godparents, Richard and Dinah."*

Sally paused a moment, glancing at me.
I said softly, "Go ahead, Sweetie."
She smiled and continued.

> *"In Deuteronomy 6:4-7, we read these ancient words of instruction:*
> *"Hear O Israel: The Lord our God is one. Love the Lord your God with all your heart, and*

*with all your soul, and with all your strength.
These commandments that I give you today are
to be upon your hearts. Impress them on their
children. Talk about them when you sit at home
and when you walk along the road, when you lie
down and when you get up."*

Sally stopped, sensing that I was ready to speak.

I raised my hands to give these words of commitment and blessing:

*"David and Daniel, I charge you as parents
to love God with all of your heart, mind, soul,
and strength, and to teach Zoya to do the same.
As you love God and one another, you will model
before Zoya a faith in God that she will want for
herself. As you stand before God and this
fellowship, do you so commit yourselves as parents?"*

David and Daniel responded together as Zoey gazed up at them. "We do."

I began to feel faint, and Richie reached forward to steady me. I paused to catch my breath and continued.

*"I call this church to bear witness to David
and Daniel and their commitment to raise their
daughter in the love of Christ. And I ask you all,
brothers and sisters of The Way, will you come
alongside this family, will you bless and guide
them and be a source of strength and
encouragement as you take the journey of faith
together? If so, please say, 'We will.'"*

Those affirming words echoed through the old building.

I placed my left hand on Zoey's blond head as Sally held my arm and I raised my right hand to offer a prayer:

"Lord Jesus, who always welcomed the little children, bless this child, Zoya Sheldon, with your grace and love. You have preserved her life in difficult and tragic circumstances, and brought her into this home and family, and this family of faith. Hold her in the palm of your hand, Lord. Protect her from all harm and bless her with health and wholeness. Let your light and love grow in her tender heart.

"Bless, O Lord, these parents, David and Daniel, two men who have committed themselves to follow you and build a godly home and family. Give them strength and wisdom, and all the faith, hope, and love that flow from your presence in their lives. May they leave footprints of faithfulness all along the journey, so that Zoya may find her way to you. Bless... Bless them, Lord... Amen."

I couldn't stand any longer. Sally and Richie caught me as my knees buckled, and sat me down in a chair on the front row, but I couldn't sit up. I slumped over on Sally's shoulder, weak, totally spent. Dinah brought me some water.

There was a reception planned in honor of our family, but I couldn't stay any longer. Richie helped Sally get me to the car.

Zoey and the boys came out to the car to say goodbye, but Sally sent them back inside. "We'll be fine. You guys go on, enjoy the reception. This is your day. We just gave out a little early, but you go on. Everyone is so happy for you. They want to celebrate with you."

I watched Zoey wave to us as they went back inside. Sally shut the door and leaned over with a kiss before buckling up.

"Are you going to make it, Bart? Maybe this was too much for you."

I disagreed. "Are you kidding? This was one of the best days of my life. I could see it, the years ahead, a good and godly future standing right before me. Our family, Sally. It's going to be all right, you know. It's going to be just fine."

***

"There you go, Bart. All ready for the day," Sally said as she helped me pull on my sweatpants and Georgia Bulldogs sweatshirt. "Let me get you a towel. Your hair's still wet."

The morning routine was becoming an ordeal, just a shower and shave pushing the limits of my endurance.

"I'm going to get you an electric razor so you don't have to stand at the sink."

"It's fine, no trouble. I'm fine, really." I had to confess that sometimes Sally's constant hovering care exhausted me as much as my illness. I tried to be as independent as possible, but there was scarcely anything left for me to do on my own. The hospice nurse, a matronly African American woman named Ruth, came every day now, and the boys were a huge help, too, though I hated feeling like an invalid.

"Let's go on downstairs," I said, though I knew that coming back up would be a major project. The night before, I had to stop and sit down on the stairs two times to catch my breath and gather some strength.

"Are you sure, Honey? I can bring your breakfast up here if you want? Daniel already took Zoey to school. There's nobody here."

I shook my head. "No, let's go down. I'm not bedfast. I want to be downstairs. George is coming over later to watch the game." Sally pulled me upright, her arm around waist, and as I struggled to my feet, I pulled her close and kissed her. "Besides, if I stay up here, you may try to take advantage of me or something."

She smiled and rolled her eyes. "Or something. You never know what I might try, hardware man."

As we started toward the door, I could see the weariness and worry hidden behind her smile. Such strength, surprising to me, as I had never depended on her so completely or needed her so desperately. I hated being a burden to her, yet felt such gratitude for her patience and tender care.

Fortunately, gravity offered us a big assist on the way down the stairs and we made it nonstop. Sally settled me into my recliner and brought me some eggs and a nutritional drink, which tasted like a strawberry shake with ground-up chalk in it. Then, she made sure everything I might need rested within my reach, my coffee and phone, my Bible and books, my laptop and the remote.

"I'm taking Duke for a walk," she said. "Back in a little while, Honey. I have my cell if you need anything." She pulled on her jacket for the cool autumn morning.

I nodded and waved. "Okay, don't worry. I'll be fine."

I tried to read awhile, but even that grew tiresome, and I dozed in my chair. Duke startled me awake upon his return. Nothing like a cold nose in the neck and being licked in the ear. He soon laid down on his rug by the fireplace, watching me with curiosity, still not used to me staying home all day.

George arrived before lunchtime, ignoring the doorbell and just making himself at home.

Duke didn't get up.

Those days, my visits with George served a double purpose. Though we had been close friends for many years now, he was coming to see me in a more official capacity, my hospice chaplain. I had no doubt that George would have spent just as much time with me if he wasn't my chaplain, but his ministry role allowed me to use our time to process much of what I was thinking and feeling.

"Good to see you, Bart. I hope today is a good day." He gave me a warm smile as he found a comfortable spot on the couch.

"So far, so good. I made it downstairs without breaking my neck. I swear those stairs get longer every day, feels like a ten-story building."

"I'll bet it does. Should've put in an elevator, I guess."

"We never thought about accessibility when we were rebuilding. I mean, we never dreamed something like this would happen. Sally wants to get a hospital bed to put in the den, or else just have me stay upstairs, but I'm not going for that till I have no choice. Maybe Duke can pull me up the stairs."

Duke perked up hearing his name, and looked us over.

George chuckled and said, "Hell, you could probably ride him upstairs if you had a saddle. Hey, when does the game come on?"

"A little later—2:30, I think. I hope you can stick around. We'll have some lunch here in a little while."

"Sure can, Bart. Are you kidding? Hanging out with my buddy and watching football, and I get to count the hours as work. What a deal."

We laughed like boys playing hooky from school. I was grateful to have George's extra attention and appreciated the chance to talk.

"How are you feeling today? Are your meds handling your pain? Just say so if they're not."

I shrugged. "It's about the same. The pain comes and goes, or at least sometimes it's not as bad. I take more at night so I can sleep. I try to ease off during the day or I just sleep all the time, and that's no good."

"I understand. What's the doctor tell you lately? Anything new?"

"I wish he would tell me something new. He just says I'm dying. He has no doubt about that. I try to press him for details, how long or how soon, and he just shakes his head. The other day, he said weeks, maybe a month or two, no longer. So, you may have to finish this football season without me, George. I guess I'm going to be checking out soon."

He nodded and sipped his coffee, not quick to reply, just letting my words linger in the air. Finally, he asked, "How do you feel about that, Bart? How are you dealing with that reality?"

"Sometimes better than others. I mean, I've had a good life, a blessed life, Sally and the kids, and I'm truly grateful for the life I've lived. But like most people, I guess, I've got my share of regrets, too—things I wish I had known sooner, handled differently, done better. Know what I mean?"

He nodded, listening intently. "What kind of regrets? I'm curious. What would you do differently?"

"Plenty! I think about my ministry, and I feel such a sense of waste—wasted time and energy, spent on all the wrong priorities. I know we always say that nothing we do for the Lord is wasted, but I'm not anxious to explain to God why I spent all those years leading churches in all the wrong directions."

"What do you mean, Bart? What are you talking about? You make it sound like you've been leading some cult or something, but you've led some great churches, and every church you served grew stronger under your leadership, didn't it?"

"Well, bigger anyway. But that's just it. Think about it. Here in Joppa, at First Baptist, we grew and we built that new sanctuary. We didn't really need to, could've started a second service easily enough, but instead we spent 4.6 million dollars on a new state-of-the-art building. It took three capital campaigns to retire the debt, and we had a big party the day we burned the note."

"Yeah, I remember that. There were pictures in the paper, a big deal."

"I guess it was, but now, looking back, I'm embarrassed, ashamed. You know how much money we spent during those years feeding the hungry or housing the homeless? Nothing. Not a dime. We asked our people to bring peanut butter or mac and cheese on the first Sunday of each month, and put whatever was collected in the food pantry downtown. That's it. Nothing else. Now, I don't know about you, but I don't want to try to explain that when it comes up on the big screen someday. I mean, looking back, I wonder what was I thinking."

"I see what you mean, but that was not all up to you. The church voted. A Baptist church always votes."

"Yeah, but I was their pastor, their leader, the one who was supposed to help them know the mind of God. I blew that one, and then there's about thirty years of preaching that I would change if I could, at least do a major revision. Some of those sermons were dead wrong, even hurtful, sinful. I wonder how many people I drove away. How can I not have regrets about that?"

"Well, you know how it works, Bart. We all start out ignorant and uninformed. Life is a journey of discovery, a process of maturing and learning as we go. Nobody begins with all the answers. We figure it out along the way, and that's what you did. You learned, you wised up, and in the process, you rediscovered what being the church is all about. And, you shared that vision, and it continues to take root and grow."

"I appreciate that, George, and I am grateful for these past four years and what's happened with The Way. It's the thirty years before... I wish I had those years to live over again, at home and in my ministry."

"Well, you don't, my friend. None of us do. You did the best you could, the best you knew how to do at the time, and you must make your peace with that reality. And, maybe—just maybe—you needed to take the whole thirty-year journey to end up where you eventually arrived. Isn't that possible?"

I had never thought about it like that, and as I pondered George's words, I felt some release and relief. It was the beginning of making peace with my past, letting go of my regrets.

***

It wasn't like Jim to be so insistent. Sally tried to politely explain that I wasn't getting out much, except to go to the doctor, and only then when it was absolutely necessary. But Jim wanted to drive me over to the store, and he wouldn't be denied.

"Is there a problem at the store, Jim? What's up?" I asked.

Jim stood in our front room in his work clothes, holding his cap in his hands, as courteous and respectful as always. "There's no problem, Bart. Everything is fine. I just need to show you something. It's important to me. Sally can come, too, of course. It won't take thirty minutes."

"Okay, Jim, we'll come along. Just gonna take me a little while. I'm not moving too quickly."

Sally helped me to my feet, and I slipped on my cardigan.

"Sally, I pulled my truck up close to the porch," Jim said. "I hope that's all right."

Sally smiled as we started to the door. "Good idea, Jim. That will make it easier."

We made it to the porch, and I had to sit in the swing for a few minutes. Then, Jim had to pick me up and put me in the truck. I felt like a helpless child, but he just laughed and smiled.

"You weigh less than a box of bolts, Bart. No trouble at all." He buckled me in next to Sally, and we were ready to go.

As we headed across town, Jim filled us in on the business. His transition to general manager had been a smooth process. In fact, he'd updated some of the ordering and stocking so that we would have a running inventory available all the time.

I appreciated his initiative to update the process while keeping the store's nostalgic flavor. "It all sounds wonderful, Jim. You're doing a great job, as I knew you would. What is it you need to show me?"

He nodded and smiled as we turned on to Maple Street. "Well, I made an executive decision about the store, one that you and Sally might not have approved in advance, so I just did it. I figured it might be easier to get forgiveness than permission on this one. Besides, I wanted it to be a surprise."

I looked at Sally, who was as baffled as I was. "What kind of decision?" I asked. "What are you talking about?"

He just smiled at us, leaving us hanging. "Probably best just to show you rather than tell you, Bart. Take a look."

We pulled up in front of the store as the afternoon sun shone bright on the big windows, the displays and advertisements all neatly in place.

Sally noticed it first and gasped in surprise. "The sign, Bart, look at the sign."

I looked up to see that Mr. Martin's original green and burgundy sign had been replaced with a new sign with the same colors, but with large block letters, "M & S," in the center, encircled by "Martin & Sheldon Hardware." Words caught in my throat. I didn't know what to say, just staring upward.

Sally found her voice first. "Jim, it's wonderful. We had no idea. What a thoughtful gesture, and you're probably right: Bart wouldn't have wanted to put his name up there if you had asked him, but that's where it belongs. Thank you so much." She leaned up and kissed Jim's cheek.

I reached my arm behind Sally and touched Jim's shoulder. "Thanks, Jim. Just to think of my name on the old store alongside Mr. Martin's means a lot to me. And, it's nice to know that my name will be on something besides a headstone," I said, as all three of us gave in to our tears.

***

Sally was determined to keep our Friday night dinners going despite my illness, but it had become more difficult, emotional, and awkward. David and Daniel and Zoey were with us all the time, so Sally had lots of help. Richie and Dinah had been coming by after work almost every day for several weeks. George and Linda's presence on Friday evenings helped to lighten the mood and broaden the conversation beyond my own pain and bodily functions. And of course, Zoey was the star of the show, her perky smile and bilingual vocabulary brightening the room.

Sitting at the table for any length of time had become increasingly difficult for me. The pain in my abdomen and lower back came in waves, increasing in frequency and intensity each day. The only effective pain medicine knocked me out, so I had to choose between pain or sleep. I chose to be awake with my family.

George came through the front door carrying a stack of large foil containers with a tray of deviled eggs riding on top. Linda followed behind with a large bowl of fruit salad and a banana cream pie. The smell of barbeque wafted through the house as George set the food on the dining room table.

"It's from Pit Stop, Bart." George smiled proudly. "Isn't that your favorite que in these parts?"

"Sure is, George. Thanks. That's thoughtful of you to bring dinner for everybody. Smells great." I did my best to ignore the queasy feeling in my stomach, the nausea that was almost constant now.

"I got ribs and pulled pork. I think he threw some sausage in there, too."

Richie was already pulling the lids from the containers, ready to dig in. In a few minutes, we were around the table, Daniel helping me get to my chair.

"Shall I ask a blessing?" I asked.

Nods all around as Sally responded. "That would be fine, Bart. Take a hand, please."

Sally reached out and we all joined hands around the table, Daniel to my left and Dinah on my right, leaning down to kiss my hand. Zoey sat between her dads, holding their hands and scrunching her eyes shut to pray.

So I prayed:

> *"O God, we thank you for this day and for this moment, for the gift of life and love, for family and friends, for good food and the opportunity to share it together. Bless our time this evening with your presence and your peace, and when we are separated, remind us of the coming day when we shall be together again at your table. In Christ's name, we pray. Amen."*

"Ah-man!" Zoey added with enthusiasm.

George and Linda filled plates rather than trying to pass the large foil pans.

My plate came first, bearing about ten times more than I could hope to eat. I did get through a couple of ribs and some pit beans before I had reached my limit.

"What a treat, a wonderful meal, and I didn't do a thing," Sally said. "Thanks to George and Linda. Bless you for this."

George shook his head and laughed. "Oh, this was nothing, no trouble at all. But God bless the hog in the smoker. Now he made a sacrifice."

We all laughed at George's twisted humor.

I watched Sally as she began to cut the pie, and I could see the weariness behind her pleasant expression. She was simply wearing down, exhausted physically and emotionally. Dinah had tried to get her out of the house from time to time, but Sally wanted to make the most of the time we had left, always rushing back ahead of schedule. Sally was watching me waste away, with a ringside seat for my gradual demise. I felt helpless to spare her the pain of watching me die a little bit each day. She caught my eye as she passed around the pie, and gave me that same tender, knowing smile. I think we both knew in that moment that this would likely be my last family night dinner.

"Gwampa, Gwampa, read books," Zoey said, standing beside my chair and tugging my sleeve. She was through eating, but still had barbeque sauce from ear to ear.

David brought a warm washcloth and did the honors, while Daniel and Richie helped me to my recliner and then situated Zoey as comfortably as possible next to me.

"Just one, Zoey. Pick one for us to read."

As I read to her, I noticed that David was taking a video with his phone, wanting to capture this moment. Yes, my moments would soon become memories, but that's always true. Time moves on for all of us. Our moments quickly become memories whether we are around to recount them or not.

***

Monday afternoon, the home health people delivered a hospital bed and set it up in the den. Navigating the stairs was out of the question by then, and just getting to the table had become too much for me. My new bed sure didn't feel like my big pillowtop mattress upstairs, and I hated the feeling of being on display as friends and family stopped by. Towards the end of the week, Sally discreetly passed the word that we could no longer handle lots of drop-by visitors. People meant well, of course, though most never knew what to say. What I hated most were the expressions of shock or revulsion when my friends saw the effects of the cancer, my hollow cheeks and dark-set yellow eyes, my skin-and-bones frame. It wasn't pleasant for them, and I hated to put them through it.

George continued to come by almost every day, and a few others persisted in their kindness and encouragement. Brian Ward stopped by a couple of times, and my pastor friend, Yvonne Meadows, sent me a psalm and a prayer each morning by email, which I treasured. What surprised me most was the mail, the sheer quantity of cards and notes arriving each day. Sally had put a small basket by my bedside so that I could look through my mail when I felt like it. In a few days, she had upsized my basket closer to the picnic variety to handle the volume. It occurred to me that I better start keeping up as much as possible.

"Can you reach me a big handful of cards, Sal? Better start with those toward the bottom of the basket. They've been here the longest. I think I can read for a while."

Sally put a stack of my mail on the bed beside me and kissed my forehead. "Happy to. It will do you good to read what people want to say. The days get long, with hardly any guests."

Sally was right about the cards. It was a real blessing to know that my friends were thinking of me, praying for me, folks from The Way, several people from First Baptist Church, and some from the congregations I had served years before. It was nice to know that so many relationships had not been forgotten. I thought we could display all my cards on the mantle of our fireplace, but no chance of that. Sally put them everywhere.

Some of the cards and letters struck me more than others, the handwritten notes more meaningful to me than the Hallmark sentiments.

I was surprised to open a note from Priscilla Larson, whom I had not seen since I left First Baptist.

> *Dear Pastor Bart,*
>
> *So sorry to hear of your illness. I'm praying that God will do a miracle in your life and heal your body. You helped me get through some tough times when my marriages broke up. You didn't give up on me even when I didn't listen to your advice. Thank you for that, Bart. You always treated me like a lady and a child of God. You never took advantage of me or let me play the same silly games that often got me in trouble. Lately, I'm trying to build a new life, hoping to become the person you treated me like. Please pray for me as I pray for you. Thank you again for being a faithful friend.*
>
> *Priscilla*

Thank God, I thought. *Maybe she can finally pull her life together and find her way.*

As I set her letter on the pile, I saw another with the return address of Bethany Baptist Church. I opened it and read the letter.

"Sally, come in here. You won't believe this one. Listen to this, from Roger Holcomb."

Sally came in from the kitchen wiping her hands on a dishtowel. "Oh my, what does it say?" she asked.

"Pastor Bart,

"I was sorry to hear of your battle with cancer. I am praying for you and your family, that you might not suffer and that you will all find some peace and comfort. While I am sincerely sorry for your situation, I cannot say that I am surprised that your ministry has been cut short. Our righteous God sometimes takes it upon Himself to silence the voices of those who seek to mislead and misrepresent the Gospel. Those who call evil good and condone immorality always risk the judgment of God, and while I do not presume to know the mind of God towards you, I do believe He always moves to protect His truth from those who would pervert it. I trust that God's Spirit will convict your heart and lead you to repent of your sins now, so that you will not be ashamed when you stand before God."

"It's signed:

"Standing for the truth of the Gospel - Rev. Roger Holcomb."

"Well, Sally, How's that for a kind word from a brother in Christ?"

Sally wiped her eyes with her dishtowel. "He might as well just say, 'Go to hell!' It makes me want to choke the life out of him. I can't believe he would write to you that way."

"That's who he is, Sal, and what he believes, that's for sure. One thing I'll say: ol' Roger sticks to his guns, true to his convictions, misguided though they may be. But I'll have the last laugh someday."

Sally gave me a puzzled look. "What do you mean? What last laugh? There's nothing funny about this."

I smiled and reached for her hand. "Someday, when we are all on the other side, me and all of us, and Roger shows up, won't he be surprised to find us there? All kinds of people, from every tongue and tribe and nation, gay and straight? And when ol' Roger is standing there with his mouth open, I'll have my laugh and I'll give him a hug, too. Someday, he'll know better."

Sally kissed my hand and stood there shaking her head. "If ol' Roger is there, I'm not so sure you'll see him after all. I'm not sure why God would want to put up with guys like that."

"Why would God put up with any of us, Sal?"

"I get it, but he's got some kind of nerve. He's lucky I'm not God," she said as she moved to the desk and opened her laptop.

I continued to sort through the mail, noticed an envelope postmarked "Athens, GA," and tore it open. As I had hoped, it was a note from Michael Peters.

> *Pastor Bart,*
>
> *I'm praying for you today, asking God to give you grace and strength. I am so thankful for your example and encouragement. Watching the changes in your life has made a huge difference in mine. When I was a boy growing up at First Baptist, I was kind of scared of you, and I never understood why you seemed angry at people outside the church. Then, after you left the church, you began to teach us what real ministry was all about, and I found myself drawn to it, wanting to follow in that same direction. The Way exists because of you, your heart, your calling from God. My only regret is that you might not be around to see this movement spread across the country,*

*and the world, but I'll always know, and God
knows you had a part in a wonderful new
beginning. God bless you for that.*
With love and prayers, Michael.

Breathing a prayer for Michael, I drifted off to sleep.

I roused when Daniel and Zoey came through the door. "Hi, Gwampa," Zoey said, climbing up to hug my neck. "Are you feeling better?" Her blues eyes always danced with curiosity.

"Yes, Zoey, today was a good day. How was school?"

"It was fine. I still have my apple in my lunch box. You want my apple, Gwampa?"

Daniel held Zoey's pink princess lunchbox, tilting it back and forth to confirm the apple inside.

"Thank you, Zoey, that's kind of you, but my tummy's full right now. Could I have a hug and a kiss instead?"

She never hesitated, reaching around my neck with both hands and mashing her lips against mine. Nobody kissed like Zoey.

I watched her climb down and run out to play on the swing with her dad, with Duke barking and chasing after her. I wondered to myself: *will she remember these few months with me, just a little window of time in her early childhood? Five years old, so... who knows? But I will remember, her smile etched on my soul.*

***

Sally asked the hospice doctor to increase my pain medication, and he doubled the dosage, with no worries about addiction in my case.

Time began to slow down for me, as every hour, every moment, seemed to drag along. Just breathing and fighting to stay awake consumed all my energy. I convinced our kids to keep going to work each day, checking on us when they got the chance. Richie and Dinah came by the house before and after work and class each day, and David came home on his lunch hour. I wanted to avoid some long, torturous, room-filled vigil around my bedside. I had sat with too many families in similar circumstances to do that again with my own.

We had said our goodbyes, recognizing the inevitable approach of death. While the pain of separation was heart-breaking for all of us, I was pleased to note the absence of fear. We grieved together, wept together, but with a sense of hope, a confidence in the promises of God. We talked openly about the future, knowing full well what I would be missing. And always in our minds was the anticipation of reunion someday in eternity. Each time the kids would leave to go to work or home, they would say, "See you later, Dad," never "Goodbye."

Perhaps 'see you later' was roughly equivalent to the biblical phrase 'until that day,' looking forward to being together again at the table of God. That was the source of our comfort.

At night, Sally slept on the couch just a few feet from me, although she didn't stay there long. I would awaken in the night to find her next to me, squeezed into my hospital bed as I was lying to one side. I felt her warmth snuggled against my back and legs, her arm gently around my waist, careful not to put pressure on my painful abdomen. I breathed in her lovely scent and took her hand in mine. The comfort of God himself could not compare with the warmth and love of my Sally. Her tenderness soothed my fading body and settled my anxious thoughts.

In and out of the darkness, the dreariness, the sleep, I heard her voice and felt her touch, her kiss on my cheek, her tears on my shoulder.

"You know I love you, hardware man, and it's going to be all right. When it's time for you to go... go with God. I'll always love you, Bart. See you later."

Epilogue

"Suffering, failure, loneliness, sorrow, discouragement, and death will be part of your journey, but the Kingdom of God will conquer all these horrors. No evil can resist grace forever."
~ Brennan Manning

I never imagined I would one day speak at my father's funeral service. It has been said that no son is fully a man until he stands beside his father's grave, the last painful step in the maturing process. Perhaps that's true, but if it is, I would rather have postponed this final step indefinitely. We hate to lose Dad now, too soon, with so much of life still ahead.

When Dinah and I were little, our family went on a summer vacation up to Sapphire Valley, North Carolina. One day, Dad and I decided to hike all the way around Whisper Lake. Mom packed our lunch in a backpack and we hiked all day, stopping along the way to skip stones and to cool our feet in the lake, and got back just before sunset. We were worn out, exhausted, but the next day, I was ready to go again.

I said, "Dad, can we walk around the world one more time?"

Today, I wish we could walk around the world one more time with Dad, but his long hike is finished. We must go on without him, and that won't be easy, especially for his one true love, our mother.

As many of you may know, Mom and Dad met in college at Union University, but I'll bet you don't know the circumstances of their first encounter. Sally Bailey was a sophomore sorority girl, and attending an intramural flag football game to cheer for the guy she was dating at the time. Bart was on the other team and was, believe it or not, the star of the game. He captured Sally's attention when he caught a pass and sprinted into the end zone, just as a defender lunged for his flag and instead ripped the seat out of Bart's shorts, leaving him celebrating his touchdown in not much more than his jock strap. This was Mom's first "exposure" to the man she would marry. Dad said he was wise to show her his best side first.

So began a journey of nearly thirty years for Sally and Bart, Mom and Dad, a journey cut short. Through all the seasons and struggles of their life together, they have been inseparable, unwavering, and passionately in love. Dinah and I are grateful for their example of faithfulness. We appreciate your prayers for Mom, and our whole family, as we adjust to life without Dad. Grief can be a long and painful path, but we will walk that road together as a family.

Most of you may have seen the little plaque, a shadow box, that Dad saw in a gift shop somewhere and brought home. It got charred badly, but survived the fire. Dad cleaned it up and touched up the words, and always kept it on his shelf. It says, "God Bless the Whole World - No Exceptions!" My dad believed those words.

"For God so loved the world," the Gospel says, and that means everybody, no exceptions. That means we are all invited to God's party. We can all come inside. We are welcomed and accepted just as we are. No one is disqualified or rejected. No one is turned away. No one is beyond the reach of God's love. God's grace and forgiveness is for everybody. We are all free to love God and love one another.

There was a time, years ago, when Dad wasn't so sure about that, when he believed differently, when he thought that God played favorites, blessing those who measured up and punishing those who didn't. Like many pastors and religious types today, Dad spent much of his ministry reciting the rules, picking and choosing scripture to suit his own views, deciding who's in and who's out, letting his own biases and customs shape his faith, instead of the other way around.

But that all changed for Dad a little over four years ago on one horrific evening at the truck stop. That terrible night triggered an unlikely series of events and changes, earth-shaking changes, in our lives, our family, our church, and our community. Since that fateful night, we have been relearning the truth of the Gospel and the nature of grace. And Dad became our teacher, our example, our model of what this grace is all about, grace as a way of life. Dad found enough grace in his heart for everyone.

Grace for me, his gay son.

Grace for Daniel, my companion, and a warm welcome to the family.

Grace for Richie, forgiveness, and a chance to leave the past behind.

Grace for Jim, returning good for evil, giving him a second chance.

Grace for Mark, loving his enemy, doing good to those who have wronged him.

Grace for Molly and Laura, caring for the least of these in Jesus' name.

And grace for little Zoey, embracing a refugee as his precious granddaughter.

Anne Lamott said, "I do not understand the mystery of grace—only that it meets us where we are and does not leave us where it found us." This was Dad's experience, and it's been true for all of us, hasn't it? Grace, God's grace, has found us and brought us to a new place, a new life, and a new church.

Dad's discovery of this Gospel of grace caused him to reconsider what a church of Jesus followers should be and do. And from his vision, The Way was brought to life here in Joppa, and has begun to spread to other towns and cities. This man who was once a determined defender of the status quo has begun a revolution. Dad has planted seeds that will bear much fruit for generations to come.

I don't know how much our daughter Zoey will remember about her *Deduska*, her grandfather. She's so young. Daniel and I will certainly talk with her when she is older, and I know Richie and Dinah will do the same when they have their family. One day, we will explain to our children what God's grace is all about, and we will tell them all about their grandfather who showed us the way.

***

The afternoon sun shone bright and clear in the crisp blue sky as the procession turned into Laurel Oaks Cemetery. The old maples were painted in bright autumn red, yellow, and orange. The procession wound its way through the old graveyard, arriving at the green tent over the burial site Mom and Dad had selected a few months before. Brian, Michael, and Jim joined Dad's golf buddies, Greg, Cory, and Steve, to serve as pallbearers. George led them to the tent, as was the custom, and found his place at the head of Dad's casket.

Mom sat next to me, with Daniel and Zoey to my right, and Richie and Dinah on her left. We waited for other family and friends to get parked and gather around the tent.

Then, Tom gave us a nod and George began:

"Now we come to this quiet, beautiful place to do all that loving hands can do, to commit the mortal part of one we have loved back to the earth, knowing that his spirit has gone on in continuing fellowship with God, who is the Author of all life. A poet, Chauncey R. Piety, described it like this:

"According to the eternal plan the body returns to the earth as it was,

"And the spirit to God who gave it.

"Of all that is material we say, 'Earth to earth, ashes to ashes, dust to dust.'

"But to the spirit we cry: 'Now you are free, free from pain and sickness and sorrow.

'Free from all physical handicaps. Free to dream and sing and work and love.

'Free to greet old friends and new and Jesus Christ, and to adventure with them forever.'

"Therefore we say, 'Goodbye, goodbye until tomorrow.' Amen.

"I've heard it said that the worth of a person's life can be best summed-up with the answer to one question: How well have I loved? By that measure, Bart Sheldon has lived well, because he has loved much. We who are gathered here have been touched by his love, blessed by his

*life, encouraged by his faith, and we are grateful
to God. Let us pray:*

*"Now let your servant depart in peace, O
God, for he has seen your great salvation.
Receive him into your care as your dearly loved
child. May he delight in your presence, free of
every burden, healed of all disease, filled with
unspeakable joy. And for we who remain, give us
your grace and comfort in our loss and your
strong peace to guard our hearts in Christ Jesus,
until that day. Amen."*

I helped Mom to the car as Dinah followed holding Zoey's hand.

"Are you going to make it all right, Mom?" I asked as I felt her leaning on me as we walked, sad and spent. She turned her face to me, a picture of grief, tears, and pain as I had never seen on my mother's face.

"I'll be okay, David. I'll be fine, I know, but not today." She stopped and buried her face in my shoulder as the tears flowed. "How can I leave him here?" I held her for a long moment until she felt a tug on her sleeve.

Zoey looked up with sad, bewildered eyes. "Gwamma, don't cwy. Gwampa is with Jesus at his house, isn't he?"

Mom turned and leaned down to take Zoey in her arms. "Yes, he is, Zoey. Thank you for reminding me. Grandpa is with Jesus now. But we're sure going to miss him, aren't we?"

Zoey nodded her head and clung to her grandmother as they mingled their tears.

I glanced back toward the tent. Daniel and Richie were standing beside Dad's casket, the only ones lingering behind. Daniel laid a rose on the top with the other flowers, as Richie gently stroked the casket with his hand.

Daniel leaned forward as his tears splashed on the polished wood, Richie's arm around his shoulder. "Thank you, Dad."

"Thank you," Richie echoed.

Standing beside the car, I watched those two unlikely brothers, arm in arm, weaving their way back through the headstones, sharing stories. I couldn't help but smile.

Nice work, Dad. Well done.

Book Club Guide

Like any good story, this novel may inspire reflection and conversation on a variety of themes, including faith and family, grace and forgiveness, courage and compromise, sexuality and marriage. The following questions are provided to spark small group discussion.

Chapter 1 – Nightmare

1. It's every parent's worst nightmare, a late-night call from first responders, a child suddenly at risk. Have you ever received such a call? How did you respond?

2. At some point in adolescence, children tend to be more influenced by their peers than their parents. What are the limits of a parent's influence? How can moms and dads keep the lines of communication open through the teenage years?

3. Sexuality tends to be one of the subjects that parents avoid discussing openly with their adolescent kids. Did your parents communicate openly about your sexuality, your feelings and development? Why are such conversations so difficult?

4. How would you describe your thoughts and understanding of homosexuality as you were growing up?

Chapter 2 – Blind Eyes

1. Every family has secrets, the stories they don't tell, the subjects to be avoided at all costs. What would you do if your family secrets were exposed for everyone to see?

2. In your experience, is the church a safe place for people to share their struggles with personal issues like sexuality?

3. Do you consider the Bible to be authoritative in your life, as Bart did? What are the challenges of applying ancient words to contemporary life?

4. Have you ever lived in a small town? Have you experienced the small-town rumor mill? Discuss the pros and cons of living in a small town.

5. What factors and influences led Bart to change his perspective about homosexuality?

Chapter 3 – Truth Bomb

1. Other than religious views, what causes some people to reject homosexuality?

2. Bart is caught between his changing views and community expectations. What kinds of pressure was Bart facing as he struggled to find his way forward?

3. How would people in your church, or churches near you, respond to a sermon like the one Bart preached on Gospel Truth Sunday? How would you respond to such a sermon?

4. Were you surprised to learn how little the Bible has to say about homosexuality? Did Bart make his case for acceptance and inclusion of committed, monogamous same-sex relationships?

Chapter 4 – Fallout

1. Can you think of a time when you changed your mind about a long-held conviction? How did your friends and family react to your changed perspective?

2. What other options did Bart have rather than preaching a sermon that he knew would be upsetting and divisive?

3. It is particularly painful to experience rejection from people we have loved and served for many years. How did Bart and his family cope with rejection and termination?

Chapter 5 – Untouchable

1. The hardest career changes are the ones we do not choose. Why did Bart have such a hard time finding a new job?

2. Have you ever been forced to move backwards economically, to downsize by necessity? What makes such circumstances so traumatic?

3. Why do you think LGBTQ people are so often victims of public shaming and violence? Why did Bart refuse to move his family away from Joppa?

4. In his desperate job search, did it strike you as ironic that Bart was rejected by the churchgoing "Christian" folks, and accepted by Mr. Martin, a harsh critic of the church?

Chapter 6 – Hardware Man

1. How did you feel about the punishment handed down to Mark Hampton and Richie Towns? Was it a just sentence, appropriate to their crime?

2. Daniel read his victim's impact statement before the two men who had attacked him. What price had he paid for their hatred and violence toward him?

3. Discuss Bart's transition from being pastor of a large church to working in a hardware store. What would he miss about his old life and enjoy about the new?

4. Mr. Martin's sudden passing and surprising generosity made Bart a new business owner. What surprised you about Hugh Martin's life as Bart shared his story?

Chapter 7 – Knitting Souls
1. What did George's friendship mean to Bart as he navigated the dramatic changes in his life?

2. What was your impression of Bart's idea, "A Church for All People"? Have you ever heard of a church with similar values?

3. Discuss Richie Towns' religious conversion. Why do we tend to be skeptical of people finding God in prison or in a sudden crisis? Have you ever known a person who experienced dramatic positive change?

4. Discuss the irony of Christians protesting Christians, on Easter morning and on David and Daniel's wedding day. Why is homosexuality such a divisive issue?

5. Some churches choose to welcome LGBTQ worshippers without allowing them to be members or leaders, or to be married in the church sanctuary. Is it possible to be genuinely welcomed but not affirmed, to be a child of God, but not fully accepted and included?

Chapter 8 – Burning Love
1. Few life experiences are as traumatizing as losing one's home in a fire. What made Bart and Sally's sudden loss so painful?

2. What's the difference between an accidental fire and an intentional act of arson? How would being personally victimized make a painful experience even worse?

3. Have you ever celebrated Christmas in the middle of a crisis or loss? How did The Way church respond to Bart and Sally on Christmas Eve?

4. Bart and Sally welcomed strangers, Molly and Laura, who were homeless and hiding out on Christmas Day. What motivated Bart and his family to practice such generous hospitality?

Chapter 9 – From the Ashes

1. What does Bart and Sally's changing housing situation from the parsonage to the rental house, to Old Blue, and finally to New Blue, say about the larger changes in their lives?

2. Discuss Bart's surprising visit from Stanley Pulliam. What caused Stanley to reconsider his condemnation of homosexual people? How does a personal connection impact one's views?

3. Describe the differences between First Baptist Church and the new church, The Way. What do you find appealing and authentic? What do you find that seems to contradict Christian teaching?

4. What strikes you about Richie and Dinah's romance and marriage? If you were Bart or Sally, could you have welcomed Richie, a convicted felon, into your family?

Chapter 10 – All Good Things

1. Over forty percent of men will develop cancer at some point in their lives. How has your family been impacted by cancer?

2. When serious illness strikes, have you ever questioned your faith and the unfairness of life? How did Bart reconcile his faith with his prognosis?

3. Discuss the loss of control and dignity that are often part of a serious hospital stay. What is the worst part of surgery and recovery?

4. What thoughts and encouragement does Bart receive from his friends as he recuperated from surgery?

5. As Bart recognizes the limits of his life, how does he invest in the next generation?

Chapter 11 – Angels

1. Have you ever questioned whether gay couples can be good, adequate parents? Can two dads or two moms provide all the love and care that a child needs? Are children somehow short-changed by not having a traditional mother and father?

2. Discuss Bart's last day at church and Zoey's dedication? Why was it important to him to be present and participate in the service? Why did Bart find the worship service that day encouraging in spite of his physical struggles?

3. Coming to the end of his life, what regrets did Bart express? How did George help him make peace with his past?

4. Discuss the hardware store as part of Bart's legacy.

5. Discuss the cards and letters that Bart received during his hospice days at home. What mixed messages did he receive?

Epilogue

1. As David delivered his father's eulogy, he highlighted his parents' romance and marriage. How would you describe their life together? What made their marriage work?

2. In your life and family, have funerals been a source of comfort or trauma? Have you found them helpful or burdensome?

3. Do you agree with David's summation of his father's life, his transition from legalism to grace?

4. Discuss the course of Richie and Daniel's relationship from the attack at the truck stop to their companionship at the cemetery.

5. How has Bart's story changed your perspective or impacted your life?

Acknowledgements

I've been asked more than a few times, "Whatever possessed you to write such a story?" It's a fair question. Why would I write a novel with such potential to offend and divide? My answer is simple enough: it's a story that needs to be told about an issue that we must address. My hope is that this novel, while it will likely offend some and anger others, can be a source of understanding, healing, and acceptance for those who have been wounded and excluded, for families torn apart, for churches struggling to open their doors to all kinds of people.

I am grateful for the love and encouragement of my family and friends, especially those early readers, and even those who tried to dissuade me from writing this story. It's all good. A big thanks to Jerry and Jan, my biggest cheerleaders, and to Neal and Ann for providing me the perfect writing retreat so many times through the years.

My wife, Suzanne, has been my faithful partner for the long haul, never anticipating that I would take on a second career in my spare time. Her understanding and love keep me going, along with our kids' surprise when they actually like something I've written. What could be better than that?

About the Author

I grew up in a small town in the Ozarks, playing baseball, riding bikes, mowing yards, and reading comic books, the youngest of eight children. Norman Rockwell could have moved in down the street and felt right at home. These days I live and write in Arlington, Virginia, with my understanding wife and a cat named Truman. Our three kids are grown, and we are begging for grandchildren.

After nearly a lifetime of writing nonfiction – essays and articles, lectures and lessons – I was rescued from my tedium and set free, liberated to explore life and faith in the realm of fiction. Unwittingly, I seem to have acquired an expansive cast of characters along the way, some begging to enter the story, others hiding in the background, hoping to go unnoticed, but I see them all. So many stories to tell.

I am, as Parker J. Palmer put it, "…one who loves to watch life become words and words become life."

For more, please visit Drew Hill online at:
Publisher Website: https://evolvedpub.com/DHill
Facebook: https://www.facebook.com/drew.hill1
LinkedIn:
https://www.linkedin.com/in/drew-hill-24305b24/

More from Evolved Publishing

We offer great books across multiple genres, featuring high-quality editing (which we believe is second-to-none) and fantastic covers.

As a hybrid small press, your support as loyal readers is so important to us, and we have strived, with tireless dedication and sheer determination, to deliver on the promise of our motto: **QUALITY IS PRIORITY #1!**

Please check out all of our great books, which you can find at this link: **www.EvolvedPub.com/Catalog/**

Thank you!